ADVANCE PRAISE FOR *BESIDE HERSELF*

"Elizabeth LaBan's characters are so immediately relatable that I defy any reader not to lose herself inside these pages. From their pain, passion, and vulnerability, I saw into the making and unmaking of a marriage—and found myself desperate to know what could come next for a loving—and daring—wife like Hannah. Whether your heart is skipping in a moment of anguish or soaring at a moment of triumph, you will be moved. Powerful and poignant, *Beside Herself* is a must-read of the year!"

—Kelly Harms, author of *The Overdue Life of Amy Byler*

"Elizabeth LaBan's chatty, familiar style instantly drew me into the drama of the story and kept me entertained throughout. A perfect poolside read!"

—Cynthia Ellingsen, Amazon Charts bestselling author of *The Lighthouse Keeper*

"*Beside Herself* is a heartwarming love story with a unique twist on the aftermath of an affair. With a full cast of sympathetic characters—and the cutest little boy, Linc—readers travel deep inside the complex layers of contemporary family life and a marriage that has lost its way. An outstanding choice for a book club."

—Barbara Claypole White, bestselling author of *The Perfect Son* and *The Promise Between Us*

"When Hannah Bent discovers her husband, Joel, has had an affair, she knows she needs to find a way to make herself feel okay again. Why not have an affair herself to even the score? Elizabeth LaBan has written a heartfelt and surprising novel about a woman's quest to restore her self-esteem and survive betrayal—as she embarks on a journey of discovering just what love really means. I could not stop turning the pages to see what was going to happen!"

—Maddie Dawson, bestselling author of *Matchmaking for Beginners*

PRAISE FOR *NOT PERFECT*

"If you haven't read Elizabeth LaBan, her latest novel, *Not Perfect*, is the perfect place to start. It's a domestic mystery starring Tabitha Brewer, a suburban housewife who wakes up one morning to find her husband gone and her life changed forever. Tabitha is a wonderfully relatable heroine, and you'll cheer her on, despite the fact that she has a few secrets—or maybe because of them! I love this book!"

—Lisa Scottoline, *New York Times* bestselling author

"With humor and elegance, Elizabeth LaBan explores the burden of perfection and the futility of seeking it in *Not Perfect.* Funny and real, poignant and charming, Tabitha is a delight as she falls from grace, from perfect mother and wife to pilfering food and money to keep her family afloat, until she realizes that perfect is overrated. This novel is a gift for anyone who has struggled to wear a mask or keep up an appearance, which is essentially all of us."

—Amulya Malladi, bestselling author of *A House for Happy Mothers* and *The Copenhagen Affair*

"*Not Perfect* is near perfect. Warm, but not cloying. Moral, but not preachy. A beautiful meditation on redemption."

—Kathy Cooperman, bestselling author of *Crimes Against a Book Club*

"*Not Perfect* is a captivating story about keeping up appearances, written with a perfect blend of humor and drama. Tabitha is delightfully human and flawed, and her struggle to preserve the balance of her world in the face of her missing husband (where *is* Stuart, anyway?) is highly relatable. A fun read that manages to also be thought provoking."

—Kerry Anne King, author of *Closer Home* and *I Wish You Happy*

PRAISE FOR *PRETTY LITTLE WORLD*

"LaBan and DePino pen an engrossing work, rife with real familial and marital issues . . . This duo is one to watch. An excellent choice for fans of Emily Giffin and Jennifer Weiner."

—*Booklist*, Starred Review

"A wonderful commentary on community, family, friendship, and questioning what these values mean in our lives."

—*Library Journal*

"*Pretty Little World* is an intriguing novel about the walls individuals put up around themselves when the physical walls come down. LaBan and DePino navigate through the lives of three families in an engaging and unconventional way, and they are not afraid to hit on hard topics . . . An interesting story that competently tackles the concept of codependency and individuality."

—*RT Book Reviews*

"When the literal walls come down among neighbors in adjoining Philadelphia row houses, three young families have the chance to create their own urban utopia. But can they pull it off? Elizabeth LaBan and Melissa DePino pack *Pretty Little World* full of gourmet meals, marital scandal, inquisitive neighbors, and friendships whose bonds are sorely tested. The result is a skilled, funny, and highly engaging examination of family, love, and marriage in the City of Brotherly Love. This book is a win."

—Meg Mitchell Moore, author of *The Admissions*

"Do good fences really make good neighbors? That's the question at the heart of LaBan and DePino's intriguing novel. Brimming with astute observations and chock full of surprises until the very last page, *Pretty Little World* offers a fresh, unexpected look at friendship and marriage."

—Camille Pagán, author of *Life and Other Near-Death Experiences*

"Hilarious, relatable, and surprisingly complex, the families in this engaging novel truly touched my heart. I laughed, I cried—I cringed!—but mostly I recognized their longing to feel true community in a world that often makes us feel so alone."

—Loretta Nyhan, author of *Digging In*, *All the Good Parts*, *Empire Girls*, and *I'll Be Seeing You*

PRAISE FOR *THE RESTAURANT CRITIC'S WIFE*

"A tender, charming, and deliciously diverting story about love, marriage, and how your restaurant-review sausage gets made. *The Restaurant Critic's Wife* is compulsively readable and richly detailed, a guilt-free treat that will have you devouring every word."

—Jennifer Weiner, #1 *New York Times* bestselling author of *Mrs. Everything*, *Good in Bed*, and *Best Friends Forever*

"Elizabeth LaBan's novel *The Restaurant Critic's Wife* stirs in love and intrigue, making for a savory delight that pairs perfectly with your armchair. Prepare to be charmed!"

—Elin Hilderbrand, author of *The Perfect Couple* and *The Rumor*

"A heartfelt and relatable look at a woman navigating the difficulties of marriage and motherhood—while struggling to maintain a sense of self. Written with charm, honesty, and an insider's eye into a usually hidden slice of the restaurant world, it's a winning recipe."

—Sarah Pekkanen, internationally bestselling author of *An Anonymous Girl*, *The Wife Between Us*, and *Things You Won't Say*

"In her debut novel for adults, Elizabeth LaBan cooks up a delectable buffet about motherhood, friendship, ambition, and romance (albeit one in need of a little more spice). She captures the essence of life with small children (smitten with a side of hysteria) and weaves a relatable, charming love story with the flair of an expert baker turning out a flawless lattice crust. LaBan's four-star story has the satisfying effect of a delicious meal shared with friends you can't wait to see again."

—Elisabeth Egan, author of *A Window Opens*

"Two things engage me when it comes to fiction—characters I want to spend more time with and details, the juicier the better, from a world I'm curious about but not likely to ever experience. Elizabeth LaBan's novel *The Restaurant Critic's Wife* has both . . . The best part? Ms. LaBan really is a restaurant critic's wife. Her husband writes for the *Philadelphia Inquirer*—which means that the wonderful details in the book both ring true and occasionally are."

—*New York Times*, *Motherlode*

"Author LaBan (*The Tragedy Paper*), who is married to a restaurant critic, excellently makes the joys and difficulties of young motherhood feel real on the page. Readers who are in the thick of raising a young family will enjoy, as will foodies looking for insight into the restaurant world."

—*Library Journal*

"The narrative flows effortlessly, and the dialogue is engaging and evocative. Lila and Sam's love and devotion, despite expected bumps along the way, provides a sensitive look at rediscovering yourself and your marriage."

—*Publishers Weekly*

"Thoroughly entertaining."

—*People*

"LaBan's writing . . . is like a dish of smooth custard—straightforward and a treat to take in. The detailed meal descriptions are likely to spark some hunger pangs, and the spicy and sympathetic Lila makes a perfect meal companion."

—*Washington Independent Review of Books*

Beside Herself

ALSO BY ELIZABETH LABAN

The Restaurant Critic's Wife

Pretty Little World

Not Perfect

Beside Herself

Elizabeth LaBan

This is a work of fiction. Names, characters, organizations, places, events, and incidents are either products of the author's imagination or are used fictitiously. Any resemblance to actual persons, living or dead, or actual events is purely coincidental.

Published by Lake Union Publishing, Seattle
www.apub.com

ISBN-13: 9781542093729
ISBN-10: 1542093724

Cover design by Caroline Teagle Johnson

Printed in the United States of America

For my longtime agent, Uwe Stender, who has seen me beside myself more times than I can count and always manages to pull me back together

PART ONE— SURPRISE!

CHAPTER ONE

"He would have loved that," Joel whispered, leaning back against the seat as the train moved slowly away from Penn Station and New York City. Hannah scowled and shook her head. How could he possibly think that? But she couldn't talk now. They had picked the quiet car on the Amtrak train back to Philadelphia on purpose, so they could read and maybe even sleep a little. She fidgeted in her seat and looked around. There was nobody behind them or in front of them.

"What do you mean, he would have loved it?" she said so quietly Joel didn't even react to her. She nudged him, and he jumped. "What do you mean, he would have loved it?" she said again, a little louder. "He would have hated it."

Joel considered what she'd said and nodded; his face said, *You're right.* He was ridiculously optimistic but also quite reasonable, two of Hannah's favorite characteristics of his. She was satisfied for a minute but then wanted to talk more. They should never have picked the quiet car. It was something they often joked about, fantasized about, really, something they could never do when the kids were with them. When they were all together, everything was always so *noisy*, constant talking, whining, laughing, crying. Right—that was why they'd picked it. Because they could. Their two kids were at home with their babysitter, Monica, waiting for them. They had only a few precious hours of peace left. But now she wanted to keep talking, mostly about the event they had just been to at NBC to honor Joel's father, Richard T. Bent, who had anchored the *NBC Nightly News* for twenty-four years. Richard wasn't well enough to make the trip, so they'd gone in his place, and it was a good thing they had. He truly would have hated it. He never wanted any of it to be about him. It was always supposed to be solely about the news. In fact, she could imagine him actually rejecting the beautiful wooden plaque they now carried back so carefully. She knew he wouldn't want to put it up on his bedroom wall at Saint Martha's Manor in South Philadelphia. He'd gone there for rehab after a small stroke and never left. That was over a year ago.

Hannah peered behind her to get a better look. It was, as far as she could tell, an empty quiet car. Did the rules apply if there was nobody there to hear you?

"He would have absolutely despised that video they played. Honestly, I liked it. I mean, you forget how much he covered. And of course ending with 'I'll see you tomorrow.' Just the other day he said again that he wished he had never started it, that it was presumptuous on so many levels. His words, obviously, not mine."

She waited again for Joel to chime in. This was a conversation they had had many times before, since it was something they never said to each other in earnest and especially never to Richard—*I'll see you tomorrow.* She turned to him now, thinking he might shush her since he probably hadn't yet noticed that they were basically alone. But he was asleep. It drove her crazy. He could fall asleep so quickly it was often a shock—one minute they were in a deep conversation, and the next he was completely checked out. For a brief second she thought about nudging him again, but the truth was this was what she had been hoping for. This was why she had suggested the quiet car in the first place.

She looked around for his phone but didn't see it. If he had it in his back pocket, that would make this impossible. She should have asked him to look up something that would have required his taking it out. She leaned over him now, not wanting to wake him, and peered in all the cracks and crannies of the seat. There it was, just slipped down on his right side. She would wait five minutes and then continue with her plan. She would let him get into a deeper sleep.

Hannah was pretty sure Joel was planning a surprise birthday party for her. All signs pointed in that direction, including a few unexplained calls and a lot of time on his computer, during which she imagined he was googling venues and contacts. About a week ago she'd caught him going through their old photo albums and her even older yearbooks, which she was fairly certain he hadn't done in years, maybe ever. She'd imagined he was looking for pictures to put on a poster board displaying her life or maybe ideas for a heartfelt, emotional speech—or, it had even occurred to her, he might have been searching for long-lost childhood friends to invite to the celebration. She would turn forty-six in four months. It might be a little soon to begin the official planning, but Hannah also guessed he would do it early, maybe even weeks or months early, to throw her off.

Last year she'd thought there might be a party, and she'd been slightly disappointed when they had gotten to their planned dinner at her favorite Greek restaurant and nobody had jumped out. There'd been no balloons or special guests. There'd been no posters and no speeches. Slightly disappointed? Make that a lot disappointed. But about halfway through that meal, she'd thought, of course, Joel would never surprise her on an obvious birthday. He was much too clever for that. He would do it on an off year, an unexpected year. In her mind, at that dinner, she'd had the very clear thought: *He will do it next year.*

A few weeks ago she'd told him that if he did intend to plan anything that involved anyone beyond their immediate four, five if Richard was up to it, she would really appreciate a little warning so she could make sure her hair was okay—fighting that gray was becoming harder and a much more frequent task—and so she could wear something nice and put on makeup. When she'd told her best friend, Kim, that she thought this was in the works, Kim hadn't let on at all that she knew anything but had suggested that Hannah be constantly ready—with colored hair and plenty of makeup—every time they went out from two months before her birthday on. It wasn't bad advice, but it also wasn't something Hannah felt up to doing. It would require way too much work. No, this was a better plan.

She glanced over at Joel and decided he was sleeping deeply enough. In fact, he was snoring. How did that factor into the rules of the quiet car? She was tempted to lift his arm the way they used to with the kids when they were tiny to see if it would drop like lead, indicating heavy sleep. But that was more likely to wake him. If he woke up and caught her, she could easily say she'd thought his phone was ringing. She reached down, trying her best to not touch his thigh—he was very ticklish—and eased his iPhone out from its hiding spot. She turned it over and placed it on the armrest, then thought better of it since that would require her to twist his arm in a funny way. Instead she held it above his knee and reached for his hand. He showed no signs of waking up. She moved the phone under his hand and pressed his thumb into the home button. She used to have his code, but he'd gotten a new phone a few months ago, and she kept forgetting to ask what the new one was, or he kept forgetting to tell her. So this was her only way in. The phone came to life, and she lifted it away from him and started looking. She wasn't sure where exactly to hunt for evidence, and there was that chance she was wrong and he hadn't actually gotten around to it yet, but if Joel was anything, he was a planner. First she went to his email and searched *Evite* and *Paperless Post*, but nothing came up. Then she searched for *Kim*—if Joel was planning something, he would likely consult with Kim. Nothing came up. She went to his texts. Tons from the kids via Monica's number, from her, from his dad—mostly about Palmolive soap, which his dad had become obsessed with lately. She kept scrolling down, looking for Kim's name or the names of any of her friends.

About twenty down she noticed a contact that just said *HOTEL*. The picture that went along with it was a red rose. That could be so many things, most likely work, but for a brief second she wondered if he was planning a getaway instead. She clicked on it.

Already thinking about the next time. Rose petals okay?

Rose petals? For what? For her? She quickly established that HOTEL had written that last text, not Joel. She scrolled down.

Checking out at seven. Will you be at the desk?

That was Joel. Oh, okay. She touched the red rose at the top of the screen to check the number. It was a 612 area code. So this must be the hotel Joel stayed at in Minnesota when he traveled for business. He was heading a team that was marketing a new hotel concept within a larger hotel chain. That made sense. He went to that hotel at least once a month, sometimes more.

She kept scrolling.

HOTEL: Not scheduled to be but I'll come in anyway. Should I come up to your room?

Joel: I'll call you.

That's a little weird, Hannah thought.

HOTEL: Eagerly awaiting your arrival.

Joel: I eagerly await my arrival too.

HOTEL: Eleven days is a long time.

Joel: Trying to move it up a day.

Hannah moved faster and faster through the texts. Some seemed like extremely normal texts from a hotel—Your room will be ready at 3:00; Room service will arrive by 8:00—but others, well, they seemed a little personal. Was she being crazy? She worried about tons of things—that her kids would get away from Monica when they were crossing the street; that Richard was slowly losing his amazing mind; that their son, Lincoln, would go down a dark, anxiety-riddled path that never led to anyplace good; that a devastating hurricane would be named after one of them, forever marring that name—but she never worried about Joel. She got out of that text stream and shut down the phone. She had a distinct feeling that she didn't want to know—whatever it was, she didn't want it. When she eased the phone back toward Joel, she was shocked to see he was wide awake and looking at her. The phone slipped out of her hand, and he reached to grab it, catching it awkwardly. They were both breathing so heavily they could hear it in the silence of the train car. Crazy words ran through her head—*before and after*, *affair*, *betrayal*—all words she did not want to say out loud. Joel looked like he was going to say something, but she shushed him under the guise of the quiet-car rules. She would figure this out, and then they would talk. This made no sense at all.

"Hannah," Joel said full out, not trying to keep his voice down at all, not honoring her unspoken request to save it for later.

"Don't," she said, also at full volume, which might as well have been yelling in the quiet car.

"Hannah," he said again, looking paler and paler as the seconds ticked by. "I never meant—I should have—I—I'm sorry."

Hannah looked at him sharply. If he was sorry, that meant there was something to be sorry about. This was exactly where she didn't want this conversation to go. She wanted it to go something like, *Oh, you saw those texts from Hotel? Those were really from Dave; we were goofing around.*

Joel continued to look at her, continued to appear to be *about* to keep talking, but he didn't. This was why she never worried about Joel. He was so tuned in to her, aware of what she needed before she even knew it half the time. Someone like that was not going to betray anyone, was he?

"About what?" she finally asked, louder than normal volume. It really *was* yelling at that point. "Who is Hotel?"

He kept staring at her. He almost looked unable to speak, like something was physically wrong. But she wasn't going to give that to him. She wasn't going to ask if he was okay.

"Who is Hotel?" she asked again, even louder this time.

"It's the quiet car," a tiny voice said from four seats back.

"I know it's the quiet car," Hannah said. "Believe me, I know."

"Come on," Joel said, coming out of his stupor, collecting his things. "Let's go to the next car."

"I don't want to," Hannah said. "I don't want to go anywhere with you."

She didn't want to. She didn't want to know. She felt—well, the best word for it was *cold*, like she had slipped into a freezing lake, and every time she moved, it felt more real and more uncomfortable. She had thought they had made it through those dangerous years when so many of their friends had been splitting up after discovering infidelities or realizing that they really didn't like each other. Some of those breakups had made sense, and some had been completely shocking. If half of all marriages ended in divorce, she often thought, then half of all marriages stayed intact. She'd been certain they were in the second half—the half that was lucky, the half that didn't have to set up two households and figure out a schedule for the kids. Had she been wrong?

"Who is Hotel?" she said again. Screw the quiet car.

"Hotel is Tara," he said quietly. "I'm so—"

"No," she said, putting up her hand. She did not want to hear it. "No," she said firmly.

He turned in his seat so he was facing forward. She could still hear him breathing. He looked even paler. She glanced past him and out the window. They were in North Philadelphia. They were almost home.

Hannah and Joel observed the rules of the quiet car for the next fifteen minutes as the train eased its way into 30th Street Station. They had already talked about taking an Uber home. It was later than they'd thought it would be—the ceremony had gone over, and they'd had to take a later train.

They didn't talk while they got off the train, took the escalator up into the cavernous station, and walked toward the exit. They stood there. Had he called the Uber? She didn't want to ask. Usually they might discuss which type of Uber to take. She always wanted to take the fancier Black, and he always wanted to save money by taking an X, but she didn't want to speak. She didn't want to hear him say he was sorry.

The Uber came, an X, and they got in. She looked out as they drove through the streets, at all the things she usually loved, the places that meant she was home, as they headed south toward Castle Avenue. When they crossed Washington, she decided she would deal with this tomorrow. It wasn't like she could get a divorce tonight, right? Well, there was probably some divorce lawyer you could call at all hours, but she wasn't sure how to find him or her. Was that where this was going to go? Was there a choice once you discovered something like this? *Don't get ahead of yourself,* she chanted in her mind. *Don't get ahead of yourself.* She thought of Kim and how awful the last year had been for her, how she felt so much for her but always put herself in that different category. Nothing about where Kim was now—officially divorced, lonely, and with the kids only half the week—looked better. She felt a sudden tickle in her throat and coughed. The more she thought about it, the harder it was to not cough. She coughed again, checking to see if there was a bottle of water there for her, as there would be in an Uber Black, something to wash all this away, but there wasn't. She cleared her throat. Joel looked at her, and she waved him off.

As they got closer, Hannah heard sirens. For a second she was glad someone else was having a crisis; then she scolded herself. That was not good karma. She glanced at Joel. He responded, turning toward her.

"I'm so—" he started.

"No," she said again.

"This block?" the Uber driver asked, slowing on 13th Street instead of turning onto Castle Avenue.

"Yes," Joel said.

"Can I leave you here?" he asked. "Looks like something's going on down there."

That was when Hannah realized the sirens she'd heard had been heading here. There were two fire trucks and three police cars on the usually quiet street. She could see neighbors out on the stoops and porches. The car was still inching along, but she opened the door, and the driver slammed on the brakes. They were jolted forward and back, and Hannah was out, leaving Joel to deal with the bags and the plaque. That was the least he could do.

Their house was toward the middle of the block, on the north side of the street, and she kept looking ahead to see where the problem was. She saw her neighbor Simon first. He was older, lived alone, and often opened his window to yell at someone who wasn't parking efficiently.

"Hey, what's going on?" she said to him, not quite stopping as she moved by him but hoping for a quick answer. She could see Joel now with everything over his shoulder and in his arms, looking concerned, shutting the door with his foot, and then having to do it again.

"Smoke," Simon said. "At the Kingdans'."

"Yikes," she said, still moving. The Kingdans were their next-door neighbors, and they shared a wall. The houses on the north side of Castle Avenue were twins, different from the usual row homes of Philadelphia. The south side of the street had the more typical row houses.

She could see the Kingdans' door was open, and there was smoke, not so much thick smoke but the sort of smoke you might see coming off a barbecue. A fireman was knocking on Hannah's door, and she ran the few feet to meet him.

"That's me," she said, breathless. "My kids are in there."

The door opened, and Monica looked out, confused.

"An alarm just started going off in here," she said. "I was just about to call someone—911, I guess."

Hannah wanted to say something snarky—911, she guessed? Was that even a question? Who else was she going to call?

The fireman went inside, Hannah was right behind him and Joel behind her. He piled everything from his arms onto the table near the front door.

"I think it's the smoke alarm," Hannah said.

"No," Joel said quickly, leaning over to steady the plaque, which was threatening to slip down a teetering pile of mail. "That's carbon monoxide."

"Okay, we need to get everyone out," the fireman said.

They scattered. Monica grabbed Lincoln, who was on the couch reading, and took him out the door. Joel and Hannah ran upstairs, and then Joel backed off, letting Hannah go for Ridley. She met him back at the top of the stairs, and Joel waited so Hannah could go first. They were all out the door in seconds, it seemed. By then more people were out; the block was full of neighbors. Smoke was still coming from the Kingdans', but there were no flames that Hannah could see. There were so many alarms going off in all the different houses it was hard to know where to turn. Ridley's eyes were wide, and she was looking around. Monica had put Lincoln down and was holding his hand, leaning over and talking to him.

"Where's Stinker?" Ridley asked. She was five and loved her stuffed skunk more than she loved pretty much any of them.

Hannah had no choice but to talk to Joel.

"We left Stinker inside," she said, pointing into their now apparently off-limits house.

"On it," Joel said, as she'd known he would. He waited until the fireman's back was turned, then sprinted in the open door, up the stairs, and back down in what seemed like under a minute with the scraggly black-and-white stuffed animal. Ridley reached out and grabbed it.

Joel walked over to one of the police officers. Hannah had the strangest feeling of comfort from his taking charge and horror that he was likely not hers in the same way anymore. Was that really going to be true? Maybe not. She hadn't heard about it yet. Maybe it wasn't as bad as it seemed. It was just like her to jump to conclusions.

"What do you think, Officer?" Joel asked in his jovial way.

"Not sure," the police officer said distractedly.

"We have two kids," Joel said warmly. "I'm just trying to get a sense of what we should do."

"Can you hang tight for a few minutes?" the officer said. "I should know more soon."

"Yes, of course, thank you," Joel said.

They watched as firemen went in and out of their house and the houses next to theirs, moving from east to west. A bunch of Lincoln's friends came out in their pajamas, and they stood together, mesmerized. One mom approached a firefighter and asked if the kids could have a tour of the truck.

"Not while we're in the middle of an active scene, ma'am," Hannah heard him say.

"My house is okay," Simon called. "I got the all clear. Everyone is welcome."

Hannah looked to Joel with raised eyebrows before she remembered. She looked away.

"Let's head over," Joel said, not even trying to meet her gaze. "It's really hot out here."

CHAPTER TWO

They traipsed down to Simon's. Hannah didn't want to be there; she wanted to be home. No, that wasn't right, either—she wanted to be at home before she saw the texts. She wanted it to be yesterday or last week. But that wasn't even right, she realized, because if something was going on, it had been happening yesterday and last week. A whole new level of fear settled in just as they reached Simon's door.

The kids gathered together around the food Simon had put out, and Hannah and Joel just stood there.

"We might have to find a hotel for the night," he said.

Hotel.

"How could you?" she said under her breath, forgetting her decision to wait until tomorrow to deal with it. She sounded loud in Simon's living room. She knew she should be careful. She didn't need everyone to know their business. But at the mention of the word *hotel*, she couldn't hold back anymore. "What were you thinking?"

He looked at her and nodded, as if to say, *Okay, so we are going to talk about this now.* His cheeks were pink, but behind that he looked a little green. His still-thick dark hair fell over his forehead. He took a deep breath.

"Anything I say will sound like a cliché, but it's all true. I didn't ever mean for it to happen. I didn't go looking for it. It's over. It's been over for a while now. I just couldn't do it. I missed you when I was with her. I don't, I didn't, love her."

"It's over? You didn't love her?" she repeated, still too loud. But nobody was paying any attention to them. "What exactly is over? And really, you're throwing the word *love* into this?"

"No, not love, of course not," he said quickly. "I will never, ever understand why I did it, why I let it happen, how I let it happen. She was always there, she was so—forceful. And then one night—it was in May—I had way too much to drink, and . . ."

Hannah put up her hand. She wasn't ready for this. He kept talking anyway.

"And then I came home to you, and I was sick, literally, and when I went back, I was like, I don't know, like, unable to do anything, unable to see clearly, in some sort of trance. I was—look, I don't want to make excuses, but I want to somehow explain that when I was there, with her, those few times, I convinced myself she was separate from this."

When he said the word *this*, he looked around, at the kids, at her. He pointed his right arm toward the door and the block.

"Separate?" Hannah hissed, remembering that week in May. He really had been sick, barely getting off the couch. In fact, he had slept on the couch all week, saying he was too weak to go up the stairs. And she had felt sorry for him! "Like when you agreed to forsake all others when we got married, she wasn't included in that? She was separate?"

"Well, no," Joel said. Something strange crossed his face, and he looked around, slowly at first but then more frantically. Hannah thought he was looking for the kids; they had moved from standing over the table to sitting on the couch, but they were clearly there, impossible to miss. He ran out the open door and vomited all over the porch, messy vomit. He stood there, his hands on his thighs, bent over, breathing hard. Hannah knew she should go to him, but she couldn't. She couldn't move her feet. She watched as he bent even closer to the ground and vomited again. Another neighbor, Helene, came up behind him and talked quietly to him, and then a police officer was there. Hannah moved closer to the door.

"How long were you inside your house?" the officer asked.

"Not long," Joel managed. "Not long at all."

He leaned over and vomited for the third time. Hannah watched the officer look up and around, and she had to go over.

"I'm his wife," she said, and it sounded so different from how it would have sounded even just an hour ago.

"I'm concerned he took in some carbon monoxide. He should get checked out. We can take him to the ER."

"No, he didn't," Hannah said, trying not to sound annoyed. A normal wife would be concerned. But she wasn't a normal wife. Not anymore. "We were in there for almost the exact same amount of time—he might have been in there a minute or two longer—and I'm fine."

"You can't play around with this, ma'am," he said before talking into his walkie-talkie. And then someone else was there, ready to lead Joel away. "It affects everyone in different ways."

"Wait!" Hannah said and looked for Monica. She spotted her and jogged over. "Joel threw up, we're going to the ER. I really think he's fine, but they're insisting because of the carbon monoxide. Can you stay here with the kids?" It was all crazy, leaving her with them. What if they had to evacuate the entire block? What would Monica do then?

Helene came up next to them. "You go with Joel," she said. "I'll make sure they're okay. If we have to go somewhere, we'll all go together. I'll stay in touch."

"Mommy?" Lincoln whined. He was next to her, by her leg. She hadn't even seen him move toward her. "I don't want you to go."

"Oh, sweetie, it's okay," she said, kneeling down and hugging him. She still had the impulse to make sure he had Dune, his beloved stuffed black bear, but when he'd turned eight a few months ago, he had cast him off. It was mostly a relief since they were constantly worrying about where the bear was. Said bear, if anyone was wondering, was currently jammed in Lincoln's closet under all his shoes, which Lincoln said Dune liked because his back was itchy. Thinking of that now made Hannah realize he wasn't done with him yet, not even close, and she wished she had thought of Dune when Ridley had mentioned Stinker, but clearly it was way too late for that now. "Daddy felt a little sick. He's okay, but we just want to make sure, so we're going to take a quick trip to see the doctor. We'll be back soon."

"You promise?" Lincoln said.

"Yes, I promise."

"Can I call your phone whenever I want?" That was his usual refrain—he needed to know he could reach her at all times.

"Yes, of course."

"We're leaving now, ma'am," the officer called toward her. She looked out. Joel was in the back seat of the police car, which seemed oddly appropriate. He should be carted away for his actions.

She turned back toward Lincoln. "You can call my phone anytime, I'll have it with me. But you be the big brother, okay? Can you take care of Rid?"

Lincoln nodded solemnly.

"Ma'am?" the officer called. Now Joel was leaning his head against the police car window. Really? Did he have to be so dramatic? Wasn't it her life that had just been twisted and mangled? He was the one at the hotel with Tara and the rose petals while she had been here with the kids and Joel's father.

"Coming," she said.

She felt like she should be able to sit in the front seat. Joel was the criminal, after all—sick or not—but the officer held the back door open for her, and she got in. Joel moaned slightly, and she wondered if he was going to be sick again. He moved toward her, like he was going to lean on her, and she moved away, as close to the door as she could. The car lurched forward, and she wondered where they were going. She could see the front door of her house was still wide open, and somehow she didn't care.

They were quiet on the short drive to the hospital, the same one where Richard had been taken right after his stroke. Of course, when they'd been here, she hadn't realized yet that that was going to be it for him, that he would never go home again. She glanced at Joel, whose eyes were closed. She hated how things could change in an instant. She reached out her hand and grabbed his. It took a second, but then he clung on with so much strength it almost hurt.

"Can you walk in?" The officer had Joel's door open, and he was looking at them. Under different circumstances she would have thought it was funny to be in the back of a police car with Joel—memorable at least. She might have even Snapchatted it to Kim. But there was so much that wasn't funny about tonight.

Joel opened his eyes. They were still holding hands, but she pulled hers away now.

"I think so," he said.

The officer seemed to be waiting for Hannah to step up and help. She got out on her own side, not even looking before she opened the door, and a car honked and moved away from her as it sped down Spruce Street. She walked over to the sidewalk and reluctantly reached in toward Joel. Again, he grabbed on to her with such force it surprised her, and she helped ease him out. He was okay; he could walk, which she was glad about. It would suck if he were really sick now and she had to be the grown-up. She didn't want to be the grown-up.

Her phone rang. It was Monica.

"Monica, hi," she said, trying to hold her phone and support Joel at the same time.

"Mommy?"

"Hi, Lincoln," she said. "I'm here."

"Okay, just checking," he said. In the last few weeks, or really since he'd turned eight, he had sounded older, and it still surprised her.

The automatic door opened in front of them. She realized she was alone now with Joel; the police were no longer helping them. One had walked in, she noticed, maybe to announce their arrival or maybe just to use the bathroom; who knew? But now they were alone. Hannah could run. She could just leave Joel here, and nobody would know, at least not for a while.

"Mommy?" Lincoln said again, and she imagined the kids finding out that she had abandoned their father at the emergency room. She held on to Joel's elbow a little tighter.

"I'm here, sweetie," she said. "I'm just helping Daddy. Can you call me back in ten minutes?"

"Ten?" he asked.

"Yes, ten," she said. This was often the only way to get him to hang up—to set the next time they would talk, the next time he could reach out to her to make sure she was there.

"Okay, Mommy."

She waited and heard the call end. She slipped her phone into her pocket and used both hands to support Joel, even though it was really the last thing she wanted to do. What she wanted to do was spit in his ear and call him names like *cheater* and *loser*.

The waiting room was fairly crowded, but they took them back right away. The officer had, in fact, gone in ahead and explained what was going on. Joel was eased onto a gurney, and a rather serious-looking mask was put over his mouth and nose. Once that was done, they got to work on his arm, finding a vein, taking some blood, and getting him set up with an IV bag. It was the first time Hannah felt alarmed.

"What is that?" she asked.

"Oxygen," a nurse said. "To help get the carbon monoxide out of his system."

"And the IV?"

"That will help flush his system, too, and we added an antinausea medication."

"I really don't think—" she said, but nobody was listening.

She watched as the nurse labeled the tubes containing his blood. Then they were left alone. Joel's eyes were closed. Hannah could literally hear the seconds tick by. Her phone rang.

"Hi, sweetie," she said.

"Hi, Mommy."

"Can you call back in ten more minutes?" Hannah asked. "I'm waiting to talk to the doctor."

"Okay, Mommy," Lincoln said.

Finally, the nurse came back in.

"He's okay," she said. "He has trace levels of carbon monoxide but not enough to make him this sick. It must just be a bug or something. Possibly food poisoning."

Or marriage poisoning, Hannah thought as the nurse eased the big mask off his face and replaced it with a smaller plastic tube that fit into his nostrils. He didn't even stir. She wanted to talk more about the type of poisoning it might be. A poisoning of their trust. A poisoning of everything they had built over the last fifteen years. A poisoning of love. That was enough to make anyone sick. But she didn't. She didn't think it was medical enough for the nurse to care.

Her phone rang again. She looked at the time—exactly ten minutes.

"Hi, sweetie," she said. "Daddy's okay. We'll be back before you know it."

"When exactly?" he asked. He sounded like a businessman negotiating a deal.

"Well, they basically said he's fine," she said. "But I guess since we came, they have to do something official to let us go. And they might have to do one more test, I don't know. Maybe an hour?"

"An hour?" he said, like she'd just said she would see him next week.

"Maybe sooner," Hannah said, looking around and thinking it might actually be much longer. The IV was still very much connected to him, and it was dripping. More than that, though, he was completely out. She pushed his side gently now, just to see, and he didn't react at all. She pushed a little harder, then even harder. She glanced at the door to see if anyone was looking.

"Mommy? Are you there?"

Hannah took a step back, away from the gurney. "Yes, sweetie, still here."

"Can I call back in ten minutes?"

"Yes, ten minutes sounds good."

"Okay," he said and ended the call. She realized she hadn't asked where they were now or how Ridley was holding up, but she knew he would call back soon, so she would ask then—first thing. She poked Joel a little more, and he still didn't react at all. She thought about how she could hurt him if she wanted. She could do all the things she'd contemplated on their way over here—spit at him, kick him, punch him, even yank his IV out of his vein. No, she thought to herself, this could be the last time. The last time she might be this close to him. And as long as he wasn't conscious, she figured, so he wouldn't even know and interpret it as acceptance or forgiveness—neither of which this would be—she might as well take advantage of the opportunity. She shoved him over a little and climbed into bed with him.

"Can I get you anything, Mrs. Bent?" the nurse asked as she checked the IV by the side of the bed. She must have taken more blood, because she had a small full vial in her hand.

Hannah was startled and took a second to remember what had happened and why she was here. She pushed back the covers roughly, getting her hand caught in the tube that was still delivering fluids to Joel. She yanked and made it worse, and she told herself to calm down, or she would wake him, and he would know she'd slept next to him. She eased her wrist out of the twisted mess with the nurse's help and stood up. She felt so woozy she grabbed the bar of the chair next to her to steady herself.

"Are you okay, Mrs. Bent?" the nurse asked with a completely straight face, even though Hannah was sure the whole scene must have looked quite comical to her. "Maybe you're coming down with whatever Mr. Bent had."

"No, no," she said, wanting again to say that he didn't actually have *anything*. He had humiliation and regret. Well, at least that was what she imagined he had. It occurred to her then that he could be sad about the end of the affair. He could have a touch of heartbreak. God, she hoped not.

"I'm okay," she said quickly because the nurse was waiting for her to respond, even though she was pretty sure she was anything but.

She lifted her phone off the maroon vinyl chair so she wouldn't sit on it and saw the notification of nineteen missed calls from the same number—Monica's number. She shook her head as she called back. She had been sleeping for more than four hours. She realized, with some relief, that it was officially morning.

"Hello?" It was Monica, sounding groggy. She had expected Lincoln to answer, but this was better.

"Oh my God, I fell asleep, which seems impossible, but I was so sure I would hear the phone ring. Maybe the air is drugged here. How are you? I see all the calls from Lincoln."

"We're okay," she said nicely, more nicely than she had to, since Hannah knew Lincoln had probably been a terrible handful when he couldn't reach her—nineteen times!

"Where are you guys?" she asked.

"We're still at Simon's. I didn't know where else to go, and he gave us sleeping bags and pillows. I made sure your door was closed, but I had to go back twice to let them in to check the carbon monoxide levels. It was fine the last time they checked. Now Simon is making pancakes for us."

"Did they say what caused all the alarms and the smoke?"

"Oh yeah," Monica said. "Old wires were burning under the street or the sidewalk or something."

"Huh. Well, you've done so much more than you signed up for when you agreed to babysit yesterday," Hannah said. "We'll pay you overtime, double from when it all went crazy."

"No, Hannah, you don't have to do that," Monica said. "It was an emergency. I'm happy to be able to help."

"Well, I'll think of some way to repay you," Hannah said. "So how's Linc?"

She held her breath. She deserved anything she got.

"He's okay," Monica said. "He was a little sad, but I told him that sometimes the phones don't work at a hospital because there are so many machines that are there helping people. He told me that you would have told him that, which I thought was true, but I told him you might not have known the extent of it before you got there. He wanted to keep trying every ten minutes until he fell asleep—and I let him. He literally fell asleep with the phone in his hand, ringing. Also . . ." She trailed off.

"Also what?"

"He's been asking for Dune."

"Oh," Hannah said, appreciating that Monica understood the magnitude of that request. "Is he still sleeping?" She felt the burn behind her eyes but tried to keep her voice steady. How could she have doubted Monica yesterday when she'd seemed unsure about whom to call when the alarm went off? She should be nicer—and less judgmental—to everyone, except for Joel.

"No, we're all up," Monica said.

"We should be home soon," Hannah said quickly. "I never thought we'd be here this long."

"Okay," Monica said. "Should we stay here or head back to the house?"

"I guess either is fine," she said. Presumably the alarms would go off again if there was any more trouble. "Make sure the alarms are in place, though, and working."

"Okay," Monica said.

"Does Lincoln want to talk to me?"

She heard muffled sounds.

"No," Monica said.

Hannah took a deep breath. She would be paying for this for days.

"Okay," she said. "I'll call you soon. Oh, and Dune is in Lincoln's closet under his shoes if he asks again."

"Thanks," Monica said.

When Hannah glanced up, Joel was looking at her. She sat up straight and instinctually moved closer to him, then remembered and sat back. This really sucked.

"Hey," he said.

It was hard to not speak to him in this tiny room while he was hooked up to an IV and getting oxygen. She closed her eyes and pictured the texts. She shook her head.

"I know, I know," he said like he was reading her mind. "Can we just get out of here, and then we can talk about it or somehow come up with a way to deal with it or something?" He sounded croaky and sad. "How am I, by the way?"

She turned back toward him and stood. Usually that sort of remark would make her laugh. She noticed his hair was matted on his forehead, and she gave in to the urge to brush it back. He grabbed her hand.

"You're fine," she said. "I don't even know why we're here."

"I feel fine," he said, pushing up a bit and looking around. "But I'm so thirsty. Can I have something to drink? Water maybe?"

"I don't know," she said, not making any move to find out. He still had her hand.

"Can you ask?" he said. "Or I guess I can push the button for the nurse."

"Ugh, fine, I'll ask," she said, moving toward the curtained doorway. There was nobody in sight.

"I don't know," she said again when she came back in. He shook his head.

"Look," he said. "Nothing has changed. I'm still me, and you're still you. We are still the same. What happened in Minnesota . . . it was nothing."

"Literally nothing?" she asked. Had she misunderstood?

"Well, no, I mean, it was something there, in the moment, but in the greater scheme of things, it was nothing. It was so, so stupid. It was . . . the dumbest thing I've ever done."

"I'll give you that because we have a big problem. We have two kids—one who is very anxious—we have your father in the nursing home, we have our house, and we're stretched thin with the mortgage and the tax increase. So now we have to figure out a way to take care of everyone *and* pay for a second place for you to live. And who knows? If your father isn't my father-in-law anymore, maybe I won't go see him like I do. I see him more than you do! You'll have to step up."

While she said all these things, she didn't look at him, but now she did. He had his head deep against the pillow, and all the color that had come back was drained from his face. Honestly, he looked as sick as he had last night.

"We can talk about this later," she said, sorry she'd started it. At this rate they would never be able to leave. "We have to get back to the kids."

He didn't say anything. A nurse she hadn't seen before came in.

"I'm Mandy," she said. "But you almost don't even need to know that! You're being discharged. You can go home!"

Castle Avenue looked a bit worse for wear, with a dug-up sidewalk and flimsy barriers blocking a big hole. Mud covered much of the pavement, and a gas truck idled near Broad Street. Hannah knew she should help Joel get out of the car—he had needed help getting in—but she just didn't have it in her.

"Thank you," she said as the driver stopped in front of their house. She got out, closed the door, and didn't look back. She waited, but there was no movement behind her. Was she really going to have to go back and help? Not only did she have a cheating husband, she had an invalid husband, which she had absolutely no patience for. She hesitated on the porch while she fished around in her purse for her keys, and just as she found them, she could see the driver's door open. She went inside, leaving the door open, but stood just to the side of the big front window to watch the driver go around to Joel and help ease him out. He let Joel lean on him as they walked up the steps slowly.

"Thanks," Joel said weakly as he crossed over the threshold.

Hannah moved toward them, the words *He cheated on me* by way of an explanation on her lips, but then Lincoln appeared. She turned away from the driver. He didn't need an explanation. She would add a big tip when she gave her extra-high rating for the ride.

"Hi, sweetie," she said, leaning over to hug him. He smelled warm and cozy and looked like he might have grown overnight. He held Dune by the back leg, so the bear was upside down. Monica must have dug him out of the closet. "I'm so, so sorry I missed your calls."

"It was bad," he said seriously. "It's a miracle I got any sleep at all."

His newly acquired old-man way of talking was something she and Joel would usually catch eyes over, but this time she didn't even look his way.

"Well, I'm glad you did," she said. "Really glad. And we're home now, so you don't have to worry anymore."

"Are you sure you're home for good?" he asked. "You won't have to go back?"

She glanced at Joel, who was standing unsteadily by the front door. He had gone rapidly downhill since he'd been discharged, and he looked awful.

"I'm sure," she said, even though she really wasn't sure. Her phone buzzed in her pocket, and she pulled it out. It was the nursing home.

"Great, now you look at your phone," Lincoln said sarcastically.

Why did the nursing home always call her and not Joel?

"Hello?" she said.

"Mrs. Bent?"

"Yes, and you can call me Hannah," she said for the millionth time. "Is Richard okay?"

"Yes, yes, Mr. Bent is okay this morning. We just have the usual soap problem."

"Oh, of course," Hannah said. Normally she would look at Joel here, too, to let him know all was basically well. But she didn't. "I just got a bunch of Palmolive. I was going to drop it off this morning along with the plaque, but we had a hard night, and I was delayed. I'll come now."

She could almost feel everyone around her gasp: She was leaving them? But she had to. If she didn't, if Richard didn't get his preferred (or really *demanded*) soap, he wouldn't relax, which would mean nobody would relax. When he was upset, his booming and highly recognizable voice filled the whole unit.

"Okay, Hannah," the nurse said, calling her by her first name, until the next time, when she would go right back to calling her Mrs. Bent. Then she added apologetically, "He won't let us bring him out of his room until he is bathed, and he won't let us bathe him unless we have the proper soap."

"Yes, I totally understand, this is my fault. I never should have let the supply get so low. I'll be there within the hour." She hung up and looked around. "Where's Ridley?"

"She fell back to sleep," Lincoln said.

"Okay, then this might be a good time to go see Grandpa," she said to Lincoln. "Do you want to come?"

Bringing him along would slow her down, but she knew being asked might be all he needed to not feel she was abandoning him again.

"I better stay here," he said. "I'll make sure everyone is okay. I think Daddy should sit down."

She again looked toward Joel, who was still standing in the same place. Did she have to do literally everything around here?

"Joel," she called to him. "Sit on the couch."

He nodded and shuffled toward their burnt-orange corduroy couch, which they always meant to replace but loved too much to actually do it. Now she wondered if she had been sitting on that couch when he had been at the hotel with Tara. She tried not to think about that right now. She had to keep moving. She turned toward Monica just as Joel sat down, put his head back, and closed his eyes.

"You probably want to go home, right?" she said gently. "You haven't been home all night."

"I'm okay," Monica said. "I was planning on coming at noon today anyway, remember?"

"Yes, of course," Hannah said. There was no camp today, Joel was supposed to be at work, and Hannah had planned to swim before her scheduled afternoon work meeting—she was just finishing a project for the redesign of a Center City hotel lobby. Today was supposed to be the last meeting, the debriefing. "Thank you. I can't thank you enough."

Hannah walked over to Joel and sat down next to him. He didn't open his eyes, and she had to fight the urge to poke him meanly.

"Will you be okay while I take the soap?" she asked, trying not to sound hostile. She didn't want to alarm Lincoln or do anything to make Monica wonder if something was wrong, beyond the obvious.

Joel nodded but didn't say anything.

"I'll be quick," she said. She got up just as Lincoln was heading their way with a plastic cup filled with red liquid. Under normal circumstances, she might question what the red liquid was, but really, she just didn't care.

"You have to stay hydrated," she heard Lincoln say to Joel as she sprinted up the stairs. Hannah glanced in Ridley's open door and saw she was sleeping peacefully on top of her covers. She backed away quietly and was reaching for the bag full of Palmolive soap just inside her room when she had an idea. Could she fit in her swim? She would feel so much better. Maybe she would even have more patience to deal with all of this. She found her Speedo and threw it in her backpack with a towel. She made a quick call to reschedule her meeting for later in the week. Then she headed back down the stairs. Joel looked a little better now, and she wasn't sure if it was real or if he was faking it for Lincoln, but it made her feel better. Despite everything she felt bad for being cold and distant when he was so low, but he deserved it—he'd done this. If he had held up his end of the bargain, she would be her usual warm self.

"Keep drinking," she called as she moved toward the front door, hoping nobody would notice the backpack she had slung over her shoulder. Then she was out the door and free.

CHAPTER THREE

"He's there!" Dani said, slightly breathless and dripping wet.

Hannah had felt her shoulders begin to relax as soon as she'd stepped inside the Christian Street Y and smelled the chlorine from the pool. She wanted a few minutes to think and be alone; she didn't want to deal with other moms. She knew she was being irresponsible, stopping to swim before going to the nursing home, but she needed to do something to feel more grounded. Swimming wouldn't take away what had happened, what Joel had done, but at least she could escape for a few minutes. She would keep it short.

"Who?" Hannah asked as she searched for the combination lock she usually kept in the front pocket of her backpack.

"Who? Are you really asking?" Dani said, her hands on the hips of her kiwi bikini. She looked more ready for the beach than the lap lane at the Y.

Hannah slammed the locker door shut, her towel and wallet in hand. She had given up on finding the lock. "Yes, I'm really asking."

"Lance."

"Seriously?" Hannah asked, hearing the snark in her voice and regretting it immediately. Dani had a boy Ridley's age and a girl Lincoln's age. Even so, she always looked good, ready for the day, never wore yoga pants or even had her hair up, at least not that Hannah ever saw.

"You're no fun," Dani said, turning and heading to her locker. Dani was right: Hannah was no fun.

"Sorry, I'm sorry, it's been a hard day." All the moms went crazy for Lance, who was an incredibly handsome lifeguard—great body, olive skin, deep-brown eyes, thick brown hair that he kept a little longer on the top. Actually, his hair reminded her of Joel's. How many times had she had that exact thought—that she didn't have to admire Lance like everyone else did because she had the most handsome husband waiting at home for her?

Lance wasn't even much younger than they were. The story—which was widely told—was that he was a single dad who'd chosen to move to the city from the Jersey Shore to be near his parents and get help with his kids. The number of kids he had changed every time she heard the story, ranging from one daughter to two sets of twins with lots of combinations in between. At the Shore he'd headed the beach patrol, or whatever it was called there, and was an EMT during the winter, and apparently this was the closest he could get to the water. He never seemed annoyed or sad that he was in a windowless room. The mystery, which everyone guessed about but nobody had a definite explanation for, was why he was a single dad. Hannah thought he was nice enough, but he wasn't what motivated her to swim, unlike the others. One time, when he'd been on a break and gone into the sauna for a few minutes, Hannah had seen Dani and Felicia, another mom, literally follow him in. Honestly, she thought they were being ridiculous.

"Actually, on second thought, I might head back out with you," Dani said. "I still have some time."

Hannah resisted the urge to roll her eyes. "Great," she said instead, nicely this time.

Hannah let Dani go first, even though she knew the lanes could be full, and in a perfect world she would like to be back in the locker room in twenty minutes or so. She had to get to Richard.

She closed her eyes briefly as the humid air hit her face and was surprised to find the pool completely empty. She could hear the chorus of Van Morrison's "Brown Eyed Girl" playing in the background.

"Hello, ladies," Lance called from the stand. "It's so quiet in here I thought I'd play some music. But if it bothers you or it messes with your swimming mojo, I'm happy to turn it off."

"No, no," Dani called. "I love it."

Lance looked to Hannah.

"Fine with me," she said.

"Okay, ladies, well, keep in mind I welcome requests."

"Oooooh," Dani squealed. "Do you have any Bob Marley?"

"I certainly do," Lance said, scrolling through his phone.

Hannah got into the pool at the shallow end and swam under two ropes to the farthest lane. She eased on her goggles, which luckily had been left in her bag from her last visit, and began to swim. After four laps of freestyle she slowed down and did the breaststroke for a while. She noticed Dani was standing below the lifeguard stand, talking to Lance, but his eyes were on the pool and, since she was the only one swimming, on her. Now "Tupelo Honey" played on the Bluetooth speaker. Hannah had to admit she loved this song.

After six laps of the breaststroke, she moved to the backstroke, which always made her nervous that she would hit her head or her hand on the wall. She came up short every time, whipping around awkwardly to see how close she was. On her third length she saw Lance was kneeling at the edge of the pool waiting for her.

"Oh, hey," she said, startled.

"Hey," he said smoothly. He had such a calm voice. He looked tan, even though, if the story about him was correct, he hadn't been to the beach much or at all this season, and he was quite fit up close. "I hope you don't mind, but I noticed you struggling with the backstroke. Not struggling—you have nice form—but not feeling confident enough to finish the length. Am I right?"

She grabbed on to the smooth edge of the pool. Their faces were just inches apart. She smelled mint. "Yes, you're right."

The first notes of Bob Marley's "Three Little Birds" rang out, and Dani practically moaned. They both looked over at her as she stood, her eyes half-closed, swaying to the music. Hannah almost felt sorry for her and for the first time wondered what her marriage was like. Lance smiled at Dani and saluted, and she smiled at him, still moving to the music. He turned back toward Hannah.

"So this doesn't have to be a guessing game," he said in such a way that she wanted to know what came next. "Look up."

Hannah didn't understand. "What?"

"Look up," he said again, now pointing toward the high ceiling. She did, and she saw a string of red and white flags across the top of the pool. Lance pointed toward the shallow end, and she saw a similar string. She had noticed the flags before and always thought they were a nice decoration to go along with Lance's miniature fake palm tree that he had attached to the stand. She knew vaguely they also served a real purpose, but she had never bothered to learn what that was.

"The flags?" she asked.

"Exactly," he said. "They tell you you're almost there. They're placed five yards from the end of the pool. Now all we have to do is figure out how many strokes you take in that space."

We?

"Okay," she said. "How do we, or how do I, do that?"

He looked around the pool. "There's nobody here," he said. "I'll get in the pool and help you figure it out."

She moved back as he eased in, barely making a splash.

"Let's go to the shallow end," he said, heading that way. She followed, doing the breaststroke behind him. He stopped under the flags and gestured for her to go to the edge of the pool.

"Okay," he said. "I can tell you that from here to here is five yards, so just take your normal strokes, and I'll count."

She suddenly felt self-conscious but pushed onto her back and did the backstroke all out. After five strokes she was about to give up, thinking she must have misunderstood what he wanted her to do, when she felt his hand on her arm. She popped up.

"Five," he said. "For you it's five. When you see the flag overhead, do five full strokes, and you'll be there."

"Okay," she said. "Thank you."

"Don't mention it," he said, pushing himself out and up to standing in one motion. When she realized she was watching him, she turned her head sharply and pushed off, not quite ready, doing the wrong stroke, then flipped around to do the backstroke and tried his trick, which worked beautifully, though she was frazzled and out of breath. She swam four more laps, and as she stood in the shallow end to check the clock, a group of older women came in carrying small bright-pink hand weights. She guessed they were here for water aerobics.

Dani was still swaying to Bob Marley—now it was "One Love."

"Hey, are you going to swim anymore?" Hannah called to her.

She stopped moving and sighed. "No, I don't think so," she said. "It's back to reality."

"Me too," Hannah said. "I have to go visit my father-in-law at the nursing home."

"Oh, that's even more reality than I have to deal with," Dani said, following her into the locker room. Just before they turned in, they stopped and waved to Lance. He was surrounded by the older women, but he noticed them and gave them the peace sign. As they turned away, Hannah heard one woman ask if he had any Frank Sinatra songs on his thingamajig.

Ninety minutes after she had left her house under the guise of taking the soap to Richard, she arrived at Saint Martha's. Her hair was still wet, and the bag of soap blew against her in the humid breeze as she made her way to the entrance. She ignored Joel's second call since she'd left. The first had come through while she'd been swimming. She just didn't want to talk to him. She made a deal with herself—she would answer Monica's call instantly, and if Joel bothered to call five times, she would answer it then. She knew if something was really wrong, she would hear from Monica.

She tucked her phone into the back pocket of her jeans and nodded to the people in wheelchairs out on the porch and to others inside the lobby, which was still decorated for the Fourth of July. Every single person she nodded to smiled, and she got a pit in her stomach thinking how nice they were and how sad they were and how little it took to make so many older people happy. She checked in at the desk and walked around to Richard's unit. She heard his deep, reverberating voice the minute she turned the corner.

"Soap poisoning has long been a problem in our country," he boomed in what she thought of as his official tone. It was the voice he'd used for the *Nightly News*. She walked faster. "It can happen when people use a product of which they don't know the ingredients or when certain ingredients are mixed. It can also happen simply when choosing a poorly made product."

Hannah practically jogged into the common area to find Richard in his wheelchair, completely dressed and groomed and combed, wearing a suit, which he insisted upon, and his signature plaid bow tie. The only hints that he was not actually out in the real world were the subject matter and his brown fuzzy slippers. His audience surrounded him, some in wheelchairs, some on couches, and one person on what looked like a gurney, listening intently to his every word.

"Palmolive has long been a trusted brand in these United States," he continued. Hannah shook her head. She knew she couldn't interrupt him, and she also knew he knew he wasn't actually anchoring the news. This was his way of communicating with his peers, and his voice was so familiar, so mesmerizing, he could literally be saying anything, and people would listen. The last time this had happened—or at least the last time Hannah was aware of—Richard had talked about the wild quest for his slippers. Before that it was 9/11, and before that it was about when the Berlin Wall had come down. She was beginning to wonder if Richard did this more often than she realized.

"Oh, hey." Reuben came up behind her, indicating that she should follow him. He was Richard's social worker and had been since he'd arrived at Saint Martha's. If you wanted to know anything about anything, Reuben was the one to ask.

"He's dressed," she said as soon as they were away from the crowd. "I'm so surprised."

"Yeah, he was especially upset this morning; he wanted to get going, so I just ran to Rite Aid and picked up a bar of Palmolive. It was easy."

"Oh, wow," Hannah said, feeling even worse than she already had for fitting in a swim. "That seems like it's above and beyond the call of duty. Thank you. Can I pay you for it?"

"No, no," Reuben said, waving her off. "It was my pleasure. Do you want some coffee?"

"Sure," Hannah said, wondering how it was that he was always so kind and never made her feel like he should be doing something else while he talked to her, even though that was undoubtedly true.

"Follow me," he said. They walked back through the common area, where Richard was now talking about an industrial accident in a soap factory. His audience was equally as rapt as before. Hannah stopped and waved to him. Richard nodded formally and kept talking, but just before she turned to follow Reuben, she saw him smile.

At the end of the ramp leading toward the lobby, Reuben turned left, into a small conference room where they had met many times before, officially and unofficially, to talk about Richard. There was a pot of coffee and a bunch of mugs on a side table. He chose one that said *Basilica of the National Shrine of Mary, Queen of the Universe* and one that said *You Are My Sunshine*, poured coffee into each, and held them both up to let Hannah choose which one she wanted.

"I'll take *Queen of the Universe*, I guess," she said, reaching for it and taking a sip. "Where is it from?"

"Oh, I'm glad you asked," Reuben said, indicating that they should sit down. "This is actually my mug collection; I finally decided to bring it in. You know the old saying, 'If you want to say something, say it with a mug,' right?"

"Um, no," Hannah said. "I've never heard that."

"I'm just kidding," Reuben said, chuckling. "Strangely, I've found the residents love the mugs. The other day when Mrs. Sokolov was under the weather, I brought her the mug with the big umbrella on it, filled with tea, of course, and she loved it. Another time—well, you don't need to know all this. I will tell you that the mug you are holding is from a church that was started in Orlando, Florida, to serve all the tourists who came to Disney World. Cool, huh?"

"I didn't even know that was a thing," she said. "Like an amusement park church? Is there a little boat that takes you through the story of the Bible? Or some 3-D image of Easter Sunday or something? Do they strap you in and make you feel like you're flying over heaven?"

"No, nothing like that," Reuben said, chuckling again. "I think it's a real church. I haven't actually been there. But I liked the *Queen of the Universe* wording. So I bought it—ordered it online, actually."

"I was going to say that if you went to a religious service while you're on vacation, I would think you would go to a synagogue, right? I mean . . ." She trailed off. It was something they hadn't talked about—Reuben's religious beliefs. Really all she knew about him was that he worked at a Catholic nursing home and he wore a yarmulke, which made him fascinating to her. She considered asking now; what did she have to lose? But before she had a chance, his expression turned serious, and she felt that the moment had passed.

"Listen, I'm glad you came in today," he said. "I've been a little concerned about Richard."

She had worried about this, that they might say he was disruptive by holding court the way he did in the common area. Really, when he did that, nobody could talk other than him. When they did, if they even just tried to ask a question, even if it was on topic, he would talk louder and louder, basically running over their words. But he seemed so happy when he was doing it. She hated the thought of having to ask him to stop.

"Is it how he takes over the common room?" she asked. "Has someone complained?"

"Are you kidding? No, it isn't that at all. In fact, people love that. It's either him or one of those food shows droning on in the background. I'd say he is much better than that, much more stimulating for everyone. After all, how many people get to listen to Richard T. Bent in the flesh?"

"Well, not many," Hannah said, slightly relieved. "So what is it, then?"

"Well, lately when I do one last check each night and I come into his room, I don't know how to say this, but I find him crying, weeping, really," Reuben said without looking at her. "The first few times I pretended I didn't realize and just said good night. I didn't want to embarrass him, but when it went on for a third night in a row, I felt I had to say something. He won't tell me what's wrong. Basically he just keeps crying and nodding and finally says in his authoritative voice, 'I'll see you tomorrow,' so I know that's my cue, and I say good night and leave."

"Wait," Hannah said. "He says 'I'll see you tomorrow'? He never says that. I mean, not anymore, and we aren't supposed to say it."

"Well, that's what he says," Reuben said. "So that's been going on for over a week now. I just thought you should know."

Hannah's phone vibrated, and she pulled it from her back pocket. Joel again.

"Do you need to take that?"

"No," Hannah said. Then, to her absolute embarrassment, she started to cry. The burn behind her eyes came first and then intense pressure followed by the tears. It was like no buildup to crying that she had ever experienced before. Reuben sat back with such wide eyes it was almost funny.

"I'm so sorry," she blurted. "It's been a hard day. We were evacuated from our house last night because of an underground fire, and Joel had to go to the ER—long story, he's fine, but we were there most of the night. And then everyone here looked so sad when I walked in—I mean, they looked happy, so happy when I said hi and waved to them, but it made me sad—and now Richard. I mean, so weird that he's been crying, but honestly his saying 'I'll see you tomorrow' bothers me more than anything. And something else happened that I can't go into, but it is—well, it's a bit shattering, so it's been a lot."

By the time she finished talking, she had stopped crying, but she felt red and puffy. She decided she couldn't possibly be the worst Reuben had seen. "You must think we Bents are all a bunch of blubbering idiots."

"No, not at all, I'm just concerned," Reuben said. "There does appear to be a lot of crying in your family right now. How's Joel? Was he injured in the fire?"

"Oh no, nothing like that," she said quickly.

"Well, then how is he?" Reuben said tentatively when it became clear she wasn't going to say anything more.

She had to look away. How was Joel? He was bad, really, on so many levels.

"He's okay," she said, trying not to picture Joel's face in an effort to hold it together.

"Okay, well, you know I'm always here if you need anything," Reuben said before draining his mug. Hannah hadn't had much of hers, so she took a few quick sips.

She nodded and mumbled thanks, but what she wanted to say was that she imagined there would be a lot of crying in her family from here on out. But none of this had anything to do with Richard. His crying was a mystery. That was Reuben's priority, not her and Joel's marital sadness and personal heartbreak. Reuben stood up, and Hannah rushed to follow him. She didn't want him to think she was being greedy and asking for more time with him. Just before they walked out the door, Reuben turned to her.

"I'll keep an eye on Richard," he said. "But I want to keep this discussion going. We don't want him to get depressed."

"No, we don't," she said emphatically. That was one thing she was sure of.

When they got back to the common room, Richard was dozing off, and most of the other residents were still surrounding him as though they were waiting for him to start up again, a brief commercial break in the middle of the broadcast. Hannah leaned in, gently squeezing his elbow. She felt like everyone was looking at her. Richard opened his eyes and smiled, then looked around. "Can you take me back to my room?" he asked.

"Yes, of course," she said, getting in position to push his wheelchair.

"I will return," he said to the small crowd, waving. They all nodded and made quiet sounds of agreement.

"Thanks for coming," he said as soon as she got him situated in his room and sat down in the chair next to him.

"I brought soap," she said, holding up the bag.

"Thank you," he said, not quite meeting her eyes. Then he shifted in his chair and looked right at her, taking both of her hands in his.

"Family is the most important thing in the world," he said, his voice booming. "Studies have shown that loving family, spending time with family, having more of that, is the number one thing people wish for at the end of their lives. Not work, not being right, not shopping, not having a bigger house. It is family."

Hannah nodded; she was used to this, but she wondered if this had more meaning than usual. Was this why he had been crying lately?

"I know, Richard," she said, squeezing his hands. "I know."

He nodded, like he was satisfied, and broke the gaze between them. That was when she allowed herself to fall back against the chair with the realization that no matter how mad she was at Joel, no matter whether they really did start down that road of separating, she could never stop seeing Richard. She could never let him know. They would have to pretend. There was no question about it. As if on cue her phone rang again. She lifted it to see Joel's name. Four times was enough—with Richard here and everything else, she felt like she at least had to see what he wanted.

"I'm with your father," she said by way of a greeting. She wasn't cold, exactly, but she also wasn't her usual self.

"How is he?"

"He's fine," she said. "He's good."

She smiled at Richard, and he smiled back.

"Okay, well, tell him I'll come by tomorrow," Joel said. He sounded much better, but Hannah didn't want to ask, or she would have to tell Richard the whole story about the smoke and the fire and the ER, and lately they had been leaving a lot out of what they shared with him. It was just easier that way. "I wanted to tell you, we have an appointment at five thirty. Can you come home, and we'll go together?"

"An appointment?" she asked. Had she forgotten something?

"Yes," he said, talking fast. "With a highly recommended marriage counselor. She had a cancellation. I feel really lucky to get this time with her. I think it's a good sign. Will you please do this with me? Please? We would have to leave here by about five or so. Monica's staying. She's practically moved in."

Richard was looking at her, waiting for her to get off the phone. She felt she had no choice.

"Fine," she said. "I'll see you then."

CHAPTER FOUR

Hannah tried not to look at all the old people as she walked out. It was too hard. Instead she focused on her phone and pretended to be busy. But pretty quickly, looking at her phone made her think of Joel's phone, which made her more sad than the easy-to-please old people, so she glanced up at the last minute, and it was like there was a lady just waiting there for her. She was tiny and sitting in a chair, her feet not even touching the floor, and she had a crocheted lilac blanket half on her lap and half off.

"Hello, miss, can you please help me?" she said as Hannah made reluctant eye contact with her.

Hannah looked around to see if there was anyone within earshot. Her first impulse was to handle this the way she handled most interactions with people asking for help on the street. She could mumble something about not today or being in a rush or that she was sorry. Honestly, that would all be true; she had to get home. But too much time went by as she decided what to do, and the lady reached out her bony hand and tried to pull the blanket back over her lap but just couldn't get a grasp on it. Hannah was suddenly concerned that the lady might tumble out of the chair trying, so she leaned over and pulled it straight and waited for the lady to start talking about what else she needed help with—there must be something more. But the lady just sighed and smiled, closing her eyes. *That was easy,* Hannah thought as she stood to go. In the corner of the blanket, she saw a name embroidered in white—*KIM*. For the briefest second she thought how strange it was that this woman had a blanket with her friend Kim's name on it, and then she thought, *Of course, this woman's name is probably Kim too.*

Hannah looked back at the lady, whose eyes were still closed. Now it didn't seem so easy to just walk away. Was she all alone? Did she have a family? Did she have things to look forward to, or was the best, most satisfying thing she could hope for in a day simply the readjusting of her crocheted throw? This was exactly why she didn't want to engage! And—Hannah tried not to let the thought form, but it formed anyway—was this where her best friend, Kim, might be in thirty years? On its back was an even worse thought that slowly rose to the surface—was she so far away from Kim's reality that this couldn't be her in thirty years? She shook her head, deciding she would bring something for this lady next time—flowers, a book, a box of candy, maybe a bunch of bags from Nuts to You—licorice and Swedish Fish. She would ask Reuben to help her find Kim.

She waited, almost wanting the woman to open her eyes so she could ask her some of these questions. Maybe she wasn't lonely at all. Maybe her husband was around the corner waiting for her. But Hannah thought she might be asleep; she looked so peaceful, plus she really did have to go. She suddenly had the strongest urge to get to Kim. She didn't even know if she was home, but judging from her routine lately, it was likely she was. She glanced at her phone; it was just before three.

Kim lived in a big house on Broad Street, way too big for one person. Of course, when she'd moved in, she wasn't just one person—she was a family, one of four people. When Hannah arrived, she looked around. Usually, the sidewalk was swept and clean, and at this time of year the big window boxes were full of red, white, and blue flowers or some decoration appropriate for the season and whatever the current holiday might be.

But now the place basically looked abandoned, with leaves and candy wrappers blown up against the house, and scraggly purple flowers that looked like they hadn't been watered in a while in the boxes. Hannah trudged up the wide steps, noticing that the shutters were closed on the big front windows, and rang the bell. She waited a minute and rang again. Then she made a fist and banged on the door. Finally, she heard movement inside. Even then it took a while for her to hear locks being turned, and eventually the door was pulled open, and Kim stood there, squinting in the afternoon sun.

"Are you sick?" Hannah asked, taking in Kim's complete lack of makeup and her sweatpants ensemble. Her shirt had a big purple painted handprint on it, which Hannah could only hope was intentional.

"No," Kim said, seemingly surprised by the question. "Why do you ask?"

"Oh, I don't know, you just look like you haven't been out today," Hannah said.

"I haven't been," Kim said matter-of-factly.

"Do you want to go for a walk?" Hannah asked. Suddenly getting Kim outside seemed like the priority.

"Um, I don't know. I was just watching *Six Feet Under*," Kim said, rubbing her eyes.

"Didn't you see that already?"

"Yeah, but not in, like, two years," Kim said. "Did we have plans that I forgot about?"

"No," Hannah said. "I just had an urge to see you." Kim nodded and opened the door wider, indicating that Hannah should come in. She walked over the threshold and had a very clear sense that she was going from one universe, the sunny July afternoon, to another—the dark, dank house of sadness and loneliness.

"Did you make sauerkraut or something?" Hannah asked.

"No, why?"

"I don't know," she said. "I thought I smelled it."

"Oh, I was just about to have dinner," Kim said. "I got out the salsa, but it seemed a little funny. That must be what you smell. Luckily, I had another jar in the cabinet. Come, sit with me while I eat."

"Okay," Hannah said, wishing she had someone else there who could help her assess this situation. She'd known Kim was down, but she'd had no idea she was at this level. She had just seen her last week, and she'd seemed fine: maybe a little sad but fully functional.

Hannah followed Kim into the huge, grand kitchen at the back of the house. Big windows on the rear wall looked out to a charming garden, which was now full of dry plants—no red, white, or blue flowers or American flags in sight. Last year, when things had been moving sharply downhill but still going along somehow, they had all come for a festive Fourth of July barbecue, and the entire place had looked professionally decorated. Hannah realized now that that had been just weeks before it had gotten really bad for Kim and Hank.

Kim sat at a stool at the kitchen island. There were crumbs and smears all over the counter and a fairly large pile of dirty dishes in the sink. Kim worked to open a sealed jar of salsa and began to pull chips out of an open bag and dip them into the jar. She chewed noisily.

"Did you say this is your dinner?" Hannah asked.

"Yeah," Kim said with a full mouth.

"But it's not even four o'clock yet," Hannah said.

"I've been going to sleep early this week."

"Where are the kids?" Hannah asked.

"With Hank. He took them to Florida. I mean, who goes to Florida in July?"

"Oh," Hannah said, feeling terrible that she hadn't remembered that the trip was *this* week. That explained the state of the house and the depressive behavior. Kim had dreaded this, the first trip Hank took with the kids by himself, and to Disney no less. "I'm so sorry."

"Yeah, well," Kim said, taking another bite. She looked around and leaned over to pull a glass out of the crowded sink. She dumped out whatever was in it and ran the tap, filling it about halfway, and took a sip.

"Have you thought about going to a movie or something?" Hannah asked. "Or even out for dinner?"

Kim shook her head.

"It's not too late. Should I see what's playing at the Riverview?"

"Hannah, if you came over to give me a hard time, I don't need it," Kim said. "I am not going out. I'm not going anywhere. I deserve this."

"What? How can you say that? And I didn't come over to give you a hard time! I had no idea there would be so much to give you a hard time about, honestly. And why do you say you deserve this? That's crazy!"

Again, Kim shook her head.

"Why?" Hannah prompted.

"I thought I was so great," Kim said with so little emotion that Hannah didn't immediately realize she was talking about her marriage. "I thought I could play with all of it, toss it around, ask for more."

"Kim," Hannah said firmly. "Have you taken something? Some drug or something? Maybe a little too much Xanax?"

"Not yet," Kim said, with no further explanation.

"You're not going to do anything . . . permanent, are you?"

Now Kim looked at her. "Oh no, I meant I always take Xanax to sleep, but I haven't taken it yet," she said. "I'm not going to kill myself, if that's what you're asking. I would never do that to the kids."

Until recently, really since just before all this had happened, Kim had been the strong one, the always-together one. Hannah could count on her for anything. A little over a year ago, Lincoln had been having a total meltdown and refused to leave the bathroom—one of only two singles at a crowded pizzeria, and there was a rather long line. Kim had gotten him out. One night before Richard had moved to Saint Martha's, he'd been sick and couldn't get his medicine bottle open—the Bents had been in Boston—and Kim had been there in under thirty minutes, opened the bottle, and hung around long enough to give Richard dinner so he wouldn't have to take the medicine on an empty stomach. She needed that Kim now. That Kim would know what to do. This Kim couldn't even get herself a clean glass of water.

Hannah tried to remember when Kim's marriage had started to deteriorate, what the progression had been, and suddenly she felt so dizzy she had to put her head in her hands for a second. It wasn't texts, so it wasn't exactly the same, but it was Facebook, and it was discovered messages. Hank had been looking for something on Kim's Facebook page and realized, without meaning to, that she had reconnected with her old boyfriend, Wesley. Hank had long joked that he was the consolation prize. Wesley had been the golden boy, the adventurer, but he was impossible to pin down. Kim had eventually given up on him and moved on, and not too long after, she'd met Hank. But there was never any true closure, never a concrete reason to stop loving him. To make matters worse, Wesley never got married, so there wasn't even that barrier there, that clear shutting down of any future possibility. On the few nights she and Kim had too much wine and got on the subject of Wesley, Hannah would always say he was never going to settle down, that Kim would *still* be waiting. Usually Kim quietly agreed. But one night, Kim said, "I hear you, I do, but the flip side of that theory is that he would have eventually asked me if I'd given him more time. That he hasn't settled down with anyone else because he still loves me. That I was the one for him."

Hannah dismissed that, and as the years went by and the kids were born, she assumed Kim thought of him less and less. But then Hank came across their reconnection, and he flipped. He knew Kim's passwords, so he was able to see their private Facebook messages and even their emails to each other. There was never anything truly incriminating, but there was a closeness, a banter, and Hank couldn't let it go. He turned into a jealous maniac, always wanting to know what Kim was doing, never trusting her responses. And instead of working to fix it or trying to reassure Hank, Kim decided she deserved better, that she was the wronged party there. And she pushed Hank away until he was gone, out the door, taking the kids with him for half the week and sometimes the whole week, like now.

And of course Hannah had been right about Wesley. Kim hadn't asked him straight out if he wanted to rekindle their long-ago romance, but she'd hinted at it, once Hank had left, and Wesley wanted no part of it. He never had. Thinking of those secret messages, the misplaced love, Hannah couldn't stand it. Those things had never been close to home before, at least not to her home, and now they were. What she especially couldn't stand was the idea of that moment when you went from not knowing, from completely trusting, to knowing, and then to questioning everything. She took a deep breath, but the dizziness didn't dissipate at all; it just got worse. She climbed off the stool and practically crawled to the couch in the corner, where she leaned back as far as she could go.

"Are you okay?" Kim asked, seeming to be truly present for the first time since Hannah had arrived. "Are *you* sick?"

"I don't even know where to begin," Hannah said, and now Kim looked more focused, sitting up straight and bugging out her eyes, and Hannah wondered briefly if she thought she was going to tell her she had some awful disease. "A lot has happened in the last twenty-four hours, but the worst thing, the life-changing thing I discovered, is that Joel had an affair."

Kim, who had taken a big bite just before Hannah had started to go downhill, coughed, then swallowed with effort.

"Are you playing a trick on me?" she said with narrowed eyes. "To make me feel better or something?"

"A trick?" Hannah said. "Do you think I would trick about that? And honestly, would that make you feel better?"

"No, I don't. And no, of course it wouldn't. But it can't be possible. There is no way." Kim put the lid back on the salsa and came to sit on the floor below Hannah. "Are you sure?"

Hannah nodded.

"Like, Joel-admitted-to-it sure?"

Hannah nodded again.

"I am so, so sorry," Kim said, taking Hannah's hand. "Wow, I really wouldn't have ever guessed that Joel would do that. I'm shocked."

"That makes two of us."

"I have four questions," Kim said, leaning closer to Hannah. "The answers to these questions will tell me everything I need to know. Believe me, I have given infidelity and perceived infidelity and the dismantling of a marriage and family a lot of thought. First, is it still going on?"

"The affair? No," Hannah said. "At least he says it isn't."

"Is he sorry?"

"Yes, he has said he is sorry. I mean, I didn't want to hear it, but."

"Does he love her?" Kim asked, cutting her off. "I assume it was a her. Or does he seem sad that it's over? Can you tell?"

"Yes, it was a her, and he says it's over, and he actually said he didn't love her," Hannah said. "I didn't like that he used that word, but he did say it."

"And the last question: Does he want to stay married to you?" Kim asked, moving even closer. Hannah could see her hair was greasy on the top.

"Yes. I mean, yes, I think so," Hannah said. "He does not seem to want to break up. He made an appointment with a marriage counselor for tonight."

"Okay, then," Kim said, like that settled it. She sat back against her heels again. Then pushed up abruptly. "One other question, one very important one. Do you want to stay with him? I mean, I get that you must be so mad, of course, but I guess what I'm asking is, Do you see this as a ticket out? You have never, ever let on that you were anything but happy with Joel, but people keep a lot of surprising things to themselves. This is crucial: Do you see this as a possible free ride to freedom?"

"No," Hannah said quickly. "I was happy, really happy, and you know, with the kids and Richard, it would be so hard to juggle all that if we are apart, and I mean, it's Joel—I still like him. At least I did until last night. But what else can you do? Do people ever recover from this sort of thing? Every affair I've heard of has ended in divorce. Have you ever heard of one that didn't?"

"Well, no, but I think that's because those people probably don't talk about it," Kim said thoughtfully. "They probably keep it quiet."

"Maybe," Hannah said slowly, shaking her head.

"Please don't give up," Kim said so forcefully it startled Hannah. "If there is one thing I know for sure, one piece of advice I can give you, it's that things can go wrong, they can go very wrong, and you do not have to be so quick to throw it all away. There are other ways to do it. Look around. Does this look like any sort of happy to you? Do anything and everything you can to hold it together. This is no way to live."

"It's going to get better for you," Hannah said. "Lots of people are way happier once they get divorced. Mindy, for example—she's so much happier now."

"That's true," Kim said, nodding. "But she was in a terrible marriage. He was emotionally abusive."

"Yes, he was. He was such an asshole," Hannah said. "Also, Linda is much happier. I mean, it took a while, but she told me not too long ago that she's happier than she's ever been as an adult."

"Well, yes, I can see that," Kim said.

They heard something, a buzzing, and Kim got up and looked frantically for where it was coming from. She found her phone and rushed around to open all the curtains and shutters, throwing unfolded blankets and pillows on the floor behind the big couch in the living room. She literally took her arm and swiped everything that was on the coffee table—and there was a lot of stuff—off and onto the floor with her outstretched arm. She sat on the couch, fluffing her hair and trying to arrange her face to look happy, and in the time all that took, the phone stopped ringing. She took a deep breath and called back.

"Hello, honey," she said, holding her phone out in front of her and smiling at it. Hannah could see Kim's daughter, Savannah, on the screen, standing somewhere in a red bikini. "Where are you guys?"

"Volcano Bay," Savannah said enthusiastically. "It's the best! Daddy surprised us. I wanted you to see it. See the river? Can you see it? It's a lazy river but not really lazy. It moves fast. I love it. I'm going to go on it again."

"Wow," Kim said, sounding so normal Hannah almost bought it. "I can see it so clearly, and that is the coolest thing ever. Wait, is that a Disney water park?"

"No, Universal! I always wanted to go to Universal! I couldn't believe it when Daddy said we were coming here today. Oh, wait, Daddy and Michael are calling me. They want to do the not-lazy river again. We got a cabana, like, our own personal hut with an honest-to-God fruit basket! I could not believe my eyes. Okay, Mommy, I have to go."

"You go, sweetie, I'll talk to you tomorrow," Kim said, continuing to sound completely okay. "Send lots of pictures! Have a great time!"

"Bye, Mommy."

Kim held the phone up for a moment longer than she had to. She couldn't possibly have wanted more of that conversation. Finally, she put her phone down and slowly picked up all the things that she had pushed off the table—a few books, a Kleenex box, an empty coffee mug that somehow hadn't broken. She sat heavily back on the couch.

"That sucked," she said. "And really, Savannah is excited about a fruit basket? I don't think she has willingly eaten fruit since that caramel apple in October."

"I'm so sorry," Hannah said. She stood up slowly. The dizziness was gone. "Are you going to be okay? I mean, I can see you aren't okay, but I have to go and deal with the mess that is now my family. I didn't even tell you the rest of it, that we were evacuated from our house last night because of carbon monoxide, that Joel had to go to the ER."

"Is he okay?"

"Yeah, I think so. I haven't been home in hours. I really have to go. What will you do now?"

"Watch a few more episodes of *Six Feet Under*, take some Xanax, and go to sleep."

"Can you have lunch tomorrow?"

"No," Kim said. "I have a work thing I can't blow off. I am actually going to have to wash my hair and get dressed and leave the house, so don't worry. I'm not quite as bad as this looks."

The way she said it made Hannah think that despite all of this, despite the shocking sadness and the loneliness, she was all right. At least that's what Hannah had to believe to be able to leave.

"I'll call you tomorrow," Hannah said. "But call me if you want to talk sooner."

Kim walked over to her and gave her a hug, and Hannah wished she had been the one to offer the comfort.

"Do not forget what I said," Kim said. "Despite your examples of happily divorced women, I would do pretty much anything to be a whole family again."

CHAPTER FIVE

As soon as she walked in the door, the kids rushed to meet her, shoving each other out of the way to get to her. Normally she would sit down on the floor and give them an order to talk in, switching it up each time. She would listen, taking each of them onto her lap as they spoke and sniffing their heads. But she just couldn't do it now. She was going to cry, and she didn't want to scare them.

"Wait, I just need one minute," she said, pushing gently by. They looked stunned, standing side by side. She couldn't blame them for feeling dejected like that. She owed them—she had been away for hours, plus she hadn't even *talked* to Ridley yet today—but she just couldn't do it right at this moment. She still had her backpack flung over her shoulder, though her time at the Y seemed so long ago now, and she hoisted it up and walked toward the stairs. Joel was in the same place on the couch where she'd left him, and when she saw him, she wanted to scream. The rage she felt was so strong she had to force herself to keep moving, up the carpeted stairs, the kids still standing like statues, because what she wanted to do was smack him over the head with her bag and ask him how he could do this to her, how he could ruin their family, sending her down a dark path that was eerily similar to Kim's.

"Hannah," Joel called, still sounding weak, which annoyed her even more. "Can we just talk?" she heard him say, but she was up the stairs and in their room, closing the door behind her quietly and sinking to the floor and crying loud, choking tears that she tried her best to keep quiet because she guessed the kids were not too far away. She made sure the door was completely shut and moved to her bed. First she lay down, but she had a hard time breathing while she cried and tried to not make any sound, so she sat up. Seeing Kim like that had been almost scary. It was like she was trapped in her big, beautiful house, like the thing that once had been so comforting and seemed to be the perfect endgame had turned into a nightmare. She pulled out her phone and texted Joel.

> Can you keep the kids down there? I'm not feeling well but will try to get it together in time to go.

She didn't want to go, but she didn't want to stay here either. It was worse than she had expected. She showered and got dressed, thinking that her skin almost hurt and wondering if that was possible. Could skin catch all the badness and hold it inside?

Is Monica still here? she texted Joel before coming down. She knew she couldn't linger. She had to walk through and out.

Yes, and kids fed, Joel wrote back.

I'm going to come down and we have to go right out, I can't handle this, she texted.

No problem, he texted right back.

> Tell them I don't feel well and I'm sorry but I have to go right out.

No problem, he texted again.

She took one last minute to look around—it was the first time she'd done all these seemingly normal things like showering and getting dressed since she'd found out. But really what had she been doing when Joel had been with Tara, rolling around on rose petals? She had been here, taking showers and making beds and sitting on the orange couch and dealing with the kids—one after the other.

She opened the door slowly, half expecting to see the kids right out there, and went down the stairs. Joel was standing at the front door, wearing a tan corduroy blazer, looking reasonably strong and good, and she was relieved about that. She smiled at the kids, gave them a little eye roll as if to say, *Isn't this a pain,* followed by a wink to tell them it was all okay. Monica was in the kitchen, putting together bowls of ice cream.

"Be back soon," Hannah said quietly as Joel held the door for her, and she went through, waiting on the other side for him, her throat tight.

"The office is right on Broad. We can walk," Joel offered before she had to ask.

When they got to Broad, Hannah immediately thought of Kim, not too far south of where they were now, in her dark house and probably already asleep for the night, and she walked a little faster.

"Fight on!" she heard Joel say, really yell, and for a split second Hannah thought he was talking to her about them. Then she saw the couple coming toward them, both wearing gold and cardinal, the colors of USC, with big letters on the front of the man's shirt. The woman even had matching sneakers.

"Fight on!" they both called back to Joel, smiling as they passed.

"Now?" Hannah managed to say. "You have to do that now?"

"Did you see how happy that made them?" Joel said. "It was so easy."

So many things ran through her mind. Why was it so easy to make other people happy? Why couldn't he take the energy it took him to remember almost every single college rally cry in the country—she had never seen him miss one—and use it to focus on what was important: namely, not betraying his wife and family? And finally, there was that tiny piece of her that was always impressed. He was like a party trick, but instead of naming all the Kentucky Derby winners the way some people could, he could match any school to its mascot and cheer. When it suited her, she liked it. Now, though—well, now it was not only annoying but also another glimpse of what she was likely to lose in all of this.

"It's on the second floor," Joel whispered when they stepped inside. She followed him up the stairs, and at the landing she looked out the window. She was struck by how strange it was to be doing this in their neighborhood. She could see the tippy top of the tallest tree on their block.

"Hello," the woman greeted them as they took the last few steps. She was waiting in the doorway. "I'm Leslie Needway."

She reached out her hand, and Joel was right there, ready to shake.

"I'm Joel Bent," he said. "And this is my wife, Hannah. Thank you for seeing us on such short notice."

"I'm glad it worked out," Leslie said, but there was no emotion to her voice. Hannah didn't believe that she was really glad it had worked out. "Come on in."

The room was sparsely decorated, with a corporate-looking desk and a sofa and two chairs. Leslie sat on one of the chairs, and Joel sat on the couch. Hannah just stood there.

"Please, take a seat," Leslie said.

Hannah continued to stand.

Leslie shrugged and turned toward Joel. "We spoke briefly about what brought you in today. Is there more you can tell me?"

"What did he say?" Hannah erupted. "When he told you briefly about what brought us in today? Did he mention that he basically ruined everything we've built? That we have an amazing family and what I have always thought of as an amazing marriage—the actual partnership between us—and now that's all gone? That this is one hundred percent his fault?"

While Hannah spoke, Leslie had to crane her neck slightly to see her. Now she shifted and moved her chair around in jerky motions so she wouldn't have to do that.

"Something like that," Leslie said.

When nobody said anything more, Leslie cleared her throat.

"I understand this is a jolt to your system, Hannah, and that Joel has had more time to process this, to live with the choices he's made and to consider what that might mean to you, to your family," Leslie said. "I also understand Joel's hope is to make this work, to stay together."

Joel nodded vigorously. Hannah wanted to walk out. It felt like this stranger was already on Joel's side. Like she was his therapist first.

"Okay, then," Leslie said, smoothing her navy skirt with both hands, once slowly and then two quick swipes. "In order to do that we really have to get to the bottom of why Joel did this. I'm a firm believer in the concept that infidelity is a symptom of something else going on in the marriage. Was he lonely? Did he feel unloved or unfulfilled sexually?"

Hannah looked at Joel to see if he had set her up—it was something she never would have thought of before, but now she was doubting everything.

He shook his head, and his eyes were wide. "No, no," he said, waving her words away roughly with his right hand. "None of that. This had nothing to do with Hannah. Hannah is a wonderful wife, better than I deserve. She is kind and loving and caring. She is a great mother and a great daughter-in-law to my father. She always makes me feel special when I walk through the door. I would say our sex life is good—I mean, it's an effort to find time to be alone, but when we do, it is great."

By the time he reached the last sentence, he couldn't talk anymore. He was full-out crying, and Hannah's first thought was that he couldn't lose any more water; he was probably still dehydrated. Her next thought was that he could rot in hell for all she cared. She looked at the door. She was tired of standing.

Leslie reached across the table, lifting a tissue as her hand moved over the top of the Kleenex box and handing it to Joel in one well-practiced motion. She gave him a minute to calm down, but in the silence of the room, his sobs and gurgles were almost embarrassing. Finally, he wiped his eyes hard with his hands and sat up a little straighter, indicating that he was ready to listen.

"I see," Leslie said like she certainly didn't see. "Well, was there something Joel was doing or not doing to make you, Hannah, act out in any way? Was he withholding at all, or aggressive, or emotionally hard to reach? And Joel, I don't want to brush over what you just said. I did sense some disappointment when you mentioned your sex life."

"What?" he said, clearly flabbergasted. "That's not what I said. There is no disappointment."

"I'm leaving," Hannah said, cutting him off.

She expected a fight from Joel, but he was right behind her.

"I'm still going to have to charge you for the whole hour," Leslie said. "So you might as well hear this one bit of advice. Until you figure out the underlying problem that resulted in the symptom of infidelity, I don't think you are going to make much progress toward your goal."

"Thanks," Joel said over his shoulder as he followed Hannah through the door. When they were out on the street, they both started to laugh for the briefest few seconds, as though they had run away from a nasty teacher or camp counselor, but Hannah quickly caught herself, and the shocked expression on her face cut off Joel's laugh at its root.

"I'm sorry," he said. "I found her on Google. I'll do better tomorrow."

"I'm not going back tomorrow," Hannah said, turning away from Joel and moving to cross the street.

"No, not here. Not to see her," Joel said, following Hannah. "I'm going to find another therapist. A better therapist. You know how hard it is to find someone you connect with, right?"

She didn't answer.

"Well, it's hard. It's all chemistry and meshing philosophies. It's hard. I'm going to find someone better tomorrow, and if that one isn't good, I'll try again the next day and the next day and the next day."

"Fine!" Hannah said firmly. She just wanted Joel to stop saying *and the next day and the next day*.

"Okay, good," he said quietly. "Thank you."

Hannah dreaded the moment when she and Joel would be alone in their bedroom with no place to hide. She had not ruled out the possibility of sleeping on the couch, for either of them, but she also knew that could be a bad idea since they would undoubtedly be found out—the kids were up and down all night, often climbing in with them at some point, and would see that one of them wasn't sleeping in their bed. Her goal at this moment was to keep everything in their view as normal as possible.

There was no avoiding it; they ended up in bed together. Joel curled away from her, presumably asleep. She was wide awake. If it was possible to be even more awake than wide awake, that was what she was. She counted to one hundred. She silently recounted the kids' birth stories. She tried all her usual tricks, but she just couldn't get sleepy. Finally, after two hours had gone by, she pulled out her phone and set the alarm for five a.m. on the lowest possible volume. She looked over at Joel, who, she thought, had not moved at all since she'd gotten under the covers. She thought about how exhausted he must be, how just last night he'd been in the hospital. She moved over toward Joel, as close as she could get, and put her phone right next to her ear. In his sleep he turned toward her, and she relaxed when his familiar scent reached her, closing her eyes. She eased even closer, wedging herself right next to him, letting her hand touch his. And in minutes she was asleep.

When the alarm went off four hours later, it took her a minute to remember it all: the train ride, searching Joel's phone, Tara, the rose petals, Kim, Leslie Needway. Joel didn't react to the quiet but also blaring sound, which seemed to be sending an urgent message to do something bigger than just wake up, though she wasn't sure what exactly. She guessed with a sigh that that was the big question. She turned it off and, in the light of day, felt like an idiot. Why had she reached for him? Why did she still feel comforted by his physical presence in such a way that it was the only thing that would let her sleep? She was going to have to work on that—find another way—because right now, in this moment, she didn't want to ever be that close to him again. And, she wondered to herself, why was last night the first night in weeks that neither kid had joined them? Did they have a sense that there was a reason to stay away? It struck her as some sort of ironic joke. She put her phone on the bedside table and closed her eyes, knowing she would never fall back to sleep. Knowing she would soon have to start her second day on a team for which her main player, the one she most depended on, the one who always helped her when she needed it, was no longer qualified to participate. Basically, she realized, she was totally alone.

CHAPTER SIX

"That has to be the last one. I can't do this anymore," Hannah said as they drove back from their fifth unsuccessful attempt at finding a therapist. "This isn't working."

They were heading home on a particularly winding part of Kelly Drive after an especially disappointing session. This therapist had ended up answering numerous calls from his special-needs son while they were there, leaving Hannah feeling sorry for him and more alone than ever.

When Hannah drove this stretch, she had to cling especially hard to the wheel. Now she could see Joel was doing the same thing. It was just beginning to get dark, and despite what they were dealing with, it all looked so beautiful with its boathouses and amazing views of the Schuylkill River. The path was full of runners and bikers, and usually Hannah would say something like maybe on Saturday they should all come and ride their bikes. But she didn't even know if they would still be a family on Saturday.

"I just don't have it in me," she added.

Joel didn't say anything, and she sighed heavily and looked forward. Just up ahead was the turnoff for Smith Playground, where they sometimes brought the kids, and again, the same thought process—*We should*, and then *Oh, but not anymore*. Hannah was surprised when Joel put on the left signal and took the turn. He drove up and past the road to Smith Playground and eventually stopped in front of one of the historic mansions of Fairmount Park. It was painted yellow. Hannah had always meant to take a tour of the old homes, which had cool names like Lemon Hill and Strawberry Mansion, but she had never had the chance. Maybe now, on the days when the kids were with Joel, she would have that time.

He put the car in park and turned off the ignition.

"Please, please, please don't give up on me," he said. His hands were clenched, and he looked pale. It was going to be a problem if he went down the road of being sick every time they really talked about this. "I have never made a more terrible mistake in my life. I would do anything to make it not have happened."

"Well, it did happen," Hannah said. Though what exactly had happened, she still didn't know. She hadn't asked for the details, thinking maybe if she didn't have them, she could get through this, but she knew even without a therapist's help that that was shortsighted. She would always wonder. She had imagined details would emerge during one of these sessions, but so far they hadn't. She looked around. Off to one side she could see kids playing, and she had to squint to figure out they were throwing a Frisbee. The sky was turning a warm red. She took a deep breath.

"I think I need to know," she said quietly, feeling that by asking this question she was somehow allowing it to be true. She shook her head and turned slightly toward Joel. "Can you tell me exactly what happened?"

She braced herself, resisting the urge to cover her ears and hum loudly, and waited. Joel cleared his throat.

"I started going to that hotel, when? In February, I think. The end of February. Remember there was that crazy snowstorm the first time I was set to go, and I almost rescheduled? But I went, and it took forever to get there, one cancelled flight after another. By the time I arrived, I didn't feel great; I had a headache, and I don't know, I was probably just tired, but it seemed worse because I was away from you guys." Joel stopped and took a breath. He looked straight ahead as he talked. "I feel like I'm making one excuse after another here. I don't mean for it to sound that way."

"You haven't even said anything yet," Hannah snapped. "Can you just get to the bad part?"

"Well, it's all the bad part," Joel said. "But yes, I'll try. When I finally got to the hotel, I checked in normally, and then this woman came out from the back office. I don't know—for some reason she noticed me. She stopped me and asked if I needed anything. I assumed she knew I was with the hotel company and just wanted to go the extra mile. I told her it had been a tedious trip, blah, blah, blah. Anyway, about thirty minutes later there was a knock on my door. She had room service send up soup and tea." Joel stopped here. He glanced toward Hannah, then back outside. It was dark now, and the kids who had been playing on the field near them had stopped and were all heading in different directions.

"I had to thank her, of course, so I found her the next morning, and she joined me while I had coffee. It all seemed so, I don't know, professional. Like nothing out of the ordinary. And that was that. Then I came back two weeks later, and as soon as I walked in, she came to help me. She remembered everything I had told her about my last trip there and—"

"I am not going to be able to stand the play-by-play," Hannah said through gritted teeth, interrupting him. "Can you just get to it? We have to get home."

"I'm trying," Joel said quietly. "I'm sorry. So it went on like that. She had things sent to my room—first that soup, better coffee than they normally had in the rooms, a piece of cake. But then, at the end of March, maybe my fourth visit, she had champagne and strawberries sent up. I still thought it was okay, a typical thing you send to a hotel guest, like, I thought maybe she was trying to show me what the hotel could do. And here was my first big mistake: I called down to thank her, and she asked if she could come up."

Joel stopped talking. Hannah didn't want to hear any more, but she knew she might never get to this point again, the brink of Joel's betrayal, so she closed her eyes and didn't say anything.

"When she got there, she wasn't wearing her usual work clothes. She had on, I don't know, other things, revealing things, and I knew, I mean, I'm not stupid. But still, I thought I could handle it, that we were two professionals. That night, when we drank the champagne, I told her about you and the kids, and she told me about her own family. She was away from home overseeing the opening of the hotel, for months actually, with just a few trips back and forth. Her kids are older, in high school, but still, it seemed hard, and I liked talking to her about it; it made me feel less bad about being away from you, less alone. It started to feel like we were in some sort of club together. I felt closer and closer to her."

Again he stopped, took a breath.

"We texted a little after that, when I was here, and we joked about our families. One day she told me a story about a hotel guest who asked to have rose petals scattered all over the room in advance of his arrival; he said he was having a romantic tryst. We joked back and forth about that and how ridiculous that seemed. When I arrived the next time, in April, she was waiting for me in the lobby. She said she had something funny to show me. I checked in, and she came to my room with me—discreetly, of course—and my room was scattered with rose petals. Still, I laughed it off, and she let me, asking if we could meet in the bar that night. She said she had had a particularly hard few weeks. So I did. And we drank and drank, and then—"

"Okay, I get it," Hannah said. "I don't get it, but I can picture it. I—"

"Just let me finish," Joel said. "Please. So we went to my room, and we had sex. I won't emphasize how drunk I was, because I don't want it to sound like an excuse, but please know I was. And when I woke up the next morning, she was there, and I was sick. I don't know what it was, a virus, maybe, or something I ate. I felt awful. She left, had soup sent up again, and that was that. That's when I cut the trip short and came home, and I was sick that whole week. I knew I had to go back, for work, of course—I had left so many things unfinished. I also knew she would be there. I thought, *I can do this*. So many people have affairs of some sort. I thought you wouldn't know—how would you ever know?"

Hannah narrowed her eyes. She wasn't sure what she had expected.

"And so that's when I had part of that text exchange you saw. I felt better enough to travel, I went back a day earlier than planned, we joked about the rose petals. And when I got there, I don't know, I didn't like her anymore. I thought I would, but I felt nothing, except for continuing to feel sick. She came to my room, the rose petals were there, I, we . . . there was another time. And then I told her that it just wasn't for me. It just . . ."

"Drive home," Hannah said abruptly. "I need to be home."

Joel looked at her, surprised, nodded, and started the car. He took a breath.

"I know how awful this sounds," Joel said. "But I also want you to know that now you know everything. That is everything. It was the biggest mistake I have ever made. Please, let me try to figure out a way through. There must be a way through."

"I am starting to think the only way through is out," she said. "There is no going back to undo it. And now this thing that I thought we had, this unbreakable love, well, it doesn't seem so unbreakable anymore. No matter how many therapists we talk to, that will still be true."

"Out?" Joel repeated. The word sounded like it had had a hard time making its way from his voice box to her; it was twisted and strangled.

"Yeah," she said, feeling like she was gaining some momentum. She was finally doing something. "Out, like out of our bed, out of our house, out of the marriage."

"No," Joel said, and now she had that feeling again that if she pushed him too hard, he was going to lose it and throw up or worse. She didn't want to drive in the dark on the winding road.

"Please, just get us home."

"Sit with me, Mommy," Ridley said before Hannah was even fully through the door. "Be with me."

"Just for a few minutes," Hannah said, letting Joel deal with seeing Monica off. Hannah felt completely exhausted. She motioned for the kids to separate and make space for her between them on the couch. She might have been imagining it, but it seemed to her that since this had happened, they had been sitting much closer together than usual, like they were each other's only comfort. She sat down, and at the same time they snuggled in and grabbed an arm. It felt like it was choreographed. *Kids Clinging to Desperate Mother: A Musical.* Eventually Joel locked up for the night and got the kids to bed. Hannah made no move to help with any of it.

"I'll try again tomorrow," Joel said when he came back down the stairs.

"No, please, no," she said. "I told you, I can't do this anymore."

"There is going to be someone just right," Joel said almost to himself.

When he said the words *just right*, her heart sank. That was the thing they said to each other when all was well. She didn't want it to be a part of their new reality.

"I think you should sleep on the couch tonight," she said. But as soon as she said it, she wished she had left it more open. She thought of the other nights this week and how she hadn't been able to sleep until she'd moved next to Joel. What was wrong with her? She had to remind herself that he was no longer her safe place. *He got drunk with Tara and slept with her, twice.* Now he was the opposite of her safe place. And really, whether the part of her brain that allowed her to fall asleep believed that or not, she'd better start getting used to sleeping without him.

She expected him to push back, to beg her to let him sleep in their room, but he didn't say anything. He went to the kitchen and filled lunch boxes with napkins and white plastic utensils to save time in the morning. She watched from the couch, thinking, *Here is when I would usually ask if we had any yogurt*, or *Here is when I would ask Joel if he wanted to sneak some ice cream*; they had mint chocolate chip in the freezer. But they didn't talk at all—not a single word. She waited for Joel to ask if he could sleep in their bed; of course he was going to ask. But when she went up, he didn't say anything, and he didn't follow her. She could barely stand it, being alone in their room, brushing her teeth, thinking this could be her life from now on. Was that nausea she was feeling? Could she possibly be having a heart attack? It sort of felt like the symptoms she always read about. Should she ask for help? She tried to breathe through it. She almost wanted it to be true so she could have something that was more important than what they were dealing with to attend to, so she could go see Joel. But the more she focused on the symptoms, the harder they were to pinpoint. She was fairly sure she was going to be okay physically.

Ridley was the first one to come in.

"Where's Daddy?" she demanded.

"He had work to do," Hannah said, welcoming her into the bed and finally daring to turn out the light. Lincoln followed shortly after. He went right to Joel's side and looked for a long time, like maybe Joel had disappeared or was wearing a cloak of invisibility that might wear off if he looked hard enough.

Every time Hannah felt close to dozing off, she would imagine the details Joel had told her in the car, and she would be wide awake again. The hours passed slowly and miserably, but finally she could see the sky begin to lighten. When she couldn't stand it anymore, she got up and showered. She had plans to visit Richard—they had a meeting about his care—and she had an important work meeting with a company that was building a hotel on Washington Avenue in an old chocolate factory. They said their hope was to have every single thing about the hotel be local. They wanted Hannah to be in from the very beginning, to be one of the managers of the project, and to have a hand in every choice that was made. It was the sort of opportunity Hannah had always wished for. She couldn't cancel just because she hadn't slept. She couldn't cancel just because she now knew the details of the affair. She couldn't let Joel take this job away from her too.

Just as she reached for her phone to see exactly where and when her meeting was, it rang. Kim. She looked at the time. It wasn't even seven yet.

"Kim, are you okay?" she said into the phone, easing the bathroom door closed again.

"He took them to the castle," she said, like it was some riddle or fairy tale. Hannah could tell she was crying.

"The castle?"

"Cinderella's castle," she said. "I mean, of course they were going to go; you can't *not* go when you're at Disney, but for some reason I hadn't thought of that detail until Savannah posted a photo. *I* was going to take her there. Ever since they were babies, we read about Cinderella, remember? Michael even liked her. And Savannah was Cinderella for Halloween for her first three years. She is still her favorite, even though of course she would never admit it anymore. And now, well, now they've been to her home—without me."

"Kim," Hannah said, sitting on the closed toilet seat. "You know Cinderella isn't real, right? She doesn't have an actual home." But as soon as she said it, she regretted it. That wasn't the point. That didn't even begin to be the point. "Sorry," Hannah said. "Sorry."

"It's okay," Kim said, sniffling. "I'm not even calling to complain personally, if you can believe it. What I'm doing is sharing with you another devastating moment of divorce. This is it. This is divorce in all its misery. Please, Hannah, please take what I have said seriously. You do not want this to be you."

Ridley wasn't in love with Cinderella, but she did love the Minions more than anything. Well, more than most things—probably not more than Stinker. Hannah knew there was a ride at Universal Orlando that they had talked about going to—before Ridley lost interest. They had even researched the hotels in the park and decided that if they went, they would stay at the one with the Italian theme. She closed her eyes hard at the thought of missing that—of getting the call that they were all there and had just seen it while she was here alone, finishing her solitary tour of the mansions of Fairmount Park. She leaned over and took deep breaths.

"Kim, I'm so sorry you are going through this," Hannah said.

"Forget about me, it's too late for me," Kim said. "But it isn't too late for you."

"It might be," Hannah said.

When she got downstairs with the kids, they found Joel sleeping peacefully on the couch under Ridley's thin fleece *Despicable Me* blanket. *Perfect,* Hannah thought.

"Shhhhh," she said to the kids, putting her finger to her mouth. "Daddy still isn't feeling well. That's really why he slept down here. He didn't want to bother me. So let's let him sleep. Okay? Don't wake him up."

Hannah knew he had an important meeting this morning, at ten. Some of the executives from Minnesota were coming into town to discuss the finishing touches of the marketing campaign for the new Minneapolis hotel. It was a big deal that they were coming to him. She knew he wanted to impress the Minnesota office. She had the urge to yank the blanket away or, better yet, get a picture of him so the words *Despicable Me* were clear as day and send it out into the world on Facebook or Instagram. But she knew not doing anything, letting him sleep through the meeting, was the worst thing she could do, at least right now.

CHAPTER SEVEN

Hannah was surprised to find Richard still in bed, asleep, with the same peaceful-with-a-hint-of-being-tortured face she had just left on the couch at home. She turned, scowling. This was so unlike Richard, especially on the morning of his monthly care meeting. Or had the nurses fallen down on the job and not even tried to get him up yet today? As she began her angry march to the nurses' station, Reuben was there, coming up behind her in his usual way.

"Good morning," he said quietly.

She had to take a second to reshuffle. She was so ready to be combative, but she didn't want to come at Reuben with that. She cleared her throat. "He isn't up yet," she said.

"I know," Reuben said. "I was going to call you, but by the time it was all decided, I figured you were probably on your way. Is Joel here too?"

"Uh, no," she said. "He has some important meeting this morning."

"Well, then it's probably all for the best," Reuben said. He began to walk away from Richard's room back down the long hall, and Hannah followed.

"Richard was up earlier. He had breakfast, his usual big bowl of oatmeal with brown sugar and a drop of maple syrup, but then he went back to his room. He said he didn't want to talk about his care, he didn't want to talk about anything. I told him to rest a little, to think about it, but when I went to check on him—that was about fifteen minutes ago—he was back in bed asleep. He couldn't have done that by himself. He must have sweet-talked a nurse into helping him, but nobody is owning up. So I guess the meeting is cancelled. Let's go talk anyway; I just made some coffee."

"Sure, okay," Hannah said. She hadn't had coffee yet this morning. Joel usually made it. In the small conference room, Reuben handed her a full, steaming mug that said *Cup of Sunshine*.

"Oh, I'm really sorry to say this, but this is not my mug today," she said, not sure why she cared so much, but she did. "I definitely can't drink out of this mug."

"Why not?"

"I am anything but sunshine right now," she said, putting the mug on the table. "Can't we pour it into another mug?"

"Well, it doesn't say *you* are sunshine," Reuben said. "It basically says the coffee in the mug is sunshine, and that is probably true. Maybe it will improve your mood, make you feel sunnier."

"Can't do it," she said, wandering away from the mug, thinking it was probably time to go. She needed to think about her meeting later that day.

She watched as Reuben scanned his mugs and pulled one out, then smoothly poured the coffee from the first mug into that one and brought it to her.

"Thank you," she said, turning the mug so she could see the front. It said *Crappity Crap Crap*, the words surrounded by dainty painted pink flowers and leaves. "Perfect."

Reuben then poured his own coffee into the *Cup of Sunshine* mug, held it up as if to say, *Cheers*, and took a long sip.

"Can you sit?" he asked.

"I guess, for a few minutes," she said, pulling a seat away from the oval table and sitting down. She took a sip of the coffee. It was delicious.

"Well, the obvious question is, What is going on with you that you find the sunshine mug so inappropriate but the crappity mug just right?" Reuben asked, choosing the seat directly across the table from Hannah. Hannah allowed the phrase *just right* to pass over her, hearing it but letting it go.

"That is a good question but one I'm not prepared to answer," she said.

"All you Bents," Reuben said warmly. "Shutting down today."

"Speaking of which, what is going on with Richard?"

"To be perfectly honest, I think he's depressed," Reuben said seriously. "I know we talked about that possibility the other day. And this, going back to bed, not wanting to talk about his care—it's classic, really. Also, he hasn't wanted to be out in the lounge at all. People are asking for him. They miss him. On the flip side, he ate his oatmeal, so his appetite hasn't been affected. I'm relieved about that."

"Well, that's good, I guess, but I'm really worried," Hannah said. "I mean, even three weeks ago, maybe a little longer, he was really a completely different man. I can't imagine what has changed." She felt her phone buzz in her purse but ignored it. It buzzed again, and she pulled it out. Two texts from Joel. Why didn't you wake me? And I slept through my meeting. She put the phone back in her bag without responding.

She was thinking that even the *Crappity Crap Crap* mug wasn't going to cut it today. She needed something stronger.

"I should go," she said, getting up.

"I'll walk you out," Reuben said.

As they walked toward the exit, the image of the old lady, Kim, came back into Hannah's mind, since this was exactly where she had encountered her.

"Hey, I wanted to ask if you know an older lady—I think her name is Kim. At least, she had a blanket with the name Kim on it. She's tiny, and she was sitting out here by herself the last time I was here."

Hannah felt her phone begin to ring. *Joel,* she thought.

Something cloudy took over Reuben's open expression.

"Kim Sokolov?" he asked.

"I don't know, maybe," Hannah said. "She is really tiny, like, her feet don't touch the ground when she's sitting down. I want to do something for her, I don't know, maybe give her something. Or maybe just spend a little time with her if she's lonely. Is she lonely?"

"Well, no, she isn't lonely. She's dead."

Hannah took two steps back. "No. No, it must be a different Kim," she said, feeling her phone stop and then start again. "She was just here, sitting right here."

"When was that?"

"Not quite a week ago, maybe five, six days ago? Right after the last time I saw you."

"What time?"

"What time?" Hannah asked. What difference could that make? But she thought back. She had wanted to be home by about five; it had been that endless day that had begun in the emergency room and ended with that awful Leslie. She had gone swimming, then come here. She'd talked to Reuben and Richard. "Three? I think it was around three."

"I am really sorry to say that is the same Kim. She was found here around four. She was sitting right there, covered in some sort of blanket. That's right," Reuben said like it was all coming back to him now. "People thought she was asleep, so nobody said anything. But then her husband came down and figured it out. I wasn't here. I had just left. But apparently it was a very sad scene. He was distraught."

"Oh my God," Hannah said. "That is so shocking—and sad. I mean, she seemed so peaceful when I saw her. And I wondered if she had a family or if she was alone."

"Yeah, one of the few married couples we had living here," Reuben said. "Everyone loved them. They had just celebrated their seventieth wedding anniversary. We had a big cake right here. It isn't every day you can do that."

"So how's her husband now?"

"Distraught, beyond distraught," Reuben said. "We don't expect he'll be with us for too much longer."

Hannah didn't know what to say. She felt inexplicably sad considering she really didn't know either of them.

"I must have been the last person she talked to," Hannah said. "I wasn't even going to stop to help her."

"But you did!" Reuben said in his usual positive way. "Listen, let's see if we can reschedule that meeting for Richard early next week."

"That sounds good," Hannah said quietly, still thinking about Kim and her husband.

Reuben reached out and touched Hannah's arm. "Pace yourself," he said kindly.

"Thanks," she said.

Hannah continued to ignore her ringing phone, and as she backed out of her spot, she saw an old man at the far end of the porch, sobbing. Kim's husband. It had to be. He was sitting on a chair, looking straight ahead. She knew that if she lowered her window, she would be able to hear him—he looked like he was making a lot of noise. The other thing she was certain about was that if she heard him, that noise would haunt her all day. She cranked up the music and drove away. But when she was on Broad heading north, she made a jerky right turn onto Porter and drove back to the nursing home. She pulled into a spot, breathing hard, and got out of the car. He was still there, but he was quiet now, staring off. Where was everyone? Why wasn't a nurse with him? Hannah walked over slowly. She didn't think this was against the rules in any way, but she wasn't sure.

"Excuse me," she said gently when she was about two feet away. She could see his nose was running, but he made no move to wipe it. "My name is Hannah. I knew your wife, Kim."

He looked at her eagerly, and she thought she could have done that in a different way. She hadn't really *known* her.

"I met her," she continued, trying to explain. "She was such a nice lady."

The man nodded and smiled.

"I just want to say how sorry I am," she said. "I'm so sorry for your loss."

"Thank you," the man said so clearly it surprised her.

She waited, but there really didn't seem to be anything more to say. She wanted to ask if they had had a good marriage, if they had had any bumps in the road. Had either one of them ever had an affair? What did it take to be married for seventy years? But she didn't; she couldn't. Instead she bowed slightly and backed away, making it to her car before she was crying so hard it was embarrassing. She pulled out her phone. Four missed calls from Joel. She called him back.

"What?" she asked harshly when she heard his voice, certain he was calling to complain about oversleeping.

"I think I finally found a really good therapist. Really good. I think this person will help us. Her name is Marjorie Snow—she's in the Northeast, near Bustleton—and . . ."

"And what?"

"And I made an appointment for tonight, at six thirty."

Hannah was going to say no. She had had it, and she didn't believe for one second that tonight would be any different from any of the other nights. But then she looked over at Kim's husband. A nurse had finally come, and she helped him get up. It was hard, a huge effort, and Hannah could see he was crying again.

"Fine," she said. "I'll go. But this is the last time."

CHAPTER EIGHT

Hannah usually loved driving around the Northeast—it was such an interesting part of Philadelphia, with hidden parks and Russian markets and an endless stream of row homes. A few years ago, the local restaurant critic had done a roundup of restaurants in this sometimes-underappreciated part of the city, and ever since then Hannah had liked coming here even more, hoping to slowly try every single place he'd recommended. But tonight, she didn't love being here at all. In fact, she felt worse than she had in days, if that were possible. After she'd agreed to see Dr. Snow, she'd been mad at herself. She had to stand her ground. And so before her meeting she'd done a little research and found two divorce lawyers. She planned to reach out to both of them tomorrow.

They drove by a Chinese restaurant they had been to not too long ago, on a lazy, happy Saturday. She knew they were also near an Italian place the critic had raved about, one they had talked about trying soon, on a date night, without the kids. She had to close her eyes to keep the tears from falling. Finally, Joel pulled up to a house that wasn't a row home. It was more like a tiny castle standing all by itself on a corner.

"This is it," Joel said.

"What is this place?" Hannah said, then wished she hadn't. Her plan had been to not say a word until they were with the new therapist.

"Look, it has a turret," Joel said.

Hannah followed Joel up an inside staircase that wound around like in a mini lighthouse. Tiny stained glass windows lined the wall as they went up and up to a wooden door. Joel hesitated, then pushed it open, and sure enough, they found themselves in a waiting room.

"Good evening," a woman greeted them warmly. "I'm glad you found your way. Please come in. And you can leave that door open; there's a nice cross breeze, and I'm not expecting anyone else tonight."

"Thanks," they both mumbled.

Four chairs were arranged in a big square. Dr. Snow sat in one, and Joel picked the seat next to her. Hannah chose the seat across from Joel, leaving an empty chair between them on the other side, so Hannah didn't feel too close to him. Hannah sat back and took a deep breath.

"First of all, let me say welcome. Thank you for giving me a chance to help you sort out this very difficult situation you are now in," Dr. Snow said. "I understand, from what Joel told me quickly on the phone, that it has been a very hard few days. Hannah, he told me a bit about what's going on. My two takeaways from my very brief conversation with Joel are that his affair is over and that he wants to stay married to you. I mention those two things because Joel asked me to—he wanted to be very clear about them. Now I want to hear from you, if you're ready to talk. I know it is all very raw, and you may be all over the place with your thoughts. That's okay. This is a process. You can say anything here."

Joel looked at Hannah hopefully. She'd come in thinking she would just listen and let them do the work, but she was surprised to find there was something about Dr. Snow that made her want to talk.

"I realize you don't know me, you don't know us as a couple," Hannah began. "But if someone had told me before we went to New York that I would discover something like this on Joel's phone, that we would be sitting here now, that I would be thinking about what my life might be like without him in it, I would have thought that person was the craziest crayon in the box. Sorry—strange thing to say about something so serious, I know, but my kids are really into crayons right now."

"I like the analogy," Dr. Snow said. "Am I hearing you right? Are you thinking at this moment that you want to end the marriage? That you don't want to be together any longer?"

Hannah didn't answer right away. Hearing the therapist say those words made Hannah think two things. The first was that it was possible to leave Joel—in the realm of possibility in the world, that option existed. The second thing she thought was, *What are the other options?*

Hannah cleared her throat. "I feel betrayed," she said reasonably. "I feel like the person I trusted the most in the world was not actually trustworthy, which makes everything seem undependable. I feel completely blindsided. I missed any and all signs, if there were any, and it seems like the thing you do when your husband has an affair—you get a divorce. Am I wrong about that?"

Dr. Snow shook her head, and it finally occurred to Hannah who she reminded her of—Dr. Melfi on *The Sopranos*. Hannah loved the show so much. She and Joel were probably the last people in the country to watch it, which for her made it more fun somehow. They were on the last season; it was a long one, and they probably had about fifteen episodes to go. She never, ever skipped ahead or watched it without him, but now she would. She would have to.

"It's true that many people choose to end the marriage after discovered infidelity," Dr. Snow said slowly. "But some don't. Some use the chance to reevaluate their relationship and sometimes even strengthen it."

"How is that possible?" Hannah said. "That does not seem possible."

"Many therapists believe that when someone goes outside the marriage, it's a symptom of something else that isn't right between husband and wife," Dr. Snow said. "That someone isn't getting the warmth or intimacy or support or whatever it might be that they need, so they seek it out somewhere else. And that can be the case. But I personally believe that affairs can also happen in happy marriages. Someone is drawn to someone else not because they don't like their spouse but because they are just drawn to that other person—and they have a momentary or sometimes longer-than-momentary lapse of judgment. Basically they make a mistake that, in this case, they almost always come to regret. Now of course that doesn't happen when someone falls in love with the other woman or the other man, when they want to be with them only and no longer with their spouse, when they can't let them go, but that does not sound to me like what's going on here. Am I right about that, Joel?"

"Yes," he said quickly. "You are very, very right about that. I would do anything to undo it, to make it not have happened, to just say to Tara, 'No, thank you, I'm fine.'"

Joel had been looking okay, even good, but now that pale-green color passed over his face. He looked around.

"Is there a bathroom?" Hannah asked.

"Through there," Dr. Snow said, pointing. Joel jumped up and ran. They heard the door shut followed by the sound of gagging.

"He keeps throwing up," Hannah said. "Every time we really talk about it. We ended up in the emergency room the night I saw his texts."

"Did you go with him?" the doctor asked.

"To the hospital?" Hannah asked. "Yes. Reluctantly, but yes."

"And how was that?" she asked. "I mean, you had just found out, right? Were you able to care for him at all? Help him?"

"Well, yeah," Hannah said. She looked toward the bathroom door, which was still closed, and cleared her throat. She was about to tell her about climbing onto the gurney with Joel, maybe ask if she had any thoughts about that, but then she thought, *No way, I'm not going to share that, with her or with anyone.* When Hannah thought about it, she felt ashamed. Like she was weak, like she still needed Joel no matter what he did to her. Dr. Snow looked at her expectantly, but she just shook her head. Finally, they heard the toilet flush, and Joel came back out.

"Sorry, sorry," he said, his voice slightly gravelly. "That's been happening a lot lately."

"That's what Hannah said," Dr. Snow said. "Look, I don't want to push either of you too much tonight. I think this is a really good start. I'm not inside your heads, and I'm certainly not in your bedroom with you, but just the fact that you are both here tells me a lot. There's something about your body language, both of you, that makes me think we can do a lot of good work together."

"All this from a slice of, um," Hannah said, sounding somewhat hysterical. It was something Tony Soprano said to his therapist after she made an intuitive remark about him. She could not think of the word, which at that moment seemed important, like it was somehow a key to something. "A slice of . . ."

"Gabagool," Joel said quietly.

Yes, that was it. She just wished she had thought of it.

"Sort of like that madeleine of Proust's," Dr. Snow said knowingly before Hannah had a chance to explain. It was the reference Dr. Melfi made in response to Tony Soprano's gabagool comment. Hannah sat back in her seat. Whether she wanted to admit it or not, Joel had found a good therapist.

"Great show," Dr. Snow said.

"The best," Joel said.

"So what do you think?" Dr. Snow asked. "Are you willing to give it a shot? Can you come back next week?"

"Yes," Joel said quickly.

"Hannah?"

If she hadn't reminded Hannah of Dr. Melfi, she might have said no in that moment, but something stopped her from doing that.

"I'll try," Hannah said—mumbled, really.

"Okay, let's say same time next week," Dr. Snow said. "And for the record, I do think it is possible to get through this and heal from it and be at least as strong as you once were on the other side. But it isn't easy, and ultimately both of you have to want it or at least want to try. Let me leave you with one thought before we call it a night. This is important, and it is sometimes a hard thing to get your head around. Your first marriage as you know it is over. You will never again be *that* Hannah and *that* Joel, the ones who met and fell in love and never, ever betrayed the other or thought of a life without the other. You will have to put that relationship and all the expectations and rules that went with it away. But now you have a chance to embark on a second marriage together. You are different people. Hannah, your eyes are open in a way they weren't before. And Joel, you have done something you regret, and you now tangibly know what you have to lose. But you are still Hannah and Joel. You still live in your same house with your kids. And you can still love each other and be married. Think about that until next week, okay? Do you think you guys will be okay? Will you be able to move through your days until we see each other again?"

"Eventually I can see coming once a week," Joel said, his voice still raspy. "But no, I don't think we can. For this first week at least, can we come more often? Can we come every day?"

Dr. Snow reached for her appointment book. She leafed through each day, putting her finger on the page and looking up and down, mumbling to herself about moving this person here and that person there.

"Hannah." She looked up. "Are you on board, at least for now? Do you want to try this? Are you willing to come each day for a week or so before moving to a weekly schedule?"

What would Tony Soprano say? she wondered. And then she remembered he and Carmela broke up and came back together. He, of course, was a terrible example of a faithful husband—that was really the point, she guessed—but still. The whole time they were apart, she rooted for them to get back together, and when they did, despite everything, it seemed right. She knew it wasn't going to be that easy for her and Joel; she knew she wasn't a fictional wife on a fictional show where two people could get over a fictional affair with no real-life consequences, but she could give it one week before facing the inevitable. In fact, that would be her plan: one week and then she would call the divorce lawyers.

"I'm willing," she said.

Every day for the rest of that week, Hannah felt like a zombie, an extra on *The Walking Dead*, but as they made their way up I-95 to Dr. Snow's little castle, she felt herself wake up and tried to shift from the zombie apocalypse to New Jersey mob life. She thought of Tony and Carmela and Meadow and AJ, and by the time they turned onto the street and spotted the turret, Hannah felt not like herself, exactly, but like a new version of herself.

In the office at the top of the winding stairs, they talked about if it was really possible to recover from a betrayal, and Dr. Snow's never-wavering answer was always yes, it was possible, if both partners wanted it to be. While Hannah pushed to focus on the here and now, Dr. Snow spent some time wanting to understand who they had been before this had happened. What did they argue about? What was their never-ending fight, the thing that kept coming up that had no resolution? Slowly, over the course of the week, it became clear that they'd never loved each other less than they thought they had, but they had been so busy, so caught up in taking care of everyone, that sometimes a month would go by when they didn't have sex. Each time there was a tiny revelation like that, Joel always jumped in to say that was no excuse for what he had done, and Hannah firmly agreed.

"The thing is," Hannah said during one of their sessions, "that I used to always be able to defuse my anger because I knew, without question, that I wanted to be with Joel, to stay married to him, so I could ask myself, *What is your endgame?* and realize there was no need to keep the fight going."

"I never knew that," Joel said quietly. "That you had that internal dialogue, I mean."

"I did," Hannah said. "That's why this is so hard. I don't know what my endgame is anymore. Or worse, I have a different endgame now." She looked right at Joel when she said this, watching his color drain away.

Dr. Snow also talked about the different roles they might have now—how even when Joel got tired of being the sorry one and had the inevitable urge to get on with it, he couldn't, he did not have that luxury, she explained. He had to stay in that role as long as Hannah needed him to. He saw no problem with that and said he would remain in that position forever if it would keep Hannah with him. With Dr. Snow they talked and talked and talked. What they didn't do was talk when they were alone.

"Tomorrow night I'm giving you homework," Dr. Snow said as they were leaving her after their fifth visit. "I want you to have Monica come early, and I want you to have dinner, just the two of you, before our time together here. It's okay if it doesn't go well. It's okay if you fight or have nothing to say—we can talk about all of that when you get here. But just try it."

"No way," Hannah said while Dr. Snow was still talking. "Coming here is one thing, but no, I won't. That would be like agreeing that this is all okay. I'm not going to do it."

"Can we sit down again?" Joel asked.

Hannah didn't want to. She was getting tired of this. They could talk and talk and talk, and no matter what they said, Joel would still have had an affair with Tara.

"Please?" Joel said.

Dr. Snow sat down. Hannah knew they were going over their time. It was so unlike Joel to do something like that. Hannah continued to stand. Joel kept his eyes on her and moved back to his seat.

"This won't take long," he said to Dr. Snow. "I've hesitated to bring this up for so many reasons. My father asked me not to, for one. More than that, though, I don't want it to seem like I'm making an excuse, because there is no excuse for what I did. But Hannah, maybe it will give you some insight."

Hannah didn't want insight. In her mind the words *talk is cheap* ran on a loop. She had said a week, and they were almost there. Maybe it had been enough time. Maybe she would call the lawyers tomorrow, decide which one she liked best, and move forward.

"My parents had some infidelity trouble of their own," Joel said. "My mother was unfaithful, on two different occasions, if I know the whole story. It was, well, it was awful, but they got through it. It didn't break them apart."

Hannah was so stunned she had to work hard to remain standing. She hadn't really known Joel's mom well—she'd been sick when they'd started dating. But still, they'd seemed like the perfect family; there'd never been an indication that they'd been anything but.

"Does this change anything for you, Hannah?" Dr. Snow asked.

"No," Hannah said.

"Well, will you reconsider my request? Will you have dinner with Joel tomorrow night? It doesn't mean anything. It is not an admission of acceptance—I want to make that very clear right now to both of you."

Poor Richard, Hannah thought. And as if he were reading her mind, Joel said, "Please don't ever tell my father you know. Please. It would kill him."

"I'll think about dinner," Hannah said, surprising herself. "Make the plans, and I'll see how I feel."

Joel took care of it all, arranging babysitting with Monica and making a reservation at the Italian restaurant in the Northeast that Hannah had always hoped to go to. Hannah had every intention of saying no, she wasn't going to go, but she never said it, and when it was time to walk out the door and she could either make a scene or go, she just went.

Hannah had a piece of paper with the divorce lawyers' names and numbers folded in her pocket, and she decided she would talk as little as possible until they got back to Dr. Snow, at which time she was going to say she had tried her best, but she just couldn't do it anymore. Once they were seated, though, Hannah didn't want to wait a minute longer. Enough was enough.

"This was a bad idea," she said, putting down her menu and lifting her napkin off her lap. "Can you call Dr. Snow to see if we can come earlier?"

"What? No," Joel said soothingly. "We'll have a nice dinner, and then we'll go see her. We'll see her soon."

"Joel, I can't sit here next to you and pretend things are okay. I can't order spaghetti and an arugula salad and act like you didn't do a terrible, terrible thing to me. How am I supposed to do that?"

"I don't know," Joel said honestly. "I just don't know."

"This is all for nothing in the end, I'm sorry to say. I gave myself a deadline, one week, and I've sat in her office and listened to her say that infidelity doesn't have to mean the end, and I believe that she *believes* that. But what I believe is that you lied to me, you had sex with another woman, and you just must not have ever loved me as much as I thought you did."

"No," Joel said, pushing up out of his seat like there was something important to tend to and then sitting back down. "No. None of those things. I mean, yes, I did those bad things. But I love you; I have always loved you at least as much as you thought I did—more—always more."

"Then why?" Hannah asked. "No, don't answer that. We'll just go around in the same circles we've been going around in all week. Please, let's go, I don't think I can even face a server here. And I can't stand being around other people. They are either happy and unscathed or miserable and betrayed, and I can't see another couple without wondering which category they fall into. It's exhausting. If we can't make our appointment earlier, we can just wait in the car. At least we'll be there."

Joel stood up. "Let me just—at the very least, let me get us a glass of wine. I'll tell them we might not order, that I don't feel well. The place isn't crowded; they won't mind, I think. Please, just one glass?"

Joel looked pale and was getting paler by the second, and Hannah thought, *Uh-oh.* She had considered showing him the paper with the lawyers' names on it to prove she was serious, and now she was glad she hadn't. She didn't have to do that in public. This had been a mistake, clearly, but now she just had to get through it.

"Fine, fine," she said quickly. "I'll have a glass of red."

It was a relief when he left the table and walked the short distance to the bar. She settled her napkin back on her lap and took a deep breath. In a few minutes he returned with two glasses of red wine. Hannah took a long sip.

She wasn't going to talk—really, she wasn't going to—but she heard herself talking anyway.

"Here's how I know this is all a waste of time," she said. "You know how Dr. Snow said we could start our second marriage together? Really, that's the only thing that kept me going back to her this week: I was curious to see if it made any sense, if it seemed possible. But the thing is I wish we could still be the old us, so how am I supposed to get from the old us to the new us? All I feel is anger and disbelief. Oh, and I feel betrayed. And I feel like I don't know you. So the new us, our second marriage, as Dr. Snow put it, seems to be our first marriage minus all the good and plus a whole lot of bad. That doesn't seem like a good marriage to me. Does it to you?"

Joel was shaking his head. He looked as pale as she had ever seen him, and she wondered if he had already located the bathroom. She watched as he took shallow breaths through his mouth and closed his eyes for a few seconds. She sighed, thinking this was where it went downhill. He would sprint to the bathroom, and that would be that for now. In that moment she wanted him gone, from the table, from the restaurant, from her life.

She squinted her eyes and looked right at him. "Have you thought for one minute about how you would feel if the tables were turned? If I had had an affair? I should have an affair," she said, spitting out the words. "I mean, why not? You did it. Why shouldn't I? And then, when I'm done and satisfied, maybe I'll be ready to start our second marriage." She finished her wine and wished another full glass would magically appear. Her heart was beating so fast it made her feel slightly nauseated, and she was having a hard time holding Joel's gaze, but she did not want to be the first one to look away.

Finally, he shifted his eyes to the table, his face alarmingly pale. The words *I don't mean it* ran through Hannah's mind. But she willed herself to not say them. She watched as he rose from his chair and backed away, looking at her until he couldn't anymore. He bolted to the left and into the bathroom. She wondered if he had asked for a table not too far from the restrooms. The main dining room was in a completely different room; there were just a few tables near the bar. That forethought would be just like him. So why, when he'd made the monumental choice to sleep with Tara, had he not thought it through the way he did everything else?

The last thing she wanted was to have an affair, put herself out there, have to look good, have to be in such close proximity to a stranger. She had done that already when she was dating, before she'd met Joel. She was finished with that. But should she? For the first time she really let herself think about Tara. What did she look like? What was so irresistible about her? She pictured Joel naked with another woman. Had Tara run her hand over the birthmark on Joel's shoulder the way she always did? Had Joel touched Tara's breasts the way he did Hannah's? She shook her head, trying to get rid of the images, but they wouldn't leave her. Instead she shifted her thoughts to herself lying naked with another man. It was an impossible picture to conjure up, and yet was it? Yes, it was totally and completely impossible to imagine; it was ridiculous, really.

When Joel got back to the table, his forehead sweaty, he wiped his mouth with the back of his hand and sat down gingerly in his seat. No color had come back to his face.

"Are you sure?" he asked, like the last five minutes hadn't happened, like he was just continuing the conversation. "Because it sounds awful to me, but at this point I'll do anything." He closed his eyes and leaned his head back.

Hannah was going to say to forget it, that she wasn't about to stoop to his level, but now she sat up straight and looked at him. He had bluish circles under his eyes, and his skin still had that slightly green look to it. She had the urge to flick her finger at his cheek or strangle him a little, not completely, just until his eyes bulged. She didn't want to have an affair, not one bit. Though maybe it would feel good to lie on some rose petals of her own and have Joel know about it. But where the heck was she going to find someone to have an affair with? She thought of Lance, the single-dad lifeguard and his Bob Marley soundtrack. She thought of Larry, the man at the bakery who had the most beautiful gray hair and always gave her extra lemon bars. She always wondered what that was all about. Now could be her chance to find out. If Joel could do it, then she could too. Why not? And the best part was that he would suffer. He would know how bad it felt to be on that other end, wondering about another hand touching the person you thought only you would touch in that way for the rest of your lives. Yeah, she was beginning to like this idea. This was a great idea. Not everything had to be so black and white. He broke the rules, so now the rules were ripe for breaking. Plus, she was so tired of being the one wronged. This would let her take charge. She was taking back the power. She leaned toward him.

"I am one hundred percent sure," she said, knowing she might send him running right back to the bathroom, but she didn't even care. She was actually getting *used* to his throwing up. And if she did end up leaving anyway, if the road to their breaking up could not be detoured, this would make for an easier transition. She would already be back in the dating game. This was smart on so many levels, she thought. Very smart.

"I'm going to do it," she said, more confidently now. "I'm going to have an affair."

PART TWO—
BOOM!

CHAPTER NINE

Paramour or no paramour, Hannah needed a haircut.

"Do you think we can do something different?" she asked Cami, who had been cutting her hair for longer than she had been married. In fact, Cami had cut her hair for her wedding day and her engagement photos. The first time Hannah had left the house alone with Lincoln when he was an infant had been for a trip to Cami's. It had gone slowly because Cami had kept putting down the scissors to reinsert the pacifier into the crying baby's mouth. And now that she thought about it, Cami had cut her hair before her first date with Joel, which by Joel's calculations had been their third date.

"Sure," Cami said, lifting her limp hair and letting it drop. "Like what?"

"You're the professional," Hannah said. "Do you have any ideas?"

Hannah's hair had looked pretty much the same for the last fifteen years—straight, below her shoulders, without bangs, and brown, though now there was some gray. It was a teenager's hairstyle; she knew that, but most of the time she put it in a ponytail or a messy bun, which she liked being able to do. She wore it down only after it had just been washed.

"Should I cut bangs?"

"Ugh, I don't know," Hannah said. "Maybe. Do men like bangs?"

"I don't know," Cami said. "Did you ask Joel?"

"This isn't about Joel."

"What?" Cami said, standing behind her but looking her in the eyes through the mirror. "What other men do you know?"

"That's the big question," Hannah said. And then she started to cry.

Weeks had passed since she'd announced she was going to have an affair, and she hadn't done anything about it. That night, after they had gotten home from Dr. Snow, to whom they still hadn't said a word about Hannah's proposed affair, Joel had come to her with a piece of paper and a pen.

"Can we set some rules?" he had asked sheepishly.

"No," she'd said. "Did I get to set rules before you lay down with Tara?"

"No," he'd said slowly. "But can we anyway?"

It was just the sort of remark she would usually find endearing. They'd stood there, looking at each other. Joel had kept making a move to talk and then thinking better of it. *Rules?* Hannah had thought. *Aren't they all broken by this point?*

"Well," Joel had said slowly, lifting the pen as though he were getting ready to write something down. "I'll start with an easy one. The kids can't find out."

She had continued to look at him for a few seconds, and then she'd shaken her head, finally walking away from Joel and his paper and pen. Just before she'd moved up the stairs, she had turned.

"Screw you, Joel," she had said quietly. "Just screw you."

"Wait," Cami said now, coming around to face Hannah. "What's going on? Why are you crying?"

"I'm, it's, ugh," she said, glad there wasn't anyone else in the small salon at the moment.

"Take your time," Cami said soothingly. "I don't even have another appointment until after lunch. Mrs. Savage cancelled; she said her cat was too sad to leave this morning."

"Oh my God, she still comes in?" Hannah said, wiping at her eyes. "Honestly, I didn't even know she was still alive. What is she, ninety-five?"

"Ninety-one," Cami said. "But the saddest part is that her cat died a year ago."

Hannah couldn't help it—she laughed.

"That's awful," she said. "Sorry, that is really awful. My emotions are all over the place."

"Yeah, I can see that."

"Joel had an affair," Hannah said. "I found out about a month ago. Anyway, long story short, it was over when I found out. He said he never loved her. He wants to stay married to me. But it's been so hard. I'm so mad. I mean, we'll be sitting there eating pork chops with the kids, and one second I'll be thinking, *Joel was so smart to fry the onions and apples with this*, and then literally the next second I will be so overwhelmed with rage that the only thing holding me back from smacking him over the head with the cast-iron pan is not wanting to freak out the kids. But then I can't eat, and I can barely pretend to carry on a conversation. It is just so bad. I keep getting migraines because I feel so much anger, but there's no place to put it most of the time."

"Yeah, Seth had an affair," Cami said, just like she was saying, *Yeah, Seth likes coffee too.*

"What?"

"Oh yeah, I don't talk about it because I don't want people to think I'm a victim or that I'm married to someone who would rather be with someone else, but yeah, he did. That was, like, three years ago."

"And you stayed married?"

"Yeah, we did," Cami said. "We had just had Jezebel. Violet was four. It was a hard time in our marriage. You know what they say: the seven-year itch. Anyway, my next-door neighbor told me. She saw him with her—the other woman." When she said *other woman*, she used her fingers to make air quotes.

"But he wanted to stay married?"

"That's debatable," she said. "But I think he believes in hell. And the wrath of his parents. It was a very difficult time. But it's better now. I don't even think about it every day anymore. And our family is still our family. We still get to have Thanksgiving dinner together and go to Violet's softball games together. And when I'm sick, he brings me tea. That was one of the things I was most scared about: What would I do if I got sick and I was all alone with two little kids? So I don't have to worry about that."

Hannah closed her eyes, and the image of her den in the house she'd grown up in popped into her mind. She'd been about ten, and her mother had been sick and lying on the bright-yellow couch. Hannah had known she had to take care of her; there was nobody else. Her father had died the year before, and it was the first time Hannah had had that sense that it was her or nobody—there was absolutely no safety net. She shook her head; she did not like that memory at all. She opened her eyes to find Cami looking at her, clearly concerned.

"So your hair," Cami said gently. "I'm going to cut long layers. I'll make it look great. Are you thinking of stepping out on him? Is that what this is about?"

"Well, yes," Hannah said, not meeting her eyes. "I'm embarrassed to even say this, but I was so angry, so completely beside myself, that I threatened to have an affair too. And now I feel like I have to. Also, I sort of want to. I mean, I do and I don't. But I haven't dared yet."

Cami nodded, her eyes wide, and Hannah had the sense that she thought she was absolutely nuts. She never should have said anything. But in her usual way, instead of backing down and saying less, now she felt like she had to explain. So she told her about the night at the Italian restaurant with Joel and the whole thought process that had led her to the idea.

"And he said okay?" Cami asked incredulously.

"Well, he didn't like it," Hannah said. "But yeah, he basically said okay. I know it sounds completely bananas. I think so, too, but at this point I think he'll try anything to stay together."

"You're lucky," Cami said. "He must really love you."

What Hannah wanted to say was, *Really? That's your measure of love?* She wanted to add that if he really loved her, really and truly, this would never have happened in the first place. But she let it go. As bad as it was, it seemed better than what Cami had had to deal with.

"I hope so," Hannah said. "But the real truth is I was just buying time. I had set my own deadline that I would call the lawyers by a certain point—that was weeks ago—but when I said that about having an affair, in my mind, at least, I pushed that date back. But I do wonder about it, a life without him. I even looked at the real estate section the other day to just get a sense of what's out there for a single person."

They were quiet while Cami washed her hair. It felt good to have someone do something for her. She closed her eyes and tried not to think. They moved across the room to the main chair, and Hannah didn't say a word. She just let Cami cut. She almost didn't even care. But when it was done, moussed and blown, she couldn't believe how good it looked. She knew she wouldn't be able to keep it up—she never could. Until now, she hadn't felt she had to.

"I love it," she said to Cami. "Do you know any single men about our age?"

"Actually, Seth's brother," she said.

"No, that's okay," Hannah said. "I'll figure it out. I don't want to drag you into this."

"I think you should find someone today, your hair looks so good," Cami said.

"Today?" Hannah asked.

"Yeah, I mean, is there anyone you've noticed, anyone you can go flirt with? What kind of guys do you like?"

Hannah wanted to say that she liked Joel, or at least she used to, but she was trying hard to change that fact.

"Well," Hannah said slowly. "For the purposes of having an affair, I guess I want to find someone who is physically attractive to me, someone I feel some chemistry with, who isn't a jerk."

"That's pretty basic," Cami said, nodding. "So go find someone—now, while your hair looks this good."

"Maybe," Hannah said. Now that she thought about it, she was just a few blocks from the bakery where Larry—the cute, flirty gray-haired man—was, the one who always gave her extra lemon bars.

"Maybe?" Cami asked, encouraging her.

"Yeah," Hannah said, standing. "I have an idea."

"Please, please keep me posted," Cami said. "And when I make wishes with Violet tonight—we do that every night and sprinkle a little fairy dust in her room; you know, it makes the wishes come true and keeps the bad dreams away—I'm going to make a wish for you. That you have an affair with some great sex and passionate kisses but that you don't fall in love with that person. I'm going to wish that you end up staying with Joel. That is my wish for you."

Hannah was going to ask, What kind of wish was that? It sounded like a bad one, an already-giving-up one. But she let it go, knowing that Cami had to think that was the best option since it had been her own choice. She was surprised to feel the burn of tears behind her eyes. It wasn't that she necessarily believed in wishes, but she always loved the idea of them. It was like having someone say they would pray for you. She was never sure if the prayer would actually do any good, but she was always touched by it. She willed the tears away. She didn't want to have bloodshot eyes when she saw Larry.

Once she was outside again in the real world, going to see Larry seemed impossible, or at least starting something with him did. She forced herself to head south on 20th Street. Really, she didn't have to go even a block out of her way to walk by the bakery. She came upon it too soon, the chalkboard sign in front boasting about a brie-and-fig scone, which did sound good. She walked right inside. Luckily, there was a bit of a line, which gave her time to spot Larry. He looked as appealing as ever, wearing a blue button-down shirt with the sleeves rolled up to his elbows. He was still helping someone when it became clear that she was next in line, so she pretended to be looking at the menu behind her and let the next person in line slip in front of her.

"Can I help you?" Larry finally asked.

"Yes, thank you. How are you?"

"Fine, thanks," he said, not quite looking at her. Didn't he usually make a bigger deal about her coming in? That was how it always seemed to her. "What can I get for you?"

"Well," she said, taking her time. She was going to ask for his number at the end of the order. That was her plan. She knew it was crazy; she wasn't even sure about the details of his personal life, but he didn't wear a wedding ring, and she just didn't care. She was ready to do this. Plus, it was likely her hair would never look this good again.

"I know I'd like a few brie scones, they sound good," she said, making a show of looking at each confection. "You know what? I'll take one of everything else."

Just as she said the word *everything*, Larry's phone rang. He pulled it out of his pocket and turned away. *No, no, no,* she chanted to herself. She waited, acting like she wasn't in a rush at all. She could wait. But it seemed like he was just getting more absorbed in his call. Where were her lemon bars? she wanted to ask. Didn't he notice her hair? Clearly not, because a second later Larry gestured to the young man behind the counter that he should take over helping her. He moved reluctantly into place, blocking Larry almost completely.

"One of everything?" the man asked, sounding as bored as a person could sound. He didn't wait for an answer and began to place one of each item in the box Larry had pulled out. She cleared her throat and looked at Larry one more time. He was turned away and talking harshly into the phone.

"Sure," she said, feeling more and more deflated as the box filled up, all the way to the top. In fact, it was so full that it was hard to close, but the man managed, tying extra string around it.

She paid, handing over her credit card while thinking of twenty ways the money could have been better spent, and just as the transaction was complete, Larry hung up the phone and turned around.

"Hey," he said. "Did you get any lemon bars in that box of yours?"

"I did," she said. "I think." She looked at him more closely now. He was pretty old. Much older than she had realized. But really, she had barely paid attention to him before; she'd just liked the attention he gave her. Or, to be more accurate, the lemon bars. She thought of what kind of guy she'd told Cami she was looking for—good looking, not a jerk. Now she wanted to add another caveat: not too old. She shrugged and turned, knocking into someone with her unwieldy box.

"Sorry," she mumbled.

"Come in again soon," Larry called after her.

I doubt it, she thought. And as she walked out, she had the very clear realization that this was going to be even harder than she'd expected.

The reason Joel thought of their first date as their third was because he said that from the minute he'd noticed her, they'd been dating. There had never been any "before" or "leading up to"—it just was. If she accepted that theory, it would mean that their first date had been at a now-closed diner on 17th Street. At that time, she'd worked for the Hyatt Hotels chain, dealing with room details, everything from furniture to soap and shampoo. That involved replacing what was broken and constantly updating the rooms so they would be relevant, welcoming, and appealing. That morning she had proposed something crazy, something that was truly before its time, when people were not really thinking about single-use plastic. She'd proposed that the hotel move away from tiny plastic shampoo bottles and put luxury refillable glass containers of shampoo and conditioner in all the showers and possibly even similar bottles of body lotion by the sinks. She'd even had sample bottles made up. She had been shot down—hard and fast. Nothing sounded better to her than a greasy hamburger, fries, and a Coke. So she walked the few blocks west to the small diner and took a seat at the horseshoe-shaped counter with its swiveling stools. It was busy, and she chose the stool all the way in, by the window, with one empty stool next to her. If she was lucky, that would remain empty while she ate.

She ordered, and it wasn't until the server walked away that she realized how much she dreaded going back to work. She had been working up to the proposal for weeks—months, really, if she went back to her initial idea. She had been so excited when the managers had agreed to the meeting and beyond thrilled when two executives from corporate had agreed to fly in to hear what she had to say. Not only had she hoped to bring it to Philadelphia's hotels, but she'd had dreams of taking it to the whole chain. Now she was going back to nothing, at least nothing that was hers or out of the ordinary. She was going back to the usual everyday drudgery.

"Oh my God, is she okay?" someone said, pulling her out of her head. She looked across to the other side of the counter. There were people leaning down, but she couldn't tell what had happened. She heard someone say, "I think she's okay," and, "Just ease her up." She tried not to look as two people, an older man with thinning white hair and a younger man, maybe about her age, with thick, dark hair and a handsome and open face, helped a tiny older woman first to standing and then to sitting on the stool. She had short red hair that was clearly dyed, and she was wearing a navy sweatshirt that said **MICHIGAN**

Grandma in bright-yellow block letters. Hannah assumed the two men were the woman's husband and son.

"Silly me, silly me," the woman said. Hannah was so relieved it wasn't some awful thing. "I didn't know the chair swivels. I'm no good on a swivel chair."

"Did you hit your head?" the older man asked.

"No, no, nothing like that," she said, giggling nervously.

Instantly the servers were around her, along with a manager, and the booth behind them was cleaned quickly so that she and the older man could be seated. Hannah expected the younger man to slip in, but instead he stood next to them for a few seconds.

"Thanks for your help, young man," the woman said.

"My pleasure," he said. "Go Blue!"

"Go Blue!"

The man went back to his stool but didn't sit. He looked around and spotted the empty seat next to Hannah and walked over.

"I hope you don't mind," he said. "Her soup spilled back there, and I don't want to make a big deal about it."

"No, I don't mind," Hannah said. "At first I thought you were with her."

"Oh no, I was just sitting next to her. That was pretty startling. She went down hard."

"I hate when things like that happen," Hannah said, surprised she was even talking to the guy. She had just wanted to get in and out, but then she had that thought again that she really wasn't rushing back to much. The server placed her burger and fries in front of her and came back a few seconds later with a fizzing Coke.

"I'd like that too," the man said to the server. Then to Hannah, "I was just about to order when all the commotion happened. I'm Joel, by the way."

"I'm Hannah," she said, taking a bite of her juicy burger. Normally she might be inhibited eating in front of a stranger with whom that code of silence had been broken, but she just didn't feel it. "So she seems okay?"

"Yeah, I think so," Joel said. Wow, was he cute. She had recently broken up with someone and was not seriously looking to start a new relationship. At least that's what she kept telling herself so she could feel less pathetic. In fact, after today's failed meeting she had had the fleeting thought that nothing was keeping her here in Philadelphia; she could go anywhere. Maybe she should. Maybe this was the time.

"What did you say to her at the end? Something blue?"

"Oh, she was wearing a shirt from the University of Michigan. They say 'Go Blue!' Like a battle cry, a connection, you know, one Wolverine to another."

"Oh, so you went to Michigan?"

"No, I didn't, I've never even been to Michigan," Joel said. "But I know most college mascots and sayings. I mean, around here it's easy—Temple Owls, Penn Quakers—but there are so many, and I love them all. Beavers, Roll Tide, Orange Power, Blue Hens. For my dad it was the names of newspapers. He loved them. I mean, he's in the news business, so it makes sense. One of my first memories is of him reciting the names of newspapers and what cities they were in and how they had changed over time and what was defunct. It's one of his *things*; you get the point."

Hannah wasn't sure that she did.

"So far I haven't come across a shirt I can't talk to," Joel said. "You know what I mean. I like to do it. It lifts people's spirits. For a brief moment I can usually make someone smile."

The server was back in an instant with Joel's burger and their two checks, murmuring, "No rush," even though there was a line at the door. They ate in comfortable silence for a few minutes.

"Please leave that," Joel said when Hannah eventually reached for her check. "Let me get it. It has been my pleasure to sit next to you."

"What? No, that's crazy," she said. "I can't let you do that."

"Please let me. I'd like to. I was also going to offer to pay for the older couple, but I heard the manager say their lunch was on them, so please let me," Joel said, taking a huge bite of his burger. "You would be doing me a favor."

Hannah wasn't sure what to do. She could grab the check and run to the counter and pay, or she could graciously agree. Either way, she would never see him again, so what difference did it make?

"Okay, sure, thank you," she said. "I had a hard morning, and this is really nice. It balances out my day."

Joel nodded, satisfied, and took another bite of his burger. She waited, thinking he was going to ask for her number or something, but he didn't. She sat just a beat longer than she usually would before she got up and walked toward the door, hoping the server would understand that she wasn't skipping out, that he was paying for her. It seemed like nobody was going to say a word. And then . . .

"Hey, Hannah," Joel called, and it sounded to her like he had been saying her name for as long as she could remember. It sounded *right.* She took a deep breath and turned.

"Where did you go to college?"

"Penn State. Why?"

"We are," he called out, like he was at a football game, sounding completely free and natural.

And without thinking Hannah answered back, "Penn State," along with about five other people in the diner. Everyone laughed.

"You too?" Hannah asked.

"No, actually, I went to West Virginia University," he said. "We are the Mountaineers."

Hannah nodded. She had never met anyone who had gone there, and that simple fact raised so many questions, but she let them go.

"Thank you again," she said.

"My pleasure," he said, getting up off his stool and moving toward her. "I know this is so out of nowhere. I was going to just let you walk out that door. My general policy is to do something nice without asking for anything in return, but then I thought about the fact that I'm so curious about you and I might never see you again. I could come back here every day for the next month for lunch and just hope I run into you again, but what if you never came back? Or what if I kept missing you by fifteen minutes or something like that? I mean, even if I came back every day for lunch, I wouldn't be able to be here for the entirety of every possible lunch period."

"I get it," Hannah said, smiling.

"So I'm not going to ask for your number; I'm not going to put you on the spot like that, but I just wondered, Is there any place I am likely to run into you again? I mean, like a coffee shop or a bookstore or something like that?"

Hannah couldn't think straight. What she wanted to do was jot down her number—that seemed easier—but also, who was this guy? Where did he come from?

"Um, I'm selling honey with a friend this weekend," she said. "At the Fitler Square Farmers' Market, on Saturday morning."

"Great," he said. "Good. Thank you." And he went back to eating his hamburger.

CHAPTER TEN

Hannah continued to head south, moving the heavy box of pastries from hand to hand. She felt like it was her scarlet letter, which she knew was ridiculous, but still. She kept thinking she would just leave it or throw it out, but then she thought of all the good food in the box and how much money she had spent, and she decided she would go to Saint Martha's and drop it off. When she was on her way, her phone rang. It was the nursing home. Weird.

"Hello?"

"Hannah?"

"Hi, Reuben," she said, surprisingly happy to hear his voice.

"Am I getting you at a bad time?"

"No, not at all," she said. "I'm just heading over there. I come with pastries."

"Oh, great," Reuben said, like it was all going to be much easier than he had expected. "I tried Joel, but he didn't pick up, so this works out even better. Let me fill you in quick so you know what you're up against when you get here."

"That doesn't sound good," Hannah said.

"Well, Richard is having a hard day. He's been in the lounge now talking nonstop for over three hours. He's very concerned about ketchup and the moving away from traditional ketchup to different types and flavors. Apparently sriracha flavored is the worst offender," Reuben said, managing to deliver the information without sounding snarky or sarcastic. "He's also upset about the upside-down plastic bottles, which led him to a discussion about plastic in general and all that goes along with that. We've all tried to ease him away or to see if he wants to take a break. Don't get me wrong, the other residents are enthralled. They don't mind at all, and he is not being disruptive; that isn't my concern. What does concern me is that his voice is going, and this just isn't like him," Reuben said.

"Oh no," Hannah said. "I'll be right there."

"Great," Reuben said. "I'm off in five, but I'll wait until you get here."

"Okay," Hannah said. "Thanks."

When Hannah got to Saint Martha's, Richard was still talking, and the crowd he had amassed was shocking—there could have been fifty or sixty people sitting in the room, listening intently. Some of them must have come from different units and different floors.

"A tour of a ketchup facility in Pittsburgh, Pennsylvania, revealed that there was much more than simple ketchup being made there," Richard said, and his voice was so raspy Hannah was alarmed. "There are also chili sauces, steak sauces, mayonnaise, mustards, and a variety of other products being manufactured. Some are put into plastic bottles, and others are sold in glass bottles."

Hannah looked around. Weren't these people bored? He had clearly gone over this information already, from what Reuben said. Also, Hannah wondered, how did he come up with this stuff and sound so formal, like he was truly anchoring the news? She expected him to say so-and-so had the story, but he didn't; he just kept talking about plastic and glass and flavored and original. She tried to get his attention by waving to him, but he looked straight ahead and wouldn't let on that he knew she was there.

"Hi." Reuben came up behind her, as he tended to do. "I'm glad you made it. Oh, your hair looks nice. Did you just get it cut?"

Her hand went to her head, and she felt the silkiness that came with a professional blow-dry. She had forgotten about her hair. "Yeah, I just did," Hannah said. "Thanks for noticing."

"My pleasure," Reuben said. He gestured toward Richard. "See what I mean?"

"This is nuts. How did all these people get here? And he is still talking about the same thing?"

"Well, he came back to it; he's covered a lot of territory since I called you," Reuben said. "And once the word got out that he was talking, a bunch of nurses brought their people here, which is great for them. But he hasn't had anything to eat or drink since he started this. I don't want to upset him, but I think we're going to have to cut this off. Are you okay with that?"

Hannah hated to do it. Richard was so proud, sitting there in his work clothes with his bow tie, never mind the slippers. She almost couldn't bear to think about where he had once been—the television studio on the third floor of the famous building at 30 Rock in New York City—versus where he was now: the common room of a nursing home in South Philadelphia.

"Here, let me try first, before we embarrass him," Hannah said, handing Reuben the box of pastries and taking a small step toward Richard. "This makes me so sad. Do you know how in charge he was when I first met him? How sharp and witty?"

"I can only imagine," Reuben said. "But the thing is he still is incredibly commanding. I mean, look at these people. It's just all twisted and not what we think of as in charge. It is sad, but it's also okay and just the way things go."

Hannah nodded, moving toward Richard again. She tried to be subtle, but it wasn't like this was the actual news. There were no cameras; this was not something that had to be respected in that way and not interrupted. She was pretty close to him when Joel walked in, looking around frantically. Reuben must have left a message, but still she was surprised he hadn't called her to coordinate. He looked so tired, with those constant bags under his eyes these days. He saw her, and his face lit up as it always did. He nodded, as if to tell her that he didn't want to interfere with whatever she was doing. It was an accepted fact between them that she was better with Richard than he was.

"Dad," she said quietly, touching him on the shoulder. She didn't usually call him dad—she called him Richard, but on rare occasions it just came out. He looked right at her, and the spell was broken. He glanced around, nodded once formally, then looked at her again.

"Are you ready to head in for a rest?" she asked.

"I am," he said. "I guess I got carried away."

Hannah moved behind his chair and grabbed the handles. As she pushed him toward his room, he waved to the crowd. Everyone had started talking, and some of the nurses had come toward the middle from the edges of the room. The spell was broken for them, too, and she was sure there were a few people who wished she hadn't done that.

"I will be back," he said, and the words *I'll see you tomorrow* came into her head. This would be the time he would say that, when he was signing off for the night to return with more news the following day. She made a mental note to ask Reuben if he was still saying that at night. They hadn't talked about it in a few weeks or so.

Hannah had expected Reuben and Joel to follow them into the room, but she was glad when they didn't. She was happy to have a little time alone with Richard.

"I'm so thirsty," he said.

"Of course you are," Hannah said, pulling a cold water bottle out of the mini refrigerator in his room. "You just talked for over three hours straight."

"There was a lot to talk about," Richard said, not defensively, almost as though he were mocking himself.

"Well, there was, I guess," she said. "And you had a huge audience."

"They just kept coming and coming," Richard said. "Honestly, they should pay me around here."

"I was thinking the same thing."

Hannah pulled a chair over so she could be closer to Richard and sat down. Ever since Joel had told her about Celine's affair, she'd wanted to talk to Richard about it, to see how he had gotten through, but every time she thought she might have a chance, she just couldn't. Joel had asked her not to mention it, and despite her anger, she wasn't going to risk causing a rift between Joel and Richard. She couldn't do that to Richard.

"What's been going on with you, really?" she asked. "I mean, why the sudden interest in the ketchup?"

"I don't know," he said, like he was really thinking about it. "I guess it was all I could remember. Also it truly bothers me."

"I understand," she said. "But are you okay? Are you happy enough?"

"Sure," he said. "I'm happy enough. I'm also lonely and mad at myself and feel some compulsive need to keep talking, to tell people what I know. Can I tell you what I know?"

"Yes," Hannah said eagerly. "Of course."

"I see the way you look at me, like I was perfect and now I'm not, and that isn't the case," he said, sounding as lucid as ever. "I was never perfect. There are so many things I regret, that I wish I could do over. I think about them—"

"Hi," Joel called as he came into the room, interrupting Richard. Hannah realized she was scowling and had to rearrange her face or else

Joel would ask what they were discussing. But what she really wanted was to know what Richard was talking about. What did he regret? What would he do over?

"Son," Richard said quietly and formally, not even looking in Joel's direction. Was Hannah seeing that right? Usually he would reach out to him, bring him close for a hug.

"I was worried," Joel said. "How are you doing?"

"Enough about me," Richard said sternly. Hannah was not imagining it: he was definitely not looking at Joel. He turned to Hannah. "Who's with the kids? That babysitter of yours? Why don't you take advantage of this unexpected time together? Treat yourself. Better yet, let me treat you." Richard pulled out his wallet and handed Hannah his American Express card. "Really, the sky is the limit, it's on me. Do not hold back."

Hannah reached out for the card—she didn't want to be rude—and looked at Joel with a questioning expression.

"Thanks, Dad," Joel said. "That's so nice of you. But we can't tonight."

It was almost like Joel wasn't even there. Richard didn't react to him at all but turned more toward Hannah. "What do you say? Nothing would make me happier." His voice was nearly gone. He leaned his head back and closed his eyes.

"We'll go now and let you rest," Hannah said, getting up and hugging Richard. She stood with the credit card in her hand and waited for him to open his eyes. When he did, she handed it back to him. "Can we take a rain check? You are always so generous, Richard. But tonight won't work for us."

"Suit yourself," Richard said, taking back the card.

"We'll talk again soon," she said pointedly, gently squeezing his wrist. "Okay?"

"Yes, of course," Richard said, his eyes closed again. "Whenever you want."

"And can you do a little less public speaking tomorrow?" she asked. "Just to give your voice a break?"

"My voice will be fine by tomorrow," Richard said. "I'm a professional, remember?"

As soon as they were out and down the hall, Joel turned to Hannah. "Should we?"

"Should we what?"

"Blow everything off and go out, the two of us?"

"Joel, are you kidding me?" Hannah said, trying to keep her voice down. "We agreed we would be as normal as possible for everyone around us, but don't mistake that for reality. Don't forget what is actually going on here."

"Have you been . . . seeing someone?" he asked, dropping to a whisper when he said the last two words.

Hannah's mind flashed back to Larry at the bakery. She was going to have to try much harder.

"Maybe," she said coldly.

"Okay, I'll go to my meeting, then," Joel said, sounding defeated but not unkind. "But honestly, at this point I hope you are, because I can't stand this. I hate all the secrets and the eggshell walking."

Hannah almost wanted to laugh at his use of the word *secrets*. So far, the secrets had been only his.

"We have Dr. Snow later," Joel said when Hannah didn't say anything. "So I'll be home in time for a quick dinner, and then we'll go. I picked up spaghetti and meatballs from Villa di Roma, to go, so that will be easy. I'll leave in time to heat them up. We should eat by about five forty-five."

"Okay," she said. "But you know you can't buy me with meatballs, right?"

She said it like she meant it, but a tiny corner of her heart broke off. He was a smart one, that Joel, and she hated that so much.

"Yes," Joel said. "I know that."

They stood there, that awkward moment when for most of their lives together they would kiss or hug, but now she couldn't stand it, so she took a step back.

"What was going on in there?" she finally asked. "With Richard. Did you guys have a fight?"

"What?" Joel responded. "No, not at all. He's just tired. Couldn't you see that?"

"Well, yes, of course," Hannah said. Still, it seemed like something more to her. But she was probably being silly. She decided to let it go. "He was clearly exhausted."

"See you at the house," Joel said, turning and walking away. She was aware of his choice of words, *See you at the house* instead of the usual *Meet you at home.*

"See you there."

Hannah waited while Joel walked through the main room, which was now almost empty, and turned left toward the exit. She took a slow step backward, eager to ask Richard to finish the conversation he had started. She glanced in, and he was fast asleep in his wheelchair. She shook her head, then followed in the path Joel had just taken.

"Oh, hey," Reuben said, startling her. He was standing at the door to the small conference room.

"I thought you were off a long time ago," Hannah said, surprised.

"I was," he said. "But I was worried about Richard, and I had some paperwork to finish." He pointed through the window toward a stack of paper on the table. "Do you have time for a quick cup?"

"Um, sure, a quick one," she said. "Did you see Joel? He walked right by."

"He did?" Reuben said, pouring steaming coffee into a bright-pink mug. "I must have missed him."

Reuben handed the mug to Hannah, and she could see it said *Hello Beautiful.* She raised her eyebrows.

"Is this on purpose?" she asked, lifting the mug slightly.

"It most certainly is," he said. "Your hair and everything. I just thought you could use a pick-me-up."

"Thanks," she said, sitting down across from Reuben's stack of papers. She realized she was starving, so she reached for the box Reuben had placed on the table and pulled on the string until it broke. As soon as she lifted the lid, the whole room smelled like baked goods. Her hand hovered over the lemon bar, but she chose the scone instead. "Help yourself. And please give them away. But make sure Richard gets one."

"Okay. That's really nice of you," Reuben said.

"So has Richard still been saying 'I'll see you tomorrow' at night?" Hannah asked as she chewed. It was a delicious scone. Maybe she shouldn't completely write off the bakery. "I've been meaning to ask."

"Actually, I'm not sure. These last two weeks I've come in early and left early; they're shifting things around a bit, so I'm usually gone by now, and I haven't had the chance to check in on him like I'd done. But last I checked, which was probably about twelve days ago, he did."

"Is someone else checking?" she asked.

"Yes, I'm sure they are," he said, taking a sip of coffee. She had to squint to read his mug, which said *You can't make everyone happy: you're not a pizza.* "I mean, there are rounds every night to make sure people are settled. But I don't think there have been long discussions. Maybe I'll hang around tonight, do all this paperwork, and then check in on him. I don't have anywhere I need to be anyway."

"Oh, you don't have to do that," Hannah said. "That seems like too much to ask."

"I'm happy to do it," Reuben said like it had been decided.

"What do you think today was all about?" she asked, sitting back and taking a sip of coffee.

"Control," Reuben said. "I think it's Richard's way of controlling his time or at least feeling in control. Also it struck me as a little obsessive, all that talk about ketchup and plastic. We could think about an antidepressant if you want to."

"I would have to talk to Joel about that," Hannah said.

"Do you mind if I ask . . . ," Reuben began. "It's just that I've noticed you haven't been here together much—you and Joel, that is—and I sense something, a difference between you. Well, really the dynamic is different with the two of you and when you're with Richard, and I just wondered: Has anything changed?"

"That's perceptive of you," she said, testing how far she might be willing to go.

"Thanks," Reuben said. "So I'm right, something has changed?"

Hannah looked at her *Hello Beautiful* mug.

"Where did you get this one?" she asked.

"Oh," he said, looking suddenly shy. "It was actually something I got for my mother for some Mother's Day a while back. When she died, it was one of the things I kept. I knew the ladies here would love it."

"I'm so sorry," Hannah said. "I didn't know." Really, she knew almost nothing about his personal life. "Is that when you started working here? Or did you already work here?"

"I already did," he said. "I always thought I wanted to be a guidance counselor—I thought probably at a high school. But I had an internship at one, and something was missing for me. It was around the time my mother got sick, and I saw all this bias against old people, like they were worthless and just being thrown away, and it made no sense to me, so I shifted gears and ended up here."

"Huh," Hannah said, impressed.

"The other route I considered was a marriage-and-sex therapist," he said, deadpan.

"Really?"

"Well, no, not really," he said, smiling. She found herself smiling back. "I'm not so sure I would be good at that. I'm sorry. I hope you don't mind my asking about this. I do feel a little awkward about it. It's just that if I sense it, Richard probably senses it."

"A little over a month ago, I discovered that Joel had an affair," she said, looking at the mug. "It was a total and complete shock. I mean, we had always had a solid marriage; I was happy, we loved being parents together, and we still found time to, you know, be alone, though I realize now not as much as we used to—I mean, it gets so busy! And the kids are often in our bed, but it isn't like we don't want to. Sorry, that's probably too much information. My point is that I was positive we were the lucky ones. But I was wrong. Some lady who worked at a hotel Joel went to in Minnesota on business trips . . . he said he never loved her. He said it was over before I found out."

"Now it's my turn to say I'm sorry," Reuben said. "So are you guys in the process of splitting? Is that what I sense?"

"Well, I guess that's the million-dollar question."

She was building up to the next part, the part about her having an affair.

"I personally might not be the best person to give advice, but you would be blown away by the stories I hear in here. These people have perspective! So if they've been married for sixty years or longer, that usually comes with some detours along the way, some infidelity on one or both parts, some incredible hurdles that they survived."

"So are you married?" she asked. She didn't think so; he didn't wear a ring. But some people just didn't wear rings.

"Oh no, I'm not married," he said. "I have a girlfriend. Her name is Lucy. She's been in Nicaragua for three months doing research about disappearing languages. She's heading to Africa now. I haven't seen her in thirteen weeks, and there is no date set for when I might see her, but I let it happen. I just keep agreeing to it. The thing is in many ways it suits me. I'm lonely, no question, but it gives me time to work and not worry about getting anywhere by a particular time. I keep telling myself it works for both of us."

There was a light knock. They both looked toward the open door to see a nurse standing there, motioning for Reuben to come talk to her.

"One sec," Reuben said. She watched as he went out and listened, then nodded. He came back in. "Sorry, actually it's a good thing I stayed. Millie on the second floor is having a fight with her roommate, apparently a loud fight, and she's threatening her with the butter knife she slipped off her tray at breakfast this morning and hid in her sheets. I'm going to go see what I can do to defuse the situation. This is not the first time this has happened. She's been warned about this."

Hannah was disappointed. She had decided to tell Reuben everything. He was so easy to talk to. She realized there weren't many people she could share her thoughts with these days. She could use a friend like him.

"Okay," Hannah said. "We'll talk again soon. I want to come back and see Richard in the next few days probably."

"Sounds good," Reuben said. He reached for her mug, placed it on the table, and snapped a photo of it with his cell. In a few seconds Hannah got the notification of a text: a photo of the words on the mug. *Hello Beautiful.*

"Now you have it, in case you need another pick-me-up," Reuben said, gathering his stack of papers. "I'm off to hopefully save Millie from herself."

On her way out, she called Kim. She had been trying to stop by whenever she could, but now it had been almost a week since their last visit. When Kim was with the kids, she was normal, capable, relatively happy (fake or not) Kim, but when the kids were with Hank, she often sank back into that dark, sad version of herself. Hannah knew tonight was a Hank night.

When Kim answered her phone, all Hannah could hear was loud music.

"Hello?" Hannah said. "Hello?"

"Oh, hi!" Kim said, sounding far away. "Sorry, you're on speaker."

"I meant to call earlier," Hannah said, talking louder than she had to. "I got caught up with Richard."

"That's okay," Kim said. "Listen, I don't have much time. Can I call you tomorrow?"

"Oh, sure. Did the kids end up switching days? Are they there?"

"The kids? No, they're with Hank. Actually, I have a date."

"A date?" She might as well have said she had decided to become an astronaut.

"Yes, a date," Kim said, responding to the shock in Hannah's voice. "What? Did you think I couldn't get one? We connected on Bumble. But I have to meet him in twenty minutes—you know, you don't want to tell someone where you live—so we're meeting at that bar near Bainbridge? That nice cocktail bar?"

"Oh, okay," Hannah said, feeling strangely flustered. "On Bumble?"

"I really have to go," Kim said, sounding more upbeat than she had in months. "I'll tell you everything tomorrow."

CHAPTER ELEVEN

"I really want to tell Dr. Snow about our plan," Joel said as he eased into the tiny parking spot. "It seems like we should, don't you think?"

Hannah didn't want to. So far she was still the good one in Dr. Snow's eyes, the one who had not stepped out on the marriage. She just wasn't willing to give up that role. More than that, though, what if Dr. Snow advised them against it or said she thought it was a terrible idea? Hannah had grown to be somewhat excited about the idea—at least the possibility of the idea—and she didn't want to do anything to jeopardize it.

"Not tonight," Hannah said, making no move to get out of the car. "Maybe next week."

"I would really like to now," Joel said, not backing down but also keeping his voice even and kind. It was a trick he had, a way to negotiate and ask for what he needed without putting the other person on edge. It was something she'd always admired until she was clearly on the other end of it. "It's just that I have so many feelings and thoughts about it. It's on my mind most of the time, so I'd like to talk about it. Plus, it seems to me we've both been holding back a little, or at least we haven't had that much to talk about lately, and I think that's because we aren't talking about this, this important thing. Come on, we should head in."

"You know, I don't love the way that all sounded," Hannah said. "That this is what you're thinking about now. It's like you switched the focus from you to me, like I'm the one doing the bad thing now, and I don't think I like that."

"No, no, that's not what I mean at all," Joel said. "I did the bad thing. I will always be the one who did the bad thing. But of course I wonder what you're doing and with whom. I don't like that one bit. I deserve it, no question, but I don't like it."

"So if I do this and you suffer, do you think we'll be even? Because it isn't true. I would never be doing this if you hadn't done what you did. I don't think we will ever be even. You're the one who started this, you did this, and if you hadn't, I would never in a million years be having an affair with another man. In a million years."

"Yes, I know, I get that," Joel said. "Wait. You're having an affair? Currently?"

"I don't want to talk about it," she said, the familiar anger building. "I just didn't think you would ever do that to me. I would have bet on our kids' lives that you wouldn't do that to me."

A strange noise came out of Joel's throat, and at first she thought he was going to be sick, though he hadn't been in a few weeks—that had pretty much stopped. But she saw right away that wasn't it. He was crying, hard, aggressive tears, and the sobs kept getting caught in his throat as he tried to pull himself together.

"Our kids' lives," he repeated back to her, but it was hard to even understand him. He sounded messy, and for one brief second she felt embarrassed for him. She looked out the window and up toward the turret, where Dr. Snow was surely waiting for them.

She didn't say anything while his crying quieted down. She knew she should get out of the car and they should go up there and absorb the professional wisdom they so clearly needed. But she just didn't want to.

"Listen, Joel, I don't want to talk to Dr. Snow about this tonight. I'm not going to change my mind," she said. She knew she needed to find her own therapist, that that was where she should be spending her time now, because despite her little internal dialogue at the bakery, she still found herself resisting this whole idea. She had taken wedding vows, for heaven's sake! She had promised Joel, of course, but she had also promised everyone else in that room and any higher being who might or might not be paying attention. She had to get over that.

"What do you want to do?" Hannah asked. "Do you want to go in even if we aren't going to talk about it? Or do you want to call it a night?" She glanced at her watch. They'd been running late to begin with, and now they were twenty-two minutes into their fifty-minute session.

"Can you call her?" Joel said. "I can barely talk."

"Can you drive?" Hannah asked somewhat harshly. She did not want to drive home.

"Yes, I can drive," he said. "I just need a minute."

Hannah pulled out her phone. As she fumbled to bring up Dr. Snow's number, she landed on Reuben's text—the picture that said *Hello Beautiful.* She took a deep breath and said the words silently to herself. *Hello beautiful, hello beautiful, hello beautiful.* Then she found the right number and called.

"Are you guys sitting down there?" Dr. Snow asked instead of saying hello.

"Yes, we've basically had our own session in the car," Hannah said. "We just don't feel up to it tonight. I'm so sorry."

"Can I come down? Just to say hello? You know I'm going to have to charge you for this either way."

"I know," Hannah said. "I just think we're going to pass tonight. You said these things ebb and flow with false starts and barriers that appear and disappear, right?"

"I'm glad to know you've been listening to me," Dr. Snow said warmly, and Hannah closed her eyes and thought of *The Sopranos*. "Is Joel in agreement with you about this tonight?"

"Yes, we're just exhausted."

"Okay. I'm here if you need me. Just a phone call away. Take good care."

"We'll see you next week."

When Hannah woke up on the Saturday morning after she'd first met Joel at the diner, she wondered if he would show up, if he had given her any thought at all since he'd bought her burger. Maybe he was a serial burger buyer, an apparent do-gooder, always on the lookout for the next possible target but never following through with the next step. Whatever—she didn't even know him. If she never saw him again, she wouldn't miss him. But still, she took her time getting ready that day, showering and washing her hair even though she would be outside selling honey.

She arrived at ten, and Joel was already there, standing on the sidewalk and trying to blend in, moving from stand to stand, picking up a peach here, a tomato there. She shook her head and got out, heading right for the honey stand and her friend Eliza.

"Sorry I'm a little late," she said.

"No problem," Eliza said, smiling warmly and patting the seat next to her. "Thanks for coming at all."

"My pleasure," Hannah said, and she meant it. What had begun as Eliza's son's bar mitzvah project—putting a few hives on the roof of their synagogue—had grown into a family honey business, and she was always asking friends to help sell it. Hannah was happy to help, of course, but if she was honest with herself, she was doing it for selfish reasons. She was lonely since she'd become single again and dreaded her empty weekend days.

"Good morning," Joel said, stepping up to the table.

"Good morning," she said. His hair looked so shiny and his skin so clear that she had an urge to stand and touch both, which she knew was ridiculous. But really, had he been so healthy looking at the diner? So . . . shimmery and otherworldly?

"Is this your honey?" he asked, as if she didn't know he was there to see her. It could have sounded like chitchat, normal banter between a buyer and a seller, not necessarily an interaction that would eventually lead to true love and two kids.

"Actually, no," Hannah said, standing now and pointing toward Eliza. "It's really her business. Long story, but it's called Holy Honey because it started on the roof of a synagogue. L'Hive'Em." She knew she sounded crazy. It was what she usually said when someone bought a bottle. It was their slogan, but now she just sounded demented. Plus, Joel hadn't even offered to buy any.

"Nice," he said, not seeming to notice how wacky she sounded or at least not seeming bothered by it. "I'll take ten bottles."

"Great," Hannah said, collecting the bottles and looking around for a bag. What she wanted to say was that he didn't have to do that. He could buy one bottle with the same result, or none, really.

"I have a bag," Joel said, placing a reusable bag on the table, perfect for all the bottles of honey. Hannah noticed that the bag was decorated with sunflowers, her favorite. She carefully placed the bottles in the bag, one at a time, and collected his money.

"Thanks," she said. Surely he wasn't going to just walk away.

"Thank you," he said, turning. He looked back over his shoulder and raised the bag. "L'Hive'Em!" She watched as he walked to the corner of Pine and continued to walk east. Should she just stand up and go after him? How would she ever find him again? Now she was going to be the one going to the diner every day at lunch hoping to run into him. She was a total mess, so overeager. He could be mean for all she knew. He could be boring, or not smart, or not clever—or worse, maybe he had no sense of humor. She would let him go. There: he was gone. Okay, so he wasn't the one. Someone else would be.

"Who was that guy, and why did he buy so much honey?" Eliza asked.

"I don't know," Hannah said, thinking it was probably too hard to explain it and in the end not worth it. "I think he just really likes honey." But she wanted to keep talking about him; she wanted Eliza to ask questions until she was forced to confess that she had actually met him before and she thought she might like him. Eliza was already talking to another customer. As the minutes went by, Hannah felt worse and worse. He had made the effort to come to the market; maybe he was waiting for her to make the next move. Why did she always mess this up? She could go looking for him, follow the path he'd taken, and see if she might be lucky enough to run into him. She stood again, thinking she would go, but then a group of four women came to the table, and Eliza was still talking to the other person. She helped them, each wanting to talk about the honey and the project and each counting how many gifts they had to bring back for their family members—they were visiting from Missouri—and when she was done, she looked up, and there was Joel, holding a cardboard tray with four cups.

"Hi!" she said, smiling, so happy to see him. "Did you forget something?"

"Well, yeah, your phone number," he said, smiling shyly. "But I didn't really forget; I was always coming back. It's a little chilly out here, so I got some hot tea for you and your friend, and I put some of the honey in it. I hope you like it sweetened."

"Yeah," she said, dazed. "I do." She accepted the cup he held out to her. It was warm and smelled good. She took a sip. He handed one to Eliza.

"Thanks," Eliza said. She put hers down on the table and gave Hannah a look saying she was crazy; why was she accepting something from this strange man *and* ingesting it? But Hannah just looked right at her and took an even bigger sip. Clearly this was where an earlier explanation would have helped: *He wasn't a stranger exactly. He seemed really nice.*

"Here, for later," Joel said, handing over the tray with the other two cups.

"Thanks," Hannah said.

"So about your number," he said. "Any chance you'll give it to me? I wondered if you were free on Thursday night. I'd love to take you out to dinner. I don't know where you live, and I'm not asking, but depending on what's easy for you, I wondered if you would consider meeting me at Villa di Roma in the Italian Market? Maybe around six thirty so if you don't have fun, it won't ruin your night—there will still be plenty of time to do something else."

"Yes, good," she said, sounding a little like a caveman. Eliza was looking at them, from one to the other, at first appearing stern and then nodding, like the image in front of her had come into focus and she finally understood. She turned her attention to the next customer. They were almost out of honey. Hannah cleared her throat. "I'll meet you at Villa di Roma at six thirty on Thursday."

"Great," Joel said, smiling. "Um, even though we have a plan, can I still have your number? So I can say hi before then?"

"Yes, of course," Hannah said, sounding more like herself. Joel pulled out a tiny notebook and pen, and she said her number slowly while he wrote it down.

"And *Hannah*, with an *h* at the end?"

"Yes, exactly."

"See you on Thursday," Joel said. "And for the record, you made my day."

Hannah spent the next few weeks looking for someone to have an affair with. She had to get on with it, constantly talking back to that voice in her head that kept saying just because Joel had done it didn't mean she should. But she truly felt she had no choice. It was either call the divorce lawyer now or do this and probably call the lawyer later anyway, so what difference did it really make in the end?

She spent a significant amount of time when she should have been researching local items for her hotel project instead researching dating apps. She considered the League, OKCupid, Match, and Tinder but finally settled on Bumble, the one Kim had been using. She liked the swiping aspect of it—if she was going to do it, she might as well have that experience—and the upside was that the woman had to make the first move. So basically, she could match and match and match and feel no pressure until she was ready.

She had to create her profile, which involved deciding whether to be honest about her name and age and situation or to be someone completely different. Could she be someone other than who she was, and if so, who in the world did she want to be? She had extracted as much information from Kim as possible, not yet admitting exactly why she was asking, though she planned to tell her all about it soon.

When she became completely stumped, she decided to go see Richard. She felt drawn to him more than ever, and even though they couldn't talk about it, she felt like he was a survivor of a terrible disease, the one she had just come down with, and she wanted to be near him.

"Good morning," she said breezily, even though he was still in bed and she wanted to ask why he hadn't been dressed and helped into his chair yet today.

"Good morning," he said, deadpan, keeping his eyes on the window. He looked pale and uninterested. She sat on his bed and took his hand.

"To what do I owe the honor of this visit? You don't usually come so early."

"I missed you," she said. "Why are you still in bed?"

"I'm tired," he said. "Isn't bed where you go when you're tired?"

That was the thing about Richard: he was pretty much always right. Even so, she wanted him to not be tired. She wanted him to be his old self.

"Will you go into the main room at some point?" she asked.

"If they make me," he said.

"Can I ask them to get you ready, and we can sit out there?"

"No, no, then everyone expects me to say something important. It just makes me more tired," he said.

"Okay, I understand that," she said. She took a breath. "Can I ask you? I mean, I know you don't seem to want to talk about it, but I think about it a lot. A while ago, after that time you talked for so long, you told me you had regrets, do you remember?"

"You've asked me this before, and I told you I don't remember saying that," he said firmly but not unkindly. "I think you imagined it."

Now he looked her in the eyes and smirked because Richard was many things, but he was not a liar, and this was his way of telling her that he knew she hadn't imagined it.

"Okay, well, I'm always here if you want to talk," she said. "And for the record, everyone has some sort of regret, don't you think?"

"What do you mean?" he asked, pushing himself up in bed. "Who?"

"You know, everyone. Every person at some point does something that they wish they hadn't done, or had done, or had done differently," she said. "You know what I mean, right?"

"Like what?" he asked, seeming more like a little kid to her now, sitting there in his pajamas in bed, a wide-eyed look on his face. "You?"

Yes, she wanted to say, *me. I am planning to join an online-dating site to have an affair, which I will most likely regret, after your beloved son had an affair, basically tearing everything apart, which he regrets. But we aren't the only ones, apparently,* she also wanted to say. *It seems your wife, too, did something and probably had a few regrets.*

"Well, I don't know," she said instead, patting his hand and standing. "Just everyone. I'm going to see if I can find Reuben. I'll be back soon."

He narrowed his eyes at her like he thought she was withholding information. But he didn't protest. He went back to looking out the window. She walked down the hall, glancing in the rooms to see if she spotted Reuben. She finally found him in the lobby sitting across from a pretty crying lady—the daughter of a resident, Hannah thought—and touching her knee gently to calm her. The lady was looking down, tears clearly flowing, and Reuben leaned toward her, looking up at her face, trying to get her to focus on him. Shoot, how could Hannah interrupt that? She pretended to be admiring the art on the walls and walked from one framed photo to another, all the while keeping an eye on the unfolding scene in the lobby. Finally, the woman's phone rang, she answered and stood up, and Hannah watched as she nodded to Reuben and walked outside. Could she swoop in now? Take his attention? Or had the woman said she would be right back?

In the end she didn't have to do anything: Reuben saw her and walked over.

"Visiting Richard this morning?" he asked.

"Yes," she said. "He seems as down as ever, honestly."

"I know, I agree," Reuben said. The other lady's situation was behind him, and this problem was now all he was focusing on. It was a skill.

"What was going on there?" Hannah asked. "Why was she so sad?"

"That's Justine. Her mom was that woman you asked about who died, Kim, remember? Now Justine's dad has declined so much we're suggesting he have comfort care only from this point on. Our program here is called Angel's Kiss—basically it's hospice."

"So, what? You just let him die?"

"In a way," Reuben said. "Or at least we stop intervening. No more trips to the hospital, heavier drugs if needed to keep him comfortable. There is definitely a giving-up aspect to it, but it is also a kind choice to make when the time is right. It's hard to keep going and going and going. Sometimes people need permission to start letting go."

"Huh," Hannah said, not able to imagine having to make that choice about Richard.

"So what's up?" Reuben said. "Hey, I just got some new coffee that I'm very excited about. Do you have time for a cup?"

"Sure," she said.

"I know it sounds corny, but it's this brand Joffrey's from Orlando. They supply a lot of the coffee to Disney, but it isn't all Disney. They roast it for you personally once you order it, and it just arrived. It's delicious. The truth is I first got it for Mr. Reynolds on the third floor. I don't think you've met him, but I do know he and Richard have talked; he's a nice man. He always talked about a honeymoon he took to Orlando and the coffee they had in the morning and how he could never find something as good. Well, I imagined he was talking about a trip fifty years ago. Turns out it was his fifth honeymoon! He's a real character. Anyway, I tried the coffee, and I was hooked. I finally ordered myself a batch."

Hannah thought maybe Reuben had gone into the wrong line of work—maybe he should have opened a coffee shop and been the in-house concierge and sometimes therapist. But really, she guessed, that was sort of what he was doing here anyway.

As soon as they went into the room, she could smell it. There was something very hopeful about the smell of coffee. She waited while he chose a mug for her. First he held up the *Crappity Crap Crap* one, and she shook her head: the day hadn't gotten that bad yet. He smiled and put it back on the shelf. He kept looking and finally chose one that said *I Can't Adult Today* and, without clearing it with her, poured the coffee and handed it over. She smiled and took a sip—it really was delicious.

"Does this have some Disney fairy dust sprinkled in?" she asked.

"Maybe," he said, chuckling. "What I do know is that Lucy would never drink it—my girlfriend? She drinks only single-origin coffee, and she has to know the source intimately, as well as the conditions for the people hired to do the work, not to mention how it's sold on the open market. She's pretty serious about it. I guess this is my way of rebelling. Though, for the record, I do care about people's work conditions."

He had already picked a mug for the day, so he just refilled it. His said *The Doctor Is In.*

"So," she said, realizing she was going to give in to her urge to tell Reuben everything, "do you remember a while ago I told you that Joel had had an affair and we were trying to figure out how to handle it?"

"Yes, of course," he said seriously, taking a seat and indicating that she should take her usual seat across the table from him.

"Well, the way I decided to handle it was that I would also have an affair, to get even, I guess, to clear the playing field. I don't know, some sports metaphor or other. Actually, that's not even true. I think I've convinced myself that that's why. But the truth is I was so mad it was just a threat, but now for so many reasons I feel like I have to, maybe even want to, follow through. Also, I want to buy time. In the end I have no idea if it will make a difference, but I wasn't quite ready to call it quits. All of that leads me to my main point of the day—it is surprisingly hard to find someone to have an affair with."

Hannah watched as the look on Reuben's face changed from solid listening mode to surprise to a flirty smile.

He was pretty cute, and she was fascinated by him, his religious beliefs, how he gelled his Jewish background with the Catholic nursing home, but that would be crazy, way too close to home, and before she had a chance to move through all the steps of consideration, his face morphed again, this time into a jolly laugh. *Of course,* she thought, *he was just kidding.*

"So," she said. "I wanted to ask if you know anything about dating profiles? I mean, about putting one together?"

"I know a few things," he said warmly.

"I've done some research," Hannah said. "And I'm going to go with Bumble because the woman is in charge."

"Don't I know it," Reuben said.

"Do you have a profile?"

"I have had many," Reuben said, but he didn't sound defeated—he almost sounded proud. "They're all shut down now, but before I met Lucy, I was a wild man when it came to dating apps."

"Really?" she asked.

"Well, maybe not a wild man," Reuben conceded. "But I tried. And actually, that's how Lucy and I met."

"Interesting," she said. "So how much information do you share? On your profile?"

"I would say the photos you choose are the key," he said. "You want to look attractive and normal, but not so different from how you truly look that if and when you meet someone they are immediately put off, thinking you tricked them. You, of course, are quite attractive. I don't think that will be a problem."

"Oh, well, thank you," Hannah said, the slightest bit flustered. "I guess my biggest problem is that I'm not sure how to get around the lying part. I mean, I'm not looking for a spouse; I already have one, at least for now. I'm not looking for a long-term commitment. I just want to, I don't even know, connect with someone, anyone I can stand. My other problem is that I don't want people to recognize me, so I can't use my real name."

"This is all doable," Reuben said confidently. She noticed that his phone kept ringing and he kept ignoring it. "First of all, you don't have to reveal your last name. Bumble uses first names only."

"That's a relief," she said.

"But even so, I would come up with a fake last name, even though you won't share it, so you *feel* like someone else when you're doing it, if that's the experience you're after. For example, what street did you grow up on?"

"Walter Place," Hannah said.

"Perfect. So while you're writing the profile, think of yourself as Hannah Walter—maybe that will make you feel freer, and I would stick with Hannah because otherwise you're going to be forced to answer to another name, and that will get old quick. Make sense?"

"I think so," she said, not at all sure it did.

"After that I don't think there's much information to give—your age, which is easy to lie about if you want to, possibly your profession, and some put their college, though I'm guessing that might be more personal than you want to get. There might be a space to write a little something extra, if you want, or to describe what you're looking for. Honestly, there are all kinds of people on those apps. I'd be as honest as possible about what you're looking for. Or on second thought, you don't have to do that. Just be vague."

"Okay," Hannah said, nodding. "So what did Lucy put in her profile that got your attention?"

For the first time, Reuben turned slightly away, and Hannah was pretty sure he was blushing.

"Okay then," she said quickly. "What did you put in your profile that attracted her to you?"

He turned fully back toward her, and she relaxed a little.

"I kept it to a minimum," he said, sounding like his normal self. "Name, city, age. I left out the part about dropping out of rabbinical school."

"You went to rabbinical school?" she asked, scooching forward. "That is so interesting."

"I dropped out of rabbinical school," he corrected her.

"Well, in order to drop out, you had to go," Hannah said lightly. "What happened?"

"It's a long story," he said. "I never made it past the second year. I was never ordained, obviously. But I learned so much about dealing with people. I mean, there is a lot more involved in it, too—history, religious beliefs, obviously—but for me it was all about interacting with people, helping people."

"I have to ask: How did you end up at a *Catholic* nursing home?"

His phone rang again, and this time he flipped it over so he couldn't see the display. He sat back in his chair, holding his mug in front of him with both hands like he was settling in for a fireside chat.

"What I'm about to say might be controversial," he said. "Especially among people with strong faith, and many people at Saint Martha's have unwavering faith in their religion, which for most people here—though not all—is Catholicism. I respect that more than I can say. But for me, I just couldn't get my head around the idea that there was just one religion that was the true religion. Obviously, if I were to become a rabbi, I would have to believe with every part of my being that Judaism was the most important faith. And it isn't that I don't, necessarily. I identify as Jewish, I'm proud of that, I wear a yarmulke every day, so it isn't like I'm trying to keep that quiet in any way. But I love all religions. I don't think one is better than another; I just think they are all paths to a good life. I mean, as a rabbi I would be free to study all religions, of course, but there was just something in me that knew it wasn't the right fit for me. I began to feel constricted by some of the rules and traditions and found myself picking and choosing what works for me. That was sort of my clue. Sorry, I'm rambling."

"No, you're not," she said. "To be perfectly honest, I've always wondered."

"I worry a lot of people do," he said. "And I worry that the truly devout people here might have a hard time connecting with me, but so far, as they say, so good. All of this is a long way of saying I did not share that in my profile. We all have things we don't quite know how to explain."

"Yes, we do," Hannah said, placing her mug on the table in front of her. She had been so absorbed in Reuben's explanation that she'd almost forgotten what they were doing there for a second.

"So," she said.

"So," he said.

"I should go," she said. "I'm sure you have much more important things to do than help me with my dating profile."

"Well," he said. "Not necessarily more important, certainly not more interesting, but if I don't return this call, I might not be working here much longer."

"Sorry, sorry," she said, standing up. "Thank you. I think I have a handle on it now. Not too much information. Choose good photos."

"I'm here if you need me," he said. "I can take a look at it before you post it."

"Okay," Hannah said slowly. "I'll keep that in mind."

It took three days for Hannah to complete her profile. Reuben's suggestion to think of herself as Hannah Walter while she was writing it, not Hannah Bent, helped a little. She did not agree to get notifications when asked since she didn't want that sweeping across her screen when she was reading to Lincoln or getting Ridley a snack, and once her profile was up, she didn't look at the app again for three more days. She wasn't ready. Until one Thursday morning when she couldn't stand it anymore, and there, waiting for her, were men—lots and lots of men. And so on that Thursday morning, she took her phone out to her porch, her husband and her kids in the house behind her, and she started swiping. Left, left, left, left. And then a photo of a man with dark, warm eyes and a thick graying beard appeared. She wasn't usually one to go for a beard, but it was striking. It said his name was Dan. She thought about that for a minute. Dan was a solid name, a good name. She had no history with any Dans. She barely knew any Dans.

In some photos he wore glasses; in others he didn't. He looked rugged and kind and adventurous. She looked at his last photo for a long time. He was in a field, smiling wide, holding a boxer puppy. Before she swiped, she wanted to ask, *Is that your puppy, or is he a prop? Are those prescription glasses or readers? Or are they just to make a fashion statement? Have you climbed that mountain behind you, or did you choose it for the sole purpose of being the backdrop of the photo shoot?* But there was only one way to get all the answers. She swiped right.

CHAPTER TWELVE

"I'm going out tonight," Hannah said to Joel. "I'm not sure when I'll be back."

"Where?" Joel asked pointedly. She looked right back at him and pursed her lips, and he lowered his eyes. She was meeting Dan at Southwark, a bar not too far from her house but one she would never think to go to, so it seemed okay. She and Dan had chatted a little through the app, but she'd decided to hold most of her questions for the date so they would have at least something to talk about.

"Just out," she said.

Joel nodded, his head down, and walked out of the bedroom. She had to remain in her armor mode as she was thinking of it, ready to protect and defend herself. When she wasn't looking for a date, she was surprised by how relatively normal things had become between her and Joel, except for the lack of sleep—neither of them were sleeping—and the lack of sex. But how could it be any other way? She knew she couldn't sleep with Joel and have an affair at the same time, even though that was exactly what he had done. Well, maybe not quite. If she had the story right, he had come home after his first time with Tara for that in-between week, ten or eleven days, and he had been sick—or at least pretended to be, she thought now—and he'd slept on the couch. Then when he'd come back the second time, the affair was over. So technically, she guessed, he had not slept with her *while* he was sleeping with Tara.

She came down the stairs to find Joel at the kitchen table with the kids, spooning steaming meatballs onto each of their plates, and she knew exactly where he'd gotten them. *Really?* she wanted to say. *Enough with the meatballs! Why do you think meatballs are the thing that will change my mind?* And then she saw he had filled "the bowl," as they called it, with extra sauce and placed it in the middle of the table. It was their bowl, the one they had had for their entire marriage, the one that represented pretty much everything they had been through, at least until things had gone so bad, with tons of cracks from their everyday living. She had avoided using it lately. Now she wanted to smash it. She had to get out of there.

"Why do you look so pretty, Mommy?" Lincoln asked, looking up from his meatballs. She really hadn't done much more than not change into her pajamas before dinner and put on earrings, a few bracelets, and lipstick. That was it. Well, that and the nice blouse.

"I have a meeting," she said as casually as she could, lifting her purse from the table next to the door.

"At night?" Lincoln asked. He was going to be a reporter one day, Hannah thought, or a lawyer, some line of work that caught people doing things they were not supposed to be doing or did not want to get caught at and then questioned them about it.

"Yeah, the people I have to meet can only meet at night," she said, cringing a little because now she had lied. If she had said *person*, she would still be lying but only by omission. In fact, that wouldn't have been a lie at all. She was going to a meeting with one person who could meet only at night.

"Person, I mean," she mumbled. There, now she wasn't lying.

"Okay, Mommy," he said, letting her off the hook. "Will you be home before we go to sleep?"

She didn't know. She guessed it depended on how well the date went. No, that was silly—she was meeting Dan for the first time. Even if she liked him, she wouldn't be out too late with him tonight; she would just schedule another date.

"Yes, I plan to be," she said, feeling like a fraud and an interloper in her own house.

"I love you guys," she said generally as she moved toward the door, accepting a hug from Lincoln, who had jumped up and run to her. "I'll be home soon."

She was a little excited about her date with Dan, being able to present herself to someone who didn't know her, meeting someone new. She had all her questions, culled from his profile photos, ready as she walked into the bar. She hoped she would know him; she had heard so many horror stories about people not looking at all like their photos, but there he was, looking exactly as he did standing below the mountain: dark hair, beard, fit, tall, welcoming.

"Hannah?" he asked as she walked toward him, and she was relieved to know she looked enough like her pictures to be recognizable.

"Yes," she said, reaching out her hand, her delicate bracelets jangling on her wrist. She should really wear bracelets more often. "It's nice to meet you."

She followed him to the bar, and they took seats next to each other.

"What would you like?" he asked.

"I'll just have a glass of red wine," she said, looking down and seeing the tiniest splatter of sauce from the meatballs at the bottom of her shirt, undoubtedly from Lincoln's hug. She fought the urge to rub it. "What about you?"

"Sounds good," he said, gesturing to the bartender and ordering.

He was cute, and he had a kind look to his eyes. She relaxed slightly. The wine came, and he raised his glass.

"To new beginnings," he said.

"Cheers," she said, even though that wasn't why she was here at all. If she had made the toast, she might have said *To a good night* or *To a short new beginning before being forced to make the biggest, hardest decision of my life*, but she let it go. She had to stop thinking that way if she was going to make any progress at all.

"So in that photo, was that your puppy?" she asked.

"Actually, it's my son's puppy," he said. He took a deep breath. "There's not much room to say all of this in a profile, so I save it for the first date. I'm divorced; I have three sons. My ex-wife has them during the week when school is in session because that's what works logistically, so I always feel like I'm not part of their routine. Anyway, that's my son Jake's puppy. His name is Waldo."

"Is that why you put that photo in?" she asked, truly curious. "Because it sparks that conversation?"

"Actually, no, I just like it," he said. "You're the first person to ask me about it. What about you? I couldn't really see anything telling in your photos. I mean, I could see you, which was enough, of course, but nothing that told me a single thing about your life."

Hannah had decided she was going to be honest but only if the person seemed like someone she might really want to have an affair with. Then she would explain the situation. She figured there must be some men who would jump at the chance to have a quick relationship, no strings attached. Or even be willing to take a chance and see how it all played out. In order to do this at all, she found herself fantasizing more and more about the possibility that she would find not only someone to have a romantic encounter with but maybe even someone who would carry her into the future should she move forward with the divorce.

"I'll tell you about me," she said, trying to not think too much and just be there with Dan. "I promise. But I'm so interested in you. It said something about your being a guide to young people in your profile. What sort of guide?"

"Ah, okay," he said like he was gearing up for something. He took a slow sip of his wine. She noticed he was wearing jeans and leather shoes, and he had an Apple Watch that kept lighting up, but she couldn't make out any of the words. "I'm a college counselor, so I'm a guide to young people in that sense. I didn't mean to be so cryptic. I am proud to say I know every college in the United States, even Canada, backward and forward."

"Oh, that's so interesting. My hu—um, my friend knows every single mascot of every single college and university in the US," she said, knowing she was getting red in the face. Why was that where her mind had to go? She couldn't stop thinking about Joel for one hour? "He, I mean she, is never stumped."

"I bet I could stump her," he said.

"Maybe," Hannah said, trailing off. This was not where she'd meant to take the conversation. "So you, what? Help them with essays and putting college lists together? Do you work at a high school?"

"Yes, yes, and no," he said, smiling. He motioned to the bartender that he wanted another glass of wine. Hannah took another sip of hers. "I'll answer in the reverse order in which the questions were asked. I don't work for a high school; I have my own private consulting firm. I do help the students make college lists, which is a long, tedious, and also intricate process, one I like and don't like at the same time. And finally, yes, I do help them with their essays. In fact, just today I helped a student come up with a great essay topic, unique, outstanding. I think it's going to get him into his first choice—which is Georgetown."

"Wow, what is it?" Hannah asked, finding the conversation to be more interesting than she'd expected. "What was the topic?"

"Hamster hospice," Dan said proudly. "Basically, my student is going to write about starting a business in which he takes in sick and dying hamsters so the owners don't have to watch them die. Hamsters go downhill fast. It's a great subject. He's going to start with a hamster named Fred, who belonged to a ten-year-old boy, no, maybe a six-year-old boy; I'm not sure which yet. The boy will be crying as he hands over his hamster to my student, thanking him for his service."

"That must be really sad," Hannah said. "To watch so many hamsters die. What does he do with them once they're dead?"

"Oh, he doesn't actually have a hamster-hospice service," Dan said like it was no big deal. "I made it up. But the colleges will never know."

Hannah's jerk radar went up. Was lying like that jerky behavior? She was fairly sure it was.

"Isn't there a code of ethics or something?" Hannah asked. Maybe she was misunderstanding.

"Yeah, I mean, of course there is," Dan said, and Hannah relaxed slightly. "But who is ever going to know? Look, it's a competitive world out there. If you want to get ahead, sometimes you have to lie and cheat and literally claw your way in."

"Can you excuse me for a minute?" Hannah asked.

"Sure," Dan said jovially.

Hannah found her way to the bathroom. She didn't have to go, but she locked the door behind her. She wished she could talk to someone to make sure she wasn't wrong about him, but there was nobody. The idea of calling Reuben moved through her mind, but she let it go. She didn't need to ask anyone. Dan was a liar, which made him a jerk. There really wasn't any way around it. On the other hand, he was cute, so he met the first part of her wish list. And it had taken so long to get to this point. She decided she would give him another chance.

She went back to the bar and took her seat.

"Welcome back," he said, and from his tone she was certain he had no idea she was having second thoughts.

"Thanks," she said.

"So, you, I want to hear about you," he said, taking a sip of wine.

Liar, liar, liar ran through her mind. Really, if she *already* knew he was a liar, what was the point? What was she doing? And in the end, he wasn't that cute. His beard was prickly looking in person. When she looked closer, she realized she had no desire in the world to kiss him.

"I'm so sorry," she said. "I'm going to call it a night. I made a mistake. I'm so sorry."

Dan looked at her for a second, then nodded.

"No problem," he said, like he really didn't care much. "It happens."

"Okay," she said, standing. She had expected a bit more of a fight from him. "Well, thanks!"

She was home less than an hour from the time she'd left. The meatballs weren't even cleaned up yet.

As Hannah walked up 9th Street, looking for Villa di Roma to meet Joel for what she considered to be their first official date (but that, unbeknownst to her yet, Joel thought was really their third), she felt happy. That was the best, most accurate word she could find in her entire vocabulary to describe what she was feeling. It was not the usual way she approached a date, especially since her recent breakup. On the few dates she had gone on recently, she'd felt full of angst and nervousness with a distinct and serious lack of confidence. But this time was different.

It took a second for her eyes to adjust to all the activity, but once they did, she saw Joel standing at the top of the bar waving.

"You came! And you found it," he said. "I never even asked where you were coming from."

"Queen Village," she said. "This couldn't have been easier. And did you think I might not come?"

"You never know," he said warmly. "And I'm so glad you did, not just because they have the best meatballs in the city, hands down."

The host led them to the next room, which had exposed brick walls and white cloth-adorned tables. A board with movable letters spelled out the menu.

"I could eat Italian food every night," Joel said. "Really, if I had to make a choice, that's what I would pick."

"I guess I would too," she said, wondering if he was gearing up to play the desert island game—If you were stranded on a desert island, what were the things you couldn't live without? Book? Food? Cosmetic or toiletry? She had it down to a science—Stephen King's *The Shining*, bread, and her facial moisturizer, which she loved, although her real answer was toilet paper. Playing this game wasn't a terrible way to get to know someone. She looked across the table, the words to her answers ready to spill out. Maybe she would change up the book this time, offer John Irving's *The World according to Garp* instead.

"Your hair looks nice," he said. "Did you just get it cut?"

"Yes, actually," she said, readjusting to this new line of conversation. She was surprised that he noticed. He had seen her only twice before.

An older woman brought over ice water and a basket of bread. "Anything to drink?"

"Red wine?" Joel asked Hannah, who nodded. It came in small juice glasses and tasted better than any fancy red wine Hannah had ever had. Hannah broke her first-date rule and ate the garlic bread; it looked way too good not to. They had fried asparagus in butter sauce, and she took Joel's lead and dipped bread in the sauce until the plate was completely clean. They both had the spaghetti and meatballs, then tiramisu for dessert.

"You pick well," Hannah said when they were finished eating and so full. "My new favorite restaurant. I have to say, this was a great first date."

"What do you mean, first date?" Joel said, sitting forward. "This is our third date."

"Third? How do you count three dates?" she asked, sitting up, too, so she could be closer to him.

"Our first date was hamburgers. Our second date was tea and honey. This is our third date."

Hannah glanced at her watch. It was almost eight thirty. She remembered how he had said they would have an early dinner so she could get on with her night if she didn't have fun. Now all she wanted to do was kiss him and see him naked, even though they had just had a big garlicky meal. She felt a physical pull toward him.

He reached his hand out and covered hers on the table. "Definitely date number three," he said quietly.

"I think it's date number one. When you meet doesn't count as a date, since you have no idea it's going to happen; it isn't planned in any way. Tea at the market was nice but also not a date. This—what we did tonight—is an official date."

"Well," Joel said, and she knew he wasn't going to argue anymore. How could she like someone so fast? She just had a feeling. With someone else she might have thought he was upping the number of dates to get her into bed, but she didn't think that was what Joel was doing. Really, she didn't even care. In fact, if that was what he was doing, then bring it on.

"But," she said, drawing out the word, "since you think it's our third date, that does put a different spin on it all. Any interest in coming back to my apartment? We can walk there."

Joel stood up quickly, and she laughed. He sat back down and looked around frantically for the server.

"Don't worry," she said, feeling confident and pretty and, still, the whole time they were together, happy. "I'm not going to change my mind."

They paid and walked back to her tiny place, feeling less and less full with each block. As they passed a bookstore on 2nd Street, he asked if she wanted to go in. She did. They went their separate ways in the small store, and he came back to her, holding a dictionary open.

"So I looked this up not because I have to be right. It's very important to me that you believe that. But the definition of a date is a romantic appointment—so yes, that would fit your description—and also a romantic engagement, which would fit mine. I'd say we're both right."

"I'll give you that," she said, smiling.

"And one more word," he said, flipping the pages. "*Incandescent*: emitting light, passionate, brilliant. This is the word that has been going through my mind since I met you. It is you, but it is also me when I'm with you. Now take this dictionary away from me before I completely embarrass myself!"

She laughed and let him hand her the dictionary, but something flipped in her at that moment, and she knew it. Usually she would hate that kind of corny display of emotion; she would think it was forced or at the very least uncomfortable. But not with Joel. He kept surprising her, but more than that she kept surprising herself with her reactions to him.

"Wait," she said as he moved toward the door. She looked at the dictionary in her hand. It was small with a decorated blue cover. It cost twelve dollars. She took it to the cashier and bought it, and then she carried the bag home and placed it on the tiny table just inside her door. They had sex on the floor. It was her one regret, she thought later. Their first time should have been on a softer surface. But afterward they lay there, and she reached up and handed him the bag. So many words ran through her head at that moment—*finally*, *lucky*, *handsome*, *chemistry*, *too fast*, *hope*—but he paged through the book and landed on a different word, and he read it out loud: *happy*.

After the scrubbed date with Dan, Hannah spent the next six long weeks going out on dates with seven other men, and each and every time she had a moment when she knew she could not have an affair with him, when one of her three criteria proved either true or false or in some cases had to be amended.

Her third date was with a man named Wiley.

"Hello," he said, spotting her immediately when she walked into the designated meeting place, a somewhat mysterious corner establishment called the Sit on It Bar in South Philadelphia. He had explained during their chat on the app that this was his go-to first-date suggestion, and even though it seemed a little odd to her, she had agreed because she was fairly sure she wouldn't know anyone there. Wiley was cute and appeared to be trying hard, which she appreciated after her second date, which had been with a man named Juan, who hadn't reacted to one thing she'd said. It had been almost like she wasn't even there. For a few minutes she thought there was the chance that Wiley would be better.

"You look just like your picture," he said. She had come to see this was a good thing, a point worth mentioning.

"So do you," she said. But did he? When she looked closer, she could tell it was the same person, but the pictures on the site made him look slightly older. If she remembered correctly, his profile had said he was forty-four. She distinctly recalled thinking he had crow's-feet around his eyes, but close up his skin was smooth as anything, no wrinkles or crow's-feet in sight. There was no way he was forty-four, though it was pretty dark in there, so maybe she was seeing things . . . or not seeing them, as the case may have been.

"Oh, good," he said. "I do fudge it a little. I'm into older women, so I try to look older in the photos, then wow them with how young I look in person."

"What? You mean you really are younger?" she said, pulling her purse onto her lap, getting ready for the exit. She could feel it coming. It was a move that was becoming familiar. "What do you do, photoshop it in or something?"

"Yep," he said proudly, thinking she liked it, not realizing this was the deal breaker. Why, she wondered, was there always a deal breaker?

"How old are you?" she asked.

"Twenty-nine," he said, like that was a good thing. "I figure, what woman wouldn't want to be with a fit, buff younger guy if the guy was into it, right?"

For the briefest second she wondered if he was right. If it was all physical, why not go for a younger man? And he might not be looking for any sort of real connection; that would work in her favor too. But no, she couldn't do it. He was far closer in age to Monica than to her, which definitely gave her pause. He wasn't so young that it was creepy or illegal, but it wasn't what she wanted. That was when she amended the "not too old" caveat to also include "not too young." Plus, he was as much a liar as Dan was, just in a different way, so he also fell firmly into the jerk category. She finished her drink and said good night.

By the eighth bad date, when she came home by seven forty-five, again, she thought she saw a small smile on Joel's face that she didn't like. He tried to hide it, but she was pretty sure it was there. The word *happy* ran through her head. He was happy that she was having no success.

She could do this, she told herself as she went upstairs to take off her earrings and bracelets. She was a pretty, fit, smart, and interesting woman. She was determined. The next one was going to stick. It was time to get serious.

CHAPTER THIRTEEN

"Who wants pancakes?" Joel asked, coming out of the bathroom fully dressed and ready to go. They had gone back to sleeping in the same bed, most nights with both kids between them, because Hannah didn't want the kids to be upset.

"Me! I do," Ridley said, sitting up.

"Chocolate chip?" Lincoln asked with his eyes still closed. He reached over and shoved Ridley, who had gotten a little too close. She looked startled and inched away a tiny bit. She was always so easy, always accepting when someone had an issue with her. It made life simpler, certainly, but now Hannah saw it in a different way. She was going to have to talk to her about that.

"Sure," Joel said. "That sounds good. Hannah? Chocolate chip for you too? Or I think there might be some blueberries down there somewhere."

"I think I'll skip the pancakes," she said. "I was hoping to swim right after drop-off."

The truth was she had meant to be the first one out this morning. She had a mission. And this, Joel's trying to act normal and make pancakes, was exactly what she had wanted to avoid.

"Then it's three orders of pancakes," Joel said, still upbeat.

"Why don't you go get breakfast started, and I'll get the kids ready," she said, trying to sound normal, trying to hold back her urge to tell him to cut the crap. Did he think he could turn things around with pancakes and meatballs?

"Okay," Joel said.

"Any chance you can drop them today?" she asked, heading toward the bathroom. "I'm eager to get to the Y."

"Sure," he said, as she'd known he would. He was trying to do everything she asked. It was actually her day to take them, and unless something had changed, she was fairly sure Joel had a pretty early meeting. Still, she needed to do what she needed to do.

"Great, thanks," she said. She would get them ready and then focus on dressing herself. She also wanted to make sure she was all shaved and that her pedicure, which she'd gotten a few days ago in preparation for something, though she hadn't been sure exactly what, didn't need any touching up.

"Come on, you guys," she said, hurrying them along. "You don't want to miss the pancakes."

They were up and scattered into their rooms, where Lincoln pulled on light sweatpants and a Philadelphia Eagles shirt before heading to the bathroom to pee with the door open.

"Is this a good outfit?" he called proudly toward her.

"Very good," she said. "Very South Philly. Perfect."

Ridley took forever choosing a shirt, and Hannah kept thinking, *How much longer?* Which was not the way she usually thought at all. The thing was she had decided that today was the day she was going to make her move on Lance, and now she could barely breathe.

As soon as everyone was down and eating pancakes, she went back upstairs and pulled out her best bikini. She had been eating much less over the last few months, and she was fairly sure she had dropped a few pounds, not that she'd really needed to. She shaved and decided her toes still looked good enough. She put jeans and a T-shirt over her bathing suit, collected a change of clothes, and at the very last minute, slipped off her wedding ring and placed it in the pocket of her jeans. Then she headed out, stopping briefly to kiss both children on the tops of their heads. She usually breathed in their scalpy, human smell when she did this, but today, considering where she was going, she held her breath as she went from head to head. How could she begin an affair with the scent of her children lingering in her nostrils?

"Bye," she said, her hand on the doorknob, the tiniest twinge of excitement roiling deep in her belly. "Have fun at school."

Once she was outside, though, she didn't want to go. She didn't want to flirt and put herself out there and hope someone found her attractive. And who was this Lance anyway? She had built him up to be *the one* in her mind, the one she'd been saving for when she got really serious, but was he worthy of that? Maybe she should do this tomorrow. She had a big meeting about the new hotel project at eleven thirty. It had stalled pending a few important permits, and now it was back up full swing. She should be making herself presentable and doing research, but she just had a strange feeling that it was now or never with Lance.

Okay, she decided, she would walk north toward the Y and see how she felt. That way, at the very least, she would be getting exercise. She was almost there when Joel called, the sound of the ringing phone interrupting Van Morrison's "Crazy Love," which she had been playing to psych herself up. At first she considered letting it go to voice mail. She could pretend she had already gotten into the pool by the time he called, but it was so early that it wasn't out of the question that there could be a problem with one of the kids.

"Hey," she said, the words *heartbeat* and *thousand miles* running through her mind.

"Uh, hey yourself," he said. "The kids are all dropped. I was wondering if you had a few minutes to talk? Maybe we could meet for coffee?"

She was so thrown off by this request that she stopped walking abruptly, and the wheels of a jogger stroller crashed into her from behind, hard.

"I'm so sorry," a woman said, coming around to her left side. "I didn't expect you to stop, and I was just about to go around."

"It's okay," she said, wondering if the skin on her ankle had been cut. Maybe. It felt like that.

"Are you sure you're okay?" the woman asked, jogging in place next to Hannah, her hand on the stroller, clearly eager to keep going.

"Yes, I'm fine," Hannah said. If Joel hadn't been on the phone, maybe she would have said she wasn't fine—she was the opposite of fine. But at that moment it didn't seem like her heel was the biggest source of her angst.

The jogger nodded and took off.

"I'm back," Hannah said.

"What happened?" Joel said, sounding concerned.

"Nothing," she said sharply, shutting him down.

"Okay, well, look, I'm having a hard time," Joel said. "I know I'm supposed to be having a hard time, that I deserve to have a hard time, but I can't sleep, I can't eat, and while I don't want to go back on our agreement, our plan, what I would like to do is maybe talk more about, I don't even know, a time line, maybe? Or some of the details? I honestly don't know what I'm asking for—I guess to just talk to you. I miss you."

"Well, you should have thought of that before you embarked on your romantic adventure with Tara," she said, surprised by how the anger was always right there, just waiting to come out. "You didn't call me in to see if certain things worked for me or if they didn't. Take the rose petals, for example. I never would have approved those rose petals. I think we've talked about this more than enough already."

"Okay," Joel said, and she knew he wasn't going to push.

"Don't you have a meeting?" she asked, annoyed. She was sure she could feel blood trickling down her heel, but she didn't want to look. Also, it was starting to ache.

Joel didn't say anything. She could hear the sounds of traffic through the phone.

"Hello?" she said, completely out of patience.

"I'm not going to my meeting," he said. "I took myself out."

"What does that mean, you took yourself out?"

"I'm just not working on this particular phase of the project," he said, like that was perfectly reasonable, even though Hannah knew it was not—Joel would never miss any phases of a project. He was a control freak. Under no circumstances that she could think of would he ever hand anything over to someone else at work.

"Why?" Hannah asked. She was both alarmed and suspicious.

"They're dealing with the details of the color and lighting throughout the building to find the right image. It's a lot of trying and seeing with the different spaces, you know how it is, and it would mean I would have to be there, in Minnesota. I don't want to be there, I don't want to go, so I'm letting Brett handle it. He's happy to."

"I bet he is," Hannah said. Brett reported to Joel, but she always suspected that he didn't like that arrangement. "Why are you afraid to go? Are you scared you'll be tempted by Tara? That you won't be able to resist her?"

"What?" Joel said, sounding truly alarmed. "No, nothing like that. God—have you not listened to a single thing I've said? I don't want Tara. I want you."

Again, Hannah wanted to say, *Well, you should have thought about that before you did what you did,* but she didn't. How many times could she say the same thing? Instead she said, "You don't have to do that. You can still go. In fact, it would be a relief."

Joel didn't say anything.

Hannah was almost to the Y. She was bleeding, her hair was windblown, and she felt pulled down by Joel. She didn't have an ounce of sexy in her right now.

"Look, I'm not going because I don't want to leave you," Joel said. "I'm afraid of what you might do. I mean, I know you've been doing something; that's a done deal, but I don't want to be too far away, just in case I can rein it in a little or at least remind you that I'm here."

"I have to go," Hannah said. "I'm at the pool."

"Okay," Joel said, but she could tell he didn't want to hang up. "And I get that you don't want to give me the chance to talk about it. I do get that. But can I just ask you to try to get on with it? It seems to be going on forever, and it's . . . hard. I feel out of control. I'm afraid you're going to like someone, a lot. I guess that's my biggest—"

"Stop, okay?" Hannah said, interrupting him.

What had he expected? That she would mark the family calendar in the kitchen, the one with images of Ocean City, New Jersey, where they spent two weeks at the beginning of each summer? That she would find the right square, take the navy Sharpie they left on the counter to write playdates and concerts, and write *First Day of the Affair* and *Last Day of the Affair*? And of course, he didn't know that she was still looking for the right person, that everything leading up to this point equaled nothing.

Hannah walked through the heavy door and breathed in the scent of the pool. She thought she might just ask the front desk for a Band-Aid and leave, try again another day when she felt better, more confident; she couldn't risk losing this chance. But through the glass wall to the right of the desk, she saw Lance, sitting tall and strong on the guard chair, his clipped-on palm tree next to him as he mouthed the words to some song. She looked closer. The pool was completely empty. She heard Joel breathing on the other end of the call. She was glad she couldn't see him because he was probably pale, maybe trying not to throw up. *Well,* she thought, *he made his bed.*

"I'm going now," she said. "I'll talk to you later." She ended the call and handed her card over to the person behind the desk. Her heart was beating so fast she could feel it thumping.

She headed to the locker room and stripped down to her bikini. She threw her stuff in one of the many open lockers and closed it, not bothering to see if she had a lock. She glanced at herself in the mirror as she walked through the shower room. She looked good, by any standards, she thought, not just with the knowledge that she had had two kids. But Lance didn't know that. She didn't think he knew much about her at all. She wished now she had told him her name was something else. It would be so much easier to do this if she were using another name—Jasmine, maybe, or Collette. Then it might seem like acting or role-playing. Then it might not feel so real. But it was too late for that.

The humid air hit her as she walked toward Lance. Her plan was to get into the deep end slowly, maybe start up a conversation, and possibly, if she dared, ask him out. Lance smiled at her as she got closer, and she thought, *We did always have a bit of a connection; isn't it great that I can actually act on that now, see how it plays out?* She was going to use the ladder and ease in, but now she thought an elegant dive would be much better, more seductive. She walked to the back of the pool, standing just in front of Lance, so he could see all her trim curves and the way her bikini bottom fit her just so. She lifted her arms over her head.

"Excuse me, ma'am?" Lance called out rather harshly. "Ma'am, are you bleeding?"

She put her arms back at her sides and turned slowly. She looked behind her at her heel, and yes, she most certainly was bleeding. A small, watery red puddle had formed below her foot as she'd stood getting ready to dive. She looked back at the path she had taken, and sure enough, there were drops of blood here and there.

"You can't swim with an open wound," Lance said.

"Well, it's not really an open wound," she said.

Lance sat forward to get a better look, then hopped off the chair and crouched down to see.

"I can treat that," he said, but his tone was so removed, so unromantic, that he could have been talking to a kid or one of the old ladies. She wanted to ask him if he remembered showing her how to adjust her backstroke based on the overhead flags and how they'd listened to Bob Marley together that day. But she couldn't. If she talked, she would cry. So she nodded. He jumped up and grabbed a first aid kit from under the guard chair. He rifled through it and pulled out an alcohol pad and a Band-Aid. He didn't ask her to sit down or to join him on one of the benches. He knelt again and wiped the cut, which stung.

"Hmmm," he said. "That's a real bleeder. Do you tend to bleed a lot?"

Just my heart, she wanted to say.

"Not really," she managed.

"Well, this one isn't stopping," he said. "I'll put the bandage on it, but you can't get in the pool until it stops. Health-code regulations. You can wait a little, maybe elevate it."

"Okay, thanks," she said, waiting while he positioned the Band-Aid on her heel. Then he smoothed it once, twice, to make sure it would stick.

She hobbled over to the bench, even though it really hadn't hurt much after that initial ache. There was something about getting medical attention that made the focused-on body part suddenly seem even worse. She sat down and put her leg out to the side on the bench. At this point, honestly, swimming sounded better than flirting with Lance. Was he even that cute? She couldn't tell suddenly. She noticed that his back was really hairy. She'd gotten a good look when he'd leaned over to tend to her foot. Also one of his toes looked twisted. Ugh, she wasn't looking for someone else to marry, she reminded herself, just someone to have a drink with, to get back at Joel with. The pool had been quiet, but now music began to play. It took a few notes to hear it was Van Morrison, "Crazy Love." She wanted to tell him what a coincidence that was, that she'd been *just listening to it,* but she couldn't; he would think she was crazy herself. He slid off the chair again and walked over to her, and she looked away. Was she so obvious? Could he tell she was thinking about him?

"Hey, how does it feel?" he asked kindly.

"Okay," she said. "Better, I think."

"Can I take a look?" he asked, reaching out his hand. At first she wasn't sure what he was asking her to do, but he pointed to her foot and opened his hand again, so she eased it around and into his palm. He turned it over and examined it. "It looks good. It stopped. I think you can swim soon."

"Do you want to get some coffee sometime?" she blurted. "Or a drink? Have you ever been to that bar with the cowboy boot sign? I've always wanted to go there."

Honestly, he didn't even appear to be surprised. He looked at her for a beat, maybe two, and then he was nodding his head, taking in the idea.

"Sure," he said. He was still holding her foot, and now she wished she had waited until he wasn't to ask. But really she hadn't even planned to ask—it was like the words had been kidnapped from her throat and sent out into the world without her consent. "That sounds like fun. You mean the one on Broad? Yeah, I've always wanted to go there too. Do they have, like, different themes on different nights? I like to line dance. Do they have that?"

"I don't know," Hannah said, easing her foot out of his hand, placing it on the tile floor, and standing. "I'll look it up."

"Great," he said.

"Um, can I take your number? I'll text you once I do some research," she said. When she heard the word *research* resonate in the pool area, she thought of her meeting.

"Sure, it's—"

"Oh, wait," she said. "Let me get my phone from my locker."

What an idiot, she thought to herself as she walked back through the shower room, opened the unlocked locker, and found her phone in her jeans pocket. Her hand brushed against her wedding ring as she pulled it out. In that short time three women had come in and shed their clothes and were now heading out toward the pool and toward Lance. One of them wondered out loud about the blood on the floor. Hannah had the urge to push past them, to get back to Lance before they did, but she couldn't without risking slipping on the wet floor, not to mention looking insane. So she took a deep breath and went back for a paper towel, using it to clean up the drops of blood as she went. When she finally got back out, two of the women were already in the shallow end, but one had walked right up to Lance with a question. While Hannah waited, she scrolled to her contacts and simply typed *POOL*. If Tara was HOTEL, then Lance would be POOL.

It didn't take long, and he was walking toward her.

"So, my number," he said and slowly recited the numbers. She typed them in, then read them back to him.

"I'll call you," she said. "So you have mine too."

"Great," Lance said. "Thanks."

What she wanted to do was get all the small talk out of the way now, to make sure this wasn't just a completely bad idea. For example, were all the rumors true, and why was he a single dad? Had he ever been married? If so, what had happened to his spouse? But she couldn't. All of that would have to wait to be answered during breaks between the Macarena and the Cupid Shuffle.

"I'll text you," she said quietly. "Later."

"I'll look forward to it," he said.

Okay, she thought as she turned away, letting her number ring through to his before ending the call, was this the beginning of the real part of her affair? Maybe. She walked into the locker room again. She imagined herself using the Sharpie by the calendar and drawing a tiny heart in the square that represented today. She smiled at the ridiculousness of it. As she slowly got dressed, pulling her clothes on over her still-dry bikini, she hoped Lance hadn't noticed that she'd ended up not getting in the pool at all. Should she go back and explain? Say she was afraid her heel would bleed in the pool? She shook her head. She was as bad at this dating stuff as she always had been. Clearly, it never got easier.

Hannah had just gotten home and was heading to the computer to do research when she heard her phone ping with a text.

The text was from POOL. She smiled, then immediately worried he had thought better of it.

Line dancing?

Phew.

Still looking into it. Will write again soon.

She considered her text for a long time, wondering how she could make it sexier, more fun. She could add a smiley face; clearly a heart or a kissy face was way too much. Flowers? No. In the end she found a red cowboy boot emoji and added that. She sent it, hoping the red didn't connote something she didn't know about. It was surprisingly complicated to have an affair, even when you were allowed to do it.

She sat down at the computer, intending to do research about all-day cafés and what people wanted from their hotel stays. Really, her plan was to read almost every single review she could find for similar hotels. What they wanted to do, what she was so excited to be a part of, was to create the perfect hotel. But instead of going to TripAdvisor, she tried to find the name of the bar with the cowboy boot. It was called Boot and Saddle and turned out to be more of a music venue than a western bar. So she looked for others—one called Howl at the Moon got her attention. But in the end she decided they should stick with the original plan. She would propose a night when there wasn't a band playing and just hope they were open to requests. Also, the house-made cocktails were appealing. The next open night, though, wasn't for a week and a half. That was okay—it would give her time to gear up for it all.

She picked up her phone.

Not sure about line dancing but looks nice. Called Boot and Saddle. How is a week from Wednesday? And again, she added the red cowboy boot emoji. She pressed send.

Not even a minute later, she got his text.

Sounds good! See you there at 7? And he added a cowboy hat emoji, which she really liked.

Yes! See you there at 7.

All she could do was hope her affair had finally begun.

CHAPTER FOURTEEN

Even though this one felt different to Hannah, she tried not to get too excited. She dressed in dark jeans and a flowy white shirt. She had stuffed a red bandana in her purse. Frankly, she felt like she was going to a sorority barn dance.

"I'll be back soon," she called toward the dinner table, waving over her shoulder. "You guys be good."

She left off the *for Daddy* that she would usually say. She couldn't even look at them as she walked out. When her cab dropped her at the iconic boot sign, she really did feel like she was acting. How many times had she wondered what it was like in there? How many times had she said to Joel, "We should go there sometime"? She walked in, and it was quiet. She looked around but didn't see Lance. She took a seat at the bar.

"What are you having?" the young, muscular bartender asked. Maybe she could date him if things didn't work out with Lance.

She tried to remember the mixed drinks that she'd read about on the website. There was one with rum—what was that called?

"I'll have a Night Out, please," she said. "The one with rum?"

"You mean the Good Night. Sure," the bartender said. But she wasn't sure—should she be waiting for Lance before she ordered? She really could use a drink. Even a few sips might help her relax a little.

"What's in that again?" she asked as her phone rang. She looked at the hopeful bartender, who was giving her all his attention since nobody else needed it. "You know what, I'm just going to think about it for a minute," she said, and he bowed slightly and backed away.

She reached for her phone, assuming it was Lance cancelling, which would totally suck. She had come this far. But it was Joel. Shoot. She clicked ignore and stuffed it back in her purse. Was he checking up on her? A few seconds later a text came through.

I'm not really calling. Lincoln needs to talk to you. Call again?

Sure, she wrote back.

In no time her phone was ringing again. Joel's picture looked up at her. She was going to have to change that, maybe replace the photo with a generic smiley face or something. Better yet, the throwing-up emoji. She chuckled to herself quietly.

"Hi, Linc," she said.

"Mommy?" he called into the phone like she hadn't just spoken.

"I'm here, sweetie. What's up?" Hannah asked.

"Mommy, when are you coming home? We have a problem," he said in his old-man way. He had been so good, barely needing to go over any timing questions with her lately, rarely calling repeatedly. Honestly, most of her dates had been so short he probably hadn't even realized she was gone. But the radar on this kid! Clearly he knew something was up tonight.

"What's the problem?" she asked, her eyes on the door. What would she do if Lance walked in before she could appease Lincoln?

"I want to read *Harry Potter*, but Ridley doesn't," he said seriously. "We need two adults in the house tonight. It's double reading duty."

"I get that," Hannah said, feeling annoyed and amused at the same time, if that were possible. "I really do. But can you compromise tonight? I'm out with Kim, and we're just going to have a few drinks and catch up—girl talk—but I'll be home at a reasonable hour."

It was so much harder to lie directly to Lincoln than it was to lie to Joel at this point. Before, she never would have thought that—she wasn't a very good liar, always confessing quickly when she tried to keep the truth from someone—but now she told herself she had to lie to keep Joel from throwing up constantly. It was for his own good. Also, she reminded herself, she didn't owe him total and complete honesty anymore the way she used to. But lying to Lincoln was a whole other story. It did not feel right. Then she thought, if she was really going to do this, she would have to lie to him and to Ridley, so was it worth that? Just then Lance walked into the bar. He stood in the doorway for a few seconds, letting his eyes adjust from the bright evening to the dark bar. He saw her and smiled. He wore jeans and a nicely worn plaid shirt with the sleeves rolled up to just under his elbow. His hair was still a little wet and neatly brushed, and as she looked at him, she realized she had never seen him in clothes before. He looked good in clothes.

She was so torn. She pointed to the phone and mouthed *my son,* which she thought was acceptable since as far as she knew he had at least one child. He nodded and gave the okay sign.

"Take your time," he said almost inaudibly, and she appreciated it so much. There was nothing for Lincoln to hear.

"Can you guys compromise tonight?" she asked again, her mind racing. How could she get him to agree to this? "Maybe you can be the one in charge and suggest a book both of you will like. I'll read you *Harry Potter* tomorrow, for an hour or more. And I'll give you twenty dollars."

"Twenty dollars?" Lincoln said incredulously. "Okay."

"Okay?"

"Sure," he said. She waited for him to ask when he could call again, but he didn't. He just stayed on the other end, singing quietly to himself, "Ring around the rosy, a pocket full of posy, ashes, ashes."

"Hey, Linc, I'm going to go now," she said. When she'd first offered the money, she'd thought, *Joel will kill me.* He hated bribery, and it was always her instinct when she was in a panic. She often ended up offering things she would come to regret—like telling one kid they could choose what the whole family was going to have for dinner if they would just please stop wailing in the grocery store and let her check out. That had backfired. Or the time she'd told Ridley she could sleep in bed alone with Mommy and Daddy if she would just please, please go to sleep. That hadn't turned out so well either. But now she realized, Who cared? Lincoln probably wouldn't tell Joel because he was smart enough to know Joel wouldn't like it, and the last thing Lincoln would want to do was lose the twenty dollars. But if he did, that would be okay. It wasn't her job anymore to consider Joel all the time; she had to keep reminding herself of that. It was really a whole new perspective on everything.

"Sorry, sorry," she said, coming up to Lance and taking the barstool next to him.

"No problem," he said so kindly. "I was just talking to Sam here, and he said he makes a mean margarita. What do you think of that?"

"I think that sounds great!" Hannah said.

"Salt?" Sam asked.

"Yes," Hannah and Lance said at the same time, and then they both laughed.

"So." Lance turned to her. She could smell a subtle soap scent and behind that the slightest hint of the chlorine from the pool. "Thanks for asking me to meet you."

"Sure," she said. "Thanks for meeting me."

"Have you been swimming at the Y long?"

"Yeah, for years, really," Hannah said. "What about you? How long have you been lifeguarding there?" She knew the answer, of course, but it was a good question.

"Exactly ten months today," he said. "I realized it this morning."

"So," she said slowly. "What was your life like one year ago today?"

"Clever," he said, not seeming to be put off by a personal question. "One year ago today I was living in Ocean City, New Jersey, with my daughter, Kathryn. She's four. I was finishing up the summer tasks and paperwork and even looking ahead to the next season—I was a head guard for the beach patrol there. My daughter went to her usual day care while I worked, which up until that time had been a great place; I never worried about her there. But then they had an incident—not with my daughter, my daughter was safe, thankfully—but it just changed everything for me. I found myself worrying about her all the time, wanting to check in on her. I wasn't as focused at work. And that is a job that demands your attention. So my parents were here in Philly, and we talked about having them move to Ocean City, but my mom is not as mobile as she used to be, and their apartment is perfect for her—they've made changes to it so she can get around no problem—so Kathryn and I came here. I don't worry about her when she's with my parents."

Hannah had so many questions, but even though Lance seemed open, she wasn't sure she dared ask them. On the other hand, why not?

"Wow," she said. "Do you miss Ocean City?"

"Yes, especially at this time of year, when it's more quiet and quite peaceful," he said. "But it's okay. I make it work."

"Is Kathryn with your parents now?"

"Yup," he said. "It is the best thing ever—for all of us."

Sam placed two beautiful cocktails in front of them.

"Cheers," he said.

"Cheers," they both said again at the same time, and once again, they laughed.

They were quiet for a moment while they each took a drink. Hannah took three big, quick sips to Lance's one slow one.

"What was the incident? At the day care? Is it okay for me to ask?"

"Oh, sure, and nobody knows exactly what happened, but a dog came into the day care facility with an adult who was there to pick up a child—presumably the dog was a family pet and was tame, but it should never have been allowed in—and it got away from the family and seriously injured one of the babies. The family claims that a child taunted it and scared it. But none of that matters. The baby was badly hurt, with bites on her face, and she lost a finger. I forgot to mention I was also an EMT when I wasn't on the beach, so I responded to the call. And Kathryn was there when it happened. It took me a long time to get that image out of my head."

"Oh, I'm so sorry," Hannah said, thinking of her own kids' tiny baby fingers and how precious they had been. "That sounds awful."

"Can I ask you some things now?" Lance said.

"Um, yes, maybe," Hannah said quickly. She had not thought this through. "Can I ask you one more question, though? And this one might be too personal because I really don't know the story, although you might have figured there are guesses among the moms at the Y. But you're a single dad, right?"

"I am," he said proudly, which surprised her. She thought there must be a sad story there, of a death or divorce, something. She pushed ahead. The longer she could avoid questions directed at her, the better.

"Can I ask why?" she said, but it sounded like an accusation, and she didn't mean for it to. "I mean, how did that come to be?"

"Sure," he said, taking out his phone and scrolling through. He held it up for her to see the image of a pretty, blonde little girl sitting on the beach with a frilly skirt spread out all around her in a big circle. "This is Kathryn, just so you can picture her while I tell the story."

"She's beautiful," Hannah said. Her impulse was to show photos of her own kids, but did she even have any that didn't include Joel on her phone? She didn't think so.

"So here's my story. About five years ago my girlfriend, Marlene, and I were living a happy, relatively carefree life. We had been dating for a few years already, and she was always lukewarm about getting married. She was very clear about that from the beginning. She is a doctor, a cardiologist, and had spent her life to that point building toward that and training for it. She was finally exactly where she wanted to be. I, too, thought I'd be okay with things staying just the way they were. We had a great time together and a very active and healthy sex life. I hope you don't mind my sharing that. We were careful, but sometimes things go awry. I'm sure you know where this is going. She got pregnant. She very thoughtfully decided she wasn't ready to have a baby, that she had just reached the exact point she was aiming for in her own life, after years and years of medical school, her residency, her fellowship, and that she wanted to be a doctor more than she wanted to be a mother. I was less sure once the possibility of having a family was actually presented to me, and I was less committed to a career. One night I had a dream about the baby, that it would be a boy and he was going to tell me the most important thing in the world on the deck of a boat. It was going to be a life-changing statement; I just had to wait for it. Anyway, that coupled with my indecision led me to a proposal—not of marriage—but that she have the baby and after the baby was born we split ways. At that point, we were falling out of love anyway. I respect her, don't get me wrong, but we were no longer in it together; we wanted different things. All my buddies told me to let it go, cut her loose, cut the baby loose, but that dream stuck with me—I had to know what the baby was going to tell me. So she had the baby, I have full custody, and we have nothing to do with Marlene. She signed away all her rights. Last I heard she was in California happily saving lives."

"That sounds complicated," Hannah said, and she could see something pass over Lance's face.

"I know, I know," he said. "This has been the hardest part of all with trying to date. I want to be upfront, but nobody believes me. Everyone thinks she's just waiting in the wings, about to come back at any time, and that I'll take her back, if not for my sake then for Kathryn's, but it isn't true. It's not going to happen. You don't have to worry about that."

Hannah finished her drink, and Sam immediately asked if she wanted another. She nodded, feeling her head get light as the tequila sank in. It seemed like Sam was their own personal bartender, their first-date Sherpa.

"Another for you?" he asked Lance.

"Sure," said Lance.

"Hey, Sam," Hannah said, and she sounded on the verge of drunk to herself. "Do you ever do any line dancing here?"

Sam smirked, then looked sideways at them and nodded.

"Not usually," he said. "But I have a feeling tonight isn't a usual night. I'll put something on."

The music until that point had been an easy mix of eighties classics, many of them acoustic versions, and some mainstream country music like Kacey Musgraves, which she liked. Kacey was singing about butterflies when the song morphed into the first few lines of a song Hannah didn't recognize but Lance clearly did—his eyes lit up, and he jumped off his stool, grabbing Hannah's hand as the lights came up on the empty dance floor.

"What is it?" she asked, laughing.

"The Cha Cha Slide," he said, leading her to the dance floor and taking the spot next to her. He knew it. He did all the moves and kept gesturing to her to follow along. Even though they were the only ones out there, she kept going in the wrong direction and bumping into him. Finally she bowed out and went to the side to watch him. He looked exasperated.

"It's not a solo dance," he said. "It's a line dance. You need a line."

"No, no," she said, feeling way more exposed than she had anticipated. She was just about to say maybe they should sit back down when she heard the first notes to a line dance she recognized—the Hoedown Throwdown from the Hannah Montana movie, Ridley's second-favorite movie after *Despicable Me*.

"I know this!" she said, rejoining him on the dance floor. She picked it up right away; she could do it all. She and Ridley had spent hours, whole afternoons, learning it. They had watched this movie so many times she couldn't even begin to count the number. Ever since Ridley was a tiny girl, she'd been drawn to the movie. It wasn't until recently that Joel had made the connection that the main character in the movie shared a first name with Hannah, and that was probably why Ridley liked it so much. But now it was coming in handy! She popped it and locked it and polka dotted it, and so did Lance. He knew the whole thing too. And by the time they were finished, they were laughing so hard she could barely breathe. They crumpled to the floor, and he reached out and touched her arm, then grabbed her hand. An unreadable expression crossed his face.

"I think I'll have to get going soon," he said, gently pulling his hand away from hers.

"What?" she said, trying not to look as shocked as she felt. "I . . . I thought it was going well. I did a line dance!"

"I know! And it is!" he said. "I'm having a great time, it's not that. It's just I don't want to get ahead of myself. What's the rush?"

Well, she wanted to say, *the rush is that I've been trying to have an affair for months now, and I think I'm finally ready. The rush is that I have to get on with it, in one way or another.*

"No rush," she said. "But can we at least finish the drinks?"

"Sure," he said, reaching for her hand again and leading her back to the bar. She wanted him to stay. She felt like she was in eighth grade and Scott Gerardo had just told her he didn't know if he liked her. She could feel all sorts of words building up that were fighting to get out. *No,* she told herself, *try to be cool.*

"I'm married," she blurted when they sat back down. It took all her energy to not smack the bar in frustration. Why had she said that?

He didn't even look surprised. "I know. I asked that other woman Dani about you a few times, and she said you were married and have two kids. I was so confused when you asked me out."

"You asked about me?" she asked.

"Well, yeah, I've always found you attractive, and you seem nice and relatively smart except for the part about not knowing how to use the flags to time your backstroke, but I figured everyone has some gap in their knowledge."

She reached out and punched his arm gently, finding herself laughing again. When was the last time she'd laughed this much? Actually, she knew. It was on the way to the train in New York right before she'd found out about the affair. Joel had kept saying the funniest things about the people around them, and she'd been howling, and each time as she'd been about to calm down, he would make some other observation that would send her back into hysterics.

"So why did you ask me out?"

"This is going to sound crazy to you, I'm sure," she said.

"Try me," he said. "I specialize in crazy."

"Do you want the truth? Or the sugarcoated version?"

"The one without the sugar," he said.

"Okay. Here goes. I found out that Joel—my husband—had an affair. It's over, and he wants to stay married, but I don't know what I want. I am just so angry I don't know if I will ever get beyond it. We kept trying to figure out how to get from this phase to the next one, and well, it just seems impossible, and out of frustration I told him I was going to have an affair too. So he knows I'm doing this; he doesn't like it, but he knows. Sorry to drag you into it."

"That was my next question," Lance said. "Why me?"

"Well, I guess I can say I saved the best for last. I've been on other dates, each one a disaster," she said. "And in the back of my mind, I always wondered about you. You're handsome, you seem nice, you're mysterious, and all the other moms are desperate to be with you. I mean, they literally follow you around. I don't know, it made sense."

"Well, I appreciate your honesty," he said. "And to reciprocate that honesty, I want to be very clear about what's going on with me. I had a good time tonight. I could imagine really liking you, and well, that's something I struggle with because so far I have not been eager to actually get attached to someone. And it sounds like things are even more complicated than I even realized, but . . ."

As he said the word *but*, he stood and took one of her arms in each hand firmly but gently and eased her up to standing. She felt like she was in a movie—*Coyote Ugly*, maybe, because it took place at a bar, but she certainly didn't feel ugly. She felt pretty. She told herself this wasn't real, that she was acting, and that was what let her stand there as he moved closer to her, and she wanted him to keep going, to reach her face and her lips. When he did, she was surprised by the urgency she felt, the craving that erupted in her. He kissed her gently, moving his mouth purposefully but not sloppily. She leaned into him, kissing back, her eyes closed. When she felt him slowing down, she kept going, but he didn't pick it up again, and she slowly backed down, letting him ease to a simple end. He was the one to take a step back.

"Thanks for a fun night," Lance said.

"That's it?" Hannah asked, trying not to sound like she had the emotions of a frantic middle schooler.

"I'm just not sure where else this night can take us," Lance said reasonably, motioning to Sam for the check. "I guess I need some time to think."

Hannah nodded. This was okay, she told herself. Really, what had she thought was going to happen? She really hadn't thought beyond this point.

"Thanks for meeting me," she said in her best adult voice. "This has been great, my most successful attempt at, well, at having an affair."

She reached into her purse for her wallet. She was the one who'd asked him, so she should pay, but he gently pushed her hand away. She waited while he paid, wondering if he might kiss her one more time. But he was moving away, not toward her now. They pushed through the door and out into the hazy night. It seemed like another world in there, one that existed separate from everything else. They stood there, and all of the ease they'd had inside was gone. Now it was awkward.

"Are you okay getting home?" he asked.

"Yes, fine. Thank you."

"I'll give you a call," he said with a smile that told her he knew how ridiculous that sounded. Great, now she was going to have to wonder if he was ever going to follow through. She certainly hadn't factored that into this whole thing.

"I'll look forward to it," she said, and she watched him walk away. At the corner he turned, his hair lifting slightly in the breeze, his dimple more pronounced than ever. She hadn't noticed it before, but he definitely had the look of a more mature Justin Bieber.

"See ya," he said, just as she realized she was staring at him.

"Yeah," she said, pulling her eyes away. "See ya."

Hannah couldn't sleep that night, wondering when and if he would call, making deals with herself about how long she should wait before she reached out to him. Two days? A week? The good news was Lance called the next morning. The bad news was he didn't want to have an affair with her.

"Look, Hannah, family life is hard enough, whatever configuration yours comes in, and whatever bumps in the road there might be, I am just not up for jumping into someone else's drama," he said kindly, the sounds of the indoor pool echoing around him.

"I understand," she said, and she really did. She just hadn't expected to like him so much.

"In another time and place . . ." He let his words trail off. Maybe he was just saying it or maybe he was really good at letting someone down, but why not take it, Hannah thought.

"Yeah, me too," she said.

CHAPTER FIFTEEN

Hannah was on her way to visit Richard when she came around the corner and saw Reuben through the window of the conference room. Older women—residents of the nursing home—sat in the seats as Reuben poured coffee into each of their mugs. A plate of colorful sprinkled cookies sat on the table. The women were talking away, and if the setting had been different, it would have seemed like Reuben was their server, not one of their caregivers. Hannah waved through the window, planning to continue on to Richard's room, but Reuben put up his finger, asking her to wait.

"Tell me something interesting that didn't happen in 1950," he said breathlessly as he came out the door and quietly closed it behind him.

"Well, I literally can't find a single person to have an affair with," Hannah said. It was the thing she was thinking about, and she just said it. "And I've tried."

"That's not really surprising," Reuben said. "I expected you would be picky—in a good way."

"What's going on in there? And isn't it a little late for them to have coffee?" Hannah asked, not sure she wanted to share the fact that she was actually *sad* about Lance's rejection, that being picky was only part of it.

"Well, first of all, it's decaf," Reuben said. "And it's Mrs. Schneider's birthday. She said the other day that she missed having coffee dates with her friends more than anything, so it's a coffee date."

"That's really nice of you," Hannah said, noticing that the woman in the middle was holding a mug that said *HAPPY BIRTHDAY!*, each letter a different color. "Really nice."

"Listen, I want to talk to you about Richard," Reuben said, lowering his voice. "I'm glad I caught you before you go in. He hasn't been talking much. It's been over two weeks since he spoke to the larger group, and they miss it. I mean, it isn't that he has to do it for them, of course, but I wonder what's going on with him. It's like he has just tuned out. I think it's time we talk seriously about an antidepressant. And there's something else."

"What is it?"

"You may or may not know this, but Joel hasn't been here at all in the last ten days. It could be longer. I keep hoping I'll see him so we can talk about the medication. I asked the staff to find me when he comes. But he just hasn't. Do you know why?"

Hannah was shocked. It was true that their personal lines of communication were bordering on nonexistent, but she'd just assumed he was visiting Richard as he usually did.

"Do you think that's why Richard is being so quiet?" Hannah asked.

"I don't know," Reuben said. "Maybe."

Just then there was a banging on the inside of the window. They both looked to see a woman holding up her empty coffee cup. It seemed rude, Hannah thought, until she realized that the woman was in a wheelchair. Actually, now that she looked at everyone, they *all* were, so she guessed they needed Reuben.

"I have to go," he said, not sounding annoyed at all. "I have a coffee date to facilitate."

Hannah looked at him, really looked at him. He was tall, with brown eyes and thinning brown hair. His yarmulke was askew and held on with a clip. His cheeks were just slightly rosy. Mostly, though, he was just so easy to be with. Really, it was a relief when she was with him.

"Hey, do you want to go to the movies with me?" she asked. It just came out. "I mean, here's the thing, I started out by going on these completely random dates. They're ridiculous, really—I might as well have been stopping people on the street and asking if they would meet me for a drink. So because the dates were consistently so awful—I mean, in some cases I knew within the first five minutes that I didn't want to spend another second with the person—anyway, because of that, I was home in less than an hour, always early. Which was good because the kids' routine wasn't disrupted, but Joel knew it, and I didn't want him to think it was so hard for me to find a date. He found one pretty easily. Then recently I went on a less random date, and I might have actually liked him, but in the end he wasn't interested in dealing with the drama, so that leads me back to the random dates, and I just don't know if I want to do that anymore. If we go to the movies, at least I'll be out longer. It will give me some time to figure out my next step. What do you think? Can you go? Maybe one night this week? Or next?"

There was another loud banging on the window. Reuben looked toward the conference room, then back at Hannah.

"I think there's a new Star Wars movie out," she said. "No, that won't work—the kids will want to see that. I can see what's playing at the Ritz."

Hannah glanced into the conference room. All the cookies were eaten, and one of the women was trying to wheel herself over to the coffeepot. The room was so small, though, and the wheels of her chair kept getting stuck on the wheels of another chair. She backed up and tried again. So far she had moved about an inch.

"You better go," Hannah said. "Think about it."

"I don't have to think about it," Reuben said. "I'll go. Why not? How's Tuesday? That's the one day I have off that I can usually depend on. And I'll check the listings. I have your cell—I'll text you."

Hannah smiled. "Great," she said. Tuesday seemed so far away. She would be happy when it got to be Tuesday. Monday was her birthday, and she was dreading it. It was hard not to think about the surprise party that wouldn't be and everything else. "That would be perfect. It's actually the day after my birthday."

"I love birthdays," he said, gesturing toward the conference room as if that were proof. "We can keep the celebration going."

"I don't know about that," she said. "But I do know I'll be happy when it's over. Thanks for wanting to go with me."

She turned to walk to Richard's room, and as she did, she heard Reuben say, "I'm back, ladies, sorry about that. I just had to take care of something important."

The main room was quiet as she moved through it. Richard's door was half-closed, so she pushed it open. He was in bed, propped up, dozing. She felt something in the pit of her stomach.

"Hey," she said. It took him a second to open his eyes and look at her. "Did you get the newspapers yet today?"

"No, I told them not to bring them anymore," he said, sounding croaky. "What's the point?"

"What do you mean? You always like to keep up with the news of the day. You have to."

"Why do I have to?" he asked seriously. "It goes on whether I pay attention to it or not."

"Well," Hannah said, not sure how to respond. That was true. That was always true, she guessed, once he'd stopped anchoring the news. "But still, you know, to be informed, to keep people here informed. It's all important."

"Bah, humbug," he said.

"Do you want me to help you get dressed? Or call one of the nurses? I can take you out to the main room. It's quiet out there. I know people would love to see you, hear what you have to say."

"Not today," he said, not looking at her. "And I have nothing to say."

"You have a lot to say, Richard," Hannah said. When he didn't answer, she asked, "Has Joel been here?"

Now he moved his eyes right to her so he was looking at her, almost through her. It took a long time for him to answer.

"Sometimes people look outward, and sometimes people look inward, and it's hard to know which is doing good and which is doing harm. One obstructs the other."

Hannah let that sit for a minute. What the heck was he talking about? Was he finally talking about his marriage? She tried to will back the tears she felt burning behind her eyes. It was at a time like this that she missed Joel more than ever.

"What do you mean, Richard?" she asked. "I'm not sure what you mean."

"Never mind," he said, sounding irritated. "Just never mind."

"Well, has Joel been here at all?"

"Why don't you know the answer to that yourself?" Richard asked, his voice angry. "Don't you live in the same house? Don't you talk to each other?"

"Well, yes, of course," Hannah said. "But you know how it is: the kids always need something, we're both working, it's really busy. So I just assumed I was coming at my usual times and he was coming at his."

"Don't you talk about me?" Richard said, sounding like a little kid and a pompous professor at the same time. "Don't you compare notes?"

Hannah realized that they had not, in a long time. They used to, but that was another casualty of this mess. She shook her head.

"I guess not as much lately," she said. "But not because we don't want to. Not because we aren't thinking about you. It's just been more hectic than usual. We've been more distracted."

Richard looked at her and pursed his lips. She could see an oil stain on his pajama top and wondered how long he had been wearing it. Had he been eating meals in bed?

"Well, if you must know," Richard said. "I told him not to come."

Hannah felt like she had to concentrate to steady herself. That was the last thing she'd expected.

"Why?" she asked.

"I just don't want to see him," Richard said, turning away.

"But," Hannah said, "you always want to see him. I don't understand."

"Ask him," Richard said. "Maybe he has more to say than I do. I'm tired. I appreciate your coming, I really do, but I want to rest now. Is that okay?"

"Yes, of course," Hannah said, standing and patting Richard on the arm. She noticed that his skin looked papery and dry. "I'll try to come back tomorrow."

"Okay," Richard said. "That would be nice."

She forced herself to leave, walk back through the lounge and toward the door. She wasn't even thinking about Reuben as she moved past the conference room, but he saw her and scooted out the door.

"Hey, sorry I had to run before. How's Richard?"

"Not great, quiet, and he said he told Joel not to come visit. I have to figure out what's going on. And I'll talk to Joel about the antidepressant."

"Okay, yes, please keep me posted. I'll check in on him as soon as the coffee date is over. I'll spend some time with him, maybe play some cards."

"That would be really great."

"Have a good day, Hannah," he said.

She nodded and walked toward the exit, wondering if he had forgotten about the movie invitation. But as soon as she stepped out onto the porch, she heard her phone ping with an incoming text.

It didn't seem like I should mention it just now, but I'm looking forward to the movie! Next to his words was an emoji of a box of popcorn. She texted back a thumbs-up, because really what else was there to do?

There was nobody out on the porch, so she took a seat in one of the white plastic rocking chairs. She had a lunch meeting today; the plans were moving ahead, and she had to prepare, not be distracted. This was what she had always wanted—to head a project like this, one that dealt with a hotel's interior and amenities, all the things she loved. It was the sort of thing she would talk endlessly to Joel about. Half the time she suspected he probably didn't listen, but the act of saying it out loud helped her work through it. Now there had been none of that. She hadn't even told him yet that she had officially accepted the position. She dialed his number.

"Hi," he said immediately. She closed her eyes for a second and pretended things were as they used to be, that his voice was her safe place, her comfort zone. Then she opened her eyes, shook her head, and forced herself to sound slightly cold, reminding herself she was not calling for any reason other than Richard.

"Hi," she said. "I just left your dad. He's acting strange, and I hear you haven't been there in over a week."

"It's true," Joel said. "I haven't been."

"Why didn't you tell me?"

"I don't know, Han," he said. "It's hard to know what we can talk about these days. To be perfectly honest, I'm a little afraid of you."

Good, she thought.

"He also said that he's the one who told you not to come," she said.

"Also true," he said.

"Well, you have to fix this," she said, exasperated. "Sometimes the child has to be the parent. I saw Reuben. He thinks it's time to talk seriously about an antidepressant."

"I was thinking the same thing. Listen, I'm around the corner, at the Oregon Diner," Joel said. "Can you come meet me? Please?"

It was literally a block away. If she could see through the building next to her, she would be able to see it.

"What?" she said. "Why?"

"I like it here," he said quietly. "It's the closest I can get to my dad without ignoring his request. I can almost see his window from here if I look really hard, through that one tall tree."

"That's creepy," she said.

"Yeah, well," he said. "Come meet me. Please come. I'll order for you. I want to see you, to sit with you. Please."

Her plan had been to go home, change, and do more research about locally focused hotels. She had heard about one in Lewes, Delaware, and she wanted to know more about it, to be able to talk specifics. But she had dressed nicely enough that if something prevented her from going home first, she would be okay; it wouldn't be a disaster. She could do this, for Richard.

"Fine," she said. "I'll be right there."

When she got to Oregon Avenue and saw the diner in front of her, the place where they often went as a family, she felt so angry all over again. She could see him sitting in the front window, waving. She thought about giving him the finger and walking away. That would feel good, for about three minutes. Then it would feel really bad, the way almost everything did these days. Instead she crossed when she had the light, walked up the ramp to the front door, and took a deep breath, smelling the diner coffee, which then reminded her of Reuben.

Joel had gotten up from the booth and was walking toward her.

"I'm so glad you came," he said, touching her arm and then pulling his hand back.

"I almost didn't," she said. "And I didn't come for you. I came for Richard."

"I know," he said. "Come on, your food just got here."

She followed him to the booth. There was a plate of barely touched scrambled eggs and toast at his place. She had noticed he looked especially thin lately and not in a particularly healthy way. He gestured toward her spot, and there was a waffle waiting for her. It was exactly what she would have ordered for herself. She sat down. She was starving.

"Thank you," she said grumpily.

"Thank *you*," he said. "Thank you for coming."

"So what's the deal?" she said, pouring the maple syrup. It felt too easy to be with him. She had to be careful. "With Richard, I mean?"

"I've been coming here every morning," Joel said quietly. "Well, since my dad told me not to come. I keep thinking I'll go in, see if I can change his mind, but you know him. He's so stubborn. There is no changing his mind."

"Well, why did he tell you not to come?" she asked. "I mean, that's the question. He loves to see you more than anyone. He never thinks you come enough. I feel like all my family members are acting the opposite of the way I would have guessed. I don't like it."

She took a quick sip of water, feeling she was giving in somehow by sitting here and indulging in the meal Joel had ordered for her. She wondered if she was always going to feel this way. If that was true, it would be impossible to stay married.

"I told him," Joel said, looking down. "I told him about what I did."

Hannah put down her fork and worked hard to swallow the big piece of waffle she had just put in her mouth.

"You told him?"

"Yes," Joel said. "Actually, I told him before. Before you found out."

"Oh my God," Hannah said. "Oh my God, so he knew, and I was just the idiot? When did you tell him? Oh my God, I'm so embarrassed.

I sat there acting like the stupid wife, doing my duty, holding up the family, and the whole time he knew! He must have thought I was so stupid."

"No. Not at all," Joel said. "You are completely misunderstanding this. That wasn't it at all. That's the last thing he would think. Remember what I said in Dr. Snow's office, about my mother? I thought, I don't know, I thought he could *help* me."

Hannah had the strongest feeling that she had to get out of there. That if she sat there and kept talking to Joel, it would all be lost somehow, all of it—her affair but ultimately their marriage. Plus, every chance he got, Joel asked to go back to Dr. Snow. They hadn't been in weeks, not since they'd sat in the parking lot and hadn't gone up, not since Hannah had started to go on dates. It seemed to Hannah that seeing her again should come after this phase, not during. One thing did not support the other, at least not in her eyes.

"I can't talk about this now," she said, scrunching up her napkin and putting it on the table.

"No, please," he begged. "I thought we were getting somewhere."

She looked at him.

"Where we are getting," she said meanly, "is that the more time goes by, the more unhappy I become. Did you hear me? *Unhappy.* In the true sense—I feel its essence. Do you have a dictionary so we can look up that word? Or was that just for when things were good, when they were easy?"

"Please," Joel said, the color draining from his face.

"I'm going," she said. "I have a meeting, and I don't want to be late for it. Also I don't want to appear unprepared. I took the job, by the way."

"Good," Joel said, and he sounded like he meant it. "You'll be great at it."

She stood, looking at him. She thought of that moment in *St. Elmo's Fire*, her absolute favorite movie from the 1980s, when the Judd

Nelson character was lurking in the apartment as Allie Sheedy's character came to pack up her things after finding out he'd had flings with other women. He threw the ball he was holding across the room and lamented about wasted love, wishing he could get it back. *So much wasted love,* Hannah thought, as the line from the movie ran through her mind. And God, she just wished she could get it back.

Before she was too far away, she turned back toward Joel.

"I think it's definitely time to put Richard on an antidepressant. Can you be in charge of that? Can you call Reuben?" Hannah said.

Joel nodded.

"At least then we'll be taking care of someone."

CHAPTER SIXTEEN

Halfway through Hannah's meeting, Reuben texted her.

> La La Land is playing at the Ritz East! Tuesday at 7:10?

They were in the middle of a discussion about soap and, while they were at it, shampoo and conditioner.

"This is an old pet cause of mine," Hannah had just said. "But I think we should absolutely have refillable containers in the showers of shampoo and conditioner, very nice, decorative—possibly glass if we can do it safely—containers. Maybe we can have the glass bottles made locally; I know there are some glassblowing studios around."

That was when she'd heard the buzz of the text coming through. She'd turned her phone as discreetly as she could and glanced to see who it was, and it had almost slipped out of her hand. She read the text quickly and put her phone back in her bag.

"I do want to add that I believe in bars of soap," she said. The three people at the table with her—one man, Ron, and one woman, Josie, who now were technically working under her, and the general manager of the imagined hotel, Stan—hadn't said a word after her first comment. Now they were nodding. She was waiting for the pushback she usually got when she brought up this idea.

"What soap, though?" Josie asked. "I think that will be an important choice. Can that be local?"

"We'll have to do some research," Hannah said. "I want everything to be local if possible, but I never want to sacrifice quality to keep something local. If we can find a good locally produced soap, then yes, absolutely. Can you be in charge of that?"

"Sure," Josie said, going on to talk about where exactly she planned to look.

Hannah was listening, she really was, but what she wanted at the moment was to text Reuben back. She liked this idea of a movie date with him. It seemed easy, no pressure, and if she was lucky, she might get to stay out later than ten o'clock.

"I plan to visit a few hotels in the area over the next few weeks," Hannah said when there was a lull in the conversation. It was very possible she had missed something. She shook her head to refocus. "I'll see how they do it, get some ideas."

Again, everyone nodded. Now Josie asked the table about other nearby towns that might be known for soap. Hannah kept one ear out while she thought about what she would say to Reuben. *Great!* Or *Is there a later show so I can help feed my kids?* Or *Is* La La Land *the only choice?* That seemed somehow too . . . she wasn't sure exactly what. Serious, maybe, or relationship focused, or romantic? A comedy might be better, or a thriller, but she didn't know of any that were currently playing.

"Hannah?" Ron said.

"Oh yes, sorry," she said. "I missed that last sentence."

"No problem," Ron said. "We were just talking about our definition of local, like, from how far away can something still be considered local? Does it have to come from within the city limits?"

"No," she said quickly. "If we do that, we miss out on things from so many places—chocolates from Hershey and West Chester, beers from all around, meat from Chester County, fruit and vegetables from South Jersey. No, I think we have a wider scope."

Again, they all nodded.

"How about this?" she said. "Let's visit the space next week, though I know there isn't much there but a shell. I also want to talk to the people designing the restaurant concept, because there might be some crossover. There's a lot to be done before we even begin to make any decisions. I'll be in touch later about our next meeting time."

"Great," Ron said, standing.

They said goodbye, and Hannah stood in the corner with her phone, reading and rereading Reuben's text. Finally she texted back.

See you there!

"So I wanted to tell you: I'm going on a fourth date with someone, tomorrow," Kim told Hannah. They were at Kim's house, the kids playing in the next room. Light came in through the open curtains and blinds. Maybe things had gotten a little brighter overall for Kim lately.

"I know," Hannah said. "You guys met on Bumble, right?"

"Yes," she said. "I think it might really be going someplace."

"Really?" Hannah asked. "Tell me everything. Who is he? What's his name? Where does he live?"

Kim looked at her, her eyes blank, and Hannah recoiled slightly, feeling she had somehow overstepped.

"Maybe later," Kim said, gesturing toward the kids, but they weren't listening to them. They were screaming and laughing.

"Okay, well, then I have to tell you something," Hannah said, sitting up straighter and leaning closer to Kim. "I've been wanting to tell you this for a while; I don't know why I didn't." She stopped talking when the kids got quiet for a few seconds and waited. Of course she knew why she hadn't. Kim would think this affair business was absolutely awful, despicable, really, and she just didn't want to hear it. But at this point she almost didn't care.

"I've also been dating," she said. "This might sound crazy, but as a way to get over Joel's betrayal, as a way to put this behind us and possibly move forward, I suggested—or more like *threatened*—I'd have my own affair. I figured, if he can do it, I can do it, right?" The more she told the story, the more convoluted it became, and she had a harder and harder time explaining why she was doing it.

Kim blinked at her. "What?" she finally said.

At that moment Lincoln ran into the room and threw himself on her lap.

"Mommy, Mommy, Savannah says her daddy isn't living here anymore," he said. "Why is this the first I'm hearing about it?"

"Oh," Hannah said, not prepared to deal with the question, for so many reasons. Also, she hoped that he had not heard a word she'd said to Kim. Now that it was just hanging there, she wished she could take it back, continue to keep it a secret.

"It's true," Kim said gently, and Hannah was relieved not to have to answer. "Sometimes mommies and daddies have fights, or misunderstandings, or just general disagreements, and they need time apart to figure it out."

"So this is your time apart?" Lincoln asked.

"Yes, exactly," Kim said, like that answered it all, like he wasn't going to have a million more questions.

"How long will your time apart last?" he asked, sitting up now, looking a little like a reporter conducting an interview at a courthouse. All he needed was a reporter's notebook or a microphone.

"That's a very good question," Kim said noncommittally.

"Savannah said it will last for six months at the most, and then everything will go back to normal. Is that true?"

Kim looked at Hannah and back at Lincoln.

"It might be," she said. "Possibly."

"Good," Lincoln said, easing himself up to standing. He ran back into the other room to rejoin the group.

"Is that what you guys are telling them?" Hannah asked. "That this is temporary?"

Kim looked like she was going to say something, but instead she started to cry. "I'm totally lying," she said through her tears, clearly trying to keep her voice down so the kids wouldn't hear.

"To the kids?"

"No, to you, to myself," she said. "It's true that I've been on a date with the same guy three times, but we haven't done anything, and he doesn't strike me as very smart. If I never saw him again, I wouldn't mind. Hannah, it's like the Wild West out there. It is not a pretty place."

"You don't have to see him again," Hannah said, knowing, though, that Kim was also talking directly to her, responding to what she had just confessed. "Just say it isn't working out for you."

"But I don't want to be alone for the rest of my life," she said miserably.

Hannah had to close her eyes. Kim had just voiced Hannah's worst fear. A moment from her childhood popped into her mind. She and her mother had been driving to her grandparents' in Tarrytown. On the highway, going by White Plains, they'd gotten a flat tire. Thank goodness they were in the right lane, her mother had said. Thank goodness they weren't speeding, she'd said. Hannah had heard the tremor in her voice, the one she'd pretended wasn't there. And while they'd waited for

AAA to come help them, since her mother didn't know how to change a tire, Hannah had had that same feeling—it was just them. There was no safety net. She shook the image away.

"There's something else," Kim said. "I know Hank has been dating."

"How do you know?"

"Well, he told me, but here is the craziest thing ever, or the worst thing. I saw him on Bumble, so he must have seen me too. I mean, I swiped left, of course—could you imagine if I swiped right and he didn't? I've seen him on other sites, too, but I got off all of those right away. I figured Bumble was okay since the woman has to make the first move, so that would always be in my court, not his. But I'm not interested in any of the guys on the site. Now I wish I could see the other women to see who he might be connecting with."

"But he's dating? Like, seeing the same person for a while?"

"Oh, I don't know," Kim said quietly, almost whispering. "All I know is that he's been on the dating sites. He's putting himself out there. He's trying." She leaned in and said, "But now something he said makes sense—oh my God, I thought he was crazy! I told him he was losing it! I asked him how long he'd been on when he dropped the kids off this morning, and he told me a little under a month, which seems reasonable, really; I deserve that. But he also told me—and I was so sure it was some sort of mistake—that he saw *you* on the site. I mean, it was the most he talked to me in a while, and I realized how much I missed him, not just the idea of him and the support of him and the togetherness of having him here, but *him*—I just purely missed talking to him. He came in and sat down and asked what I knew about you being on the site. I told him there was no way, but I also told him about you and Joel and the affair and . . ." She trailed off.

"Well, he was right," Hannah said matter-of-factly. "He saw me there."

"Did you see him?"

Hannah *had* seen Hank. In a frenzied moment of swiping left over and over again, his face had come up, and then it was gone. Afterward she had wondered, *Did I really see that?*

"I think I did," Hannah said quietly. "I know I did. I swiped left so fast that afterward I wondered if I had imagined it. But now that you say he was on, I guess I really did see him."

"And you didn't tell me?" Kim asked. Hannah could almost feel something shift between them. In a million years she never would have imagined that her heartbreak would mesh with Kim's heartbreak.

"I, well, I didn't want to tell you I *thought* I'd seen him. What if I'd been wrong?" Hannah said. "I wished I could go back and make sure, but you can't do that; once you swipe, you swipe."

"You can shake your phone," Kim said, her voice sounding strange. "You can shake it and bring it back."

"I tried," Hannah said. "But by the time I realized what had happened, or what I thought had happened, I was already three beyond. I couldn't go back."

"Mom?" Savannah called from the next room.

Hannah watched as Kim cleared her throat and straightened up. "Yes?" she called back.

"Can you make pizza rolls?"

"Sure!"

She got up and preheated the oven, grabbed a bag out of the freezer, and arranged the frozen rectangles on a tray. Kim pushed the tray into the oven, not waiting for it to fully preheat, and came back to the couch, but she didn't sit. She just stood there.

"I told you," she said, barely opening her mouth to let the words out. "That you should make it work with Joel, that you shouldn't throw away your marriage and your family. Did you not listen to a thing I said?"

"I heard you," Hannah said, feeling defensive. "But we all have to make our own choices, right? I mean, you didn't listen to me when I worried you were wondering about Wesley too much, did you? I'd say you're guilty of the pot calling the kettle black."

They stared at each other, Hannah's heart beating fast, the growing smell of the pizza rolls making her feel slightly nauseated.

"You should go," Kim said.

Despite the state of their current interaction, Hannah was surprised. She'd thought they would fight and get through it. She didn't want to leave.

"No, we can—" Hannah said.

"You should go," Kim said again, interrupting her.

"Kids, we have to go," Hannah called.

"No," they all cried. "We're starving."

They appeared in the doorway, taking up the whole frame, their little hopeful faces looking at them. If it had been another time, Hannah would have snapped a picture, and she was sure it would have been one of those photos that you passed around and reposted on birthdays and at various graduations, but she knew she would not want to remember this moment.

"I'll take you to McDonald's," she said, knowing they would agree and also knowing it was a dig at Kim, who, to her children's dismay, had put into place a family boycott of McDonald's years ago after she'd read some article or other. *So there,* Hannah thought as she gathered her things and walked to the door. The kids dutifully followed, talking quietly about hamburgers and Chicken McNuggets and caramel sundaes.

Once they were in the car, Hannah looked back at Kim's door. Normally she would wait there and wave until they drove away. But the door was already closed. Hannah pulled out her phone and deactivated her account on Bumble. She put it back in her bag, tried to shake off her anger before she started to drive, and decided to go to the better McDonald's on Oregon Avenue. Maybe she would even take the kids for a quick visit to see Richard. She wouldn't mind having a chance to say hi to Reuben—at this point, as far as she could tell, he was the easiest person to be around.

CHAPTER SEVENTEEN

"Mommy?" Lincoln called up the stairs. "Can you come read to us, please?"

Hannah was lying on her bed, thinking about calling Kim, who, for the record, had not called all day to wish her a happy birthday. She had the clear and heavy sense that all of her usual and dependable human connections had come undone in the last few months. She was sure each one must have a mystery antidote to set things right, but she just couldn't figure out how to conjure it up. She knew now that she should have told Kim right away about seeing Hank on Bumble; she *regretted* not telling her immediately, but surely Kim was going to come around. Surely they would find their way back to each other.

"Mommy?" Lincoln called again.

She sighed. Really all she wanted to do was stay in her room and let the rest of her birthday go by. She wanted to call down and say that their birthday present to her—there had been very little this year except for a few still-wet glitter cards—could be to just give her some needed time alone. But she didn't think it was worth it. That would just make the time go by even slower, waiting as they tiptoed around her because, she knew, they would agree to it.

"Coming," she called.

She ducked into Lincoln's room and grabbed the book they were in the middle of, *Harry Potter and the Chamber of Secrets*, and headed downstairs.

"Happy birthday to you . . ." The singing began before she hit the bottom step. "Happy birthday to you. Happy birthday, dear Mommy. Happy birthday to you."

She stopped short. She had thought she smelled something baking, but she was so disconnected from the activities in her own house these days that it hadn't even occurred to her to see what it was. The kids sat at the table, smiling so big, with Stinker and Dune propped up on the corner of the table and Joel in the middle hunched over a cake—the usual cake—white frosting and sprinkles, a one-layer rectangle. Just the way he always did. And she would have bet money, she would have bet anything, that inside was chocolate cake, her favorite.

"Whoa," she said. "I was not expecting this."

"But Mommy, we give you a cake every year," Lincoln correctly pointed out.

"Mommy, come sit," Ridley said.

She walked to the table and took her seat. Joel came around to her and first touched her on the shoulder, then leaned down and touched his nose to the top of her head. It wasn't a kiss, really—it was more of a sniff. She closed her eyes for the briefest moment before moving her head just enough to let him know she wanted him to move, which he did right away.

"Birthday cake, check!" Joel said as he did every single year. "Number fourteen and counting."

That was her cue to say, "Yes, sir, thank you, sir," in an extremely overexaggerated way, as she always did, their running joke. The kids loved it. But she couldn't do it.

"Mommy, now you say, *Thank you, mister,*" Lincoln prompted her after a few seconds had gone by and they were just sitting there, not doing or saying anything. It was like they couldn't move forward until she said it. This was their play, and that was the next line.

"It's okay," Joel said. "Mommy can switch it up a little. She is overwhelmed and rendered speechless."

"Okay, Mommy," Lincoln said. "But can you not be speechless? Please?"

When he said the word *speechless*, it sounded like *speaches*.

"Yes, of course I can not be speechless," she said, leaning over and hugging Lincoln. "This cake is so great, so delicious looking. I declare that it is okay to eat it before dinner!"

"Yay!" they cheered, even though she knew that was their plan anyway, whether she said it or not. Again, that was part of the tradition, more lines in their play.

Joel pulled plates and napkins out of a drawer where he must have been hiding them, and she was secretly touched to see they were unicorn themed—another favorite of hers. These weren't left over from someone else's birthday; she knew that since they were a new design still in their wrapping. He must have either ordered them or gone to the party store. And it wasn't like he was being extra nice this year because of what he'd done; he was nice every year on her birthday. Every single year.

When Joel had called Hannah's mother to ask for permission to propose, her mother had been thrilled. Her one request—really, now that Hannah thought about it, she realized her mom should have reached higher, maybe requested that Joel remain faithful—was that Joel bake a birthday cake for Hannah every year and sing to her. "Everyone should be sung to on their birthday," her mother always said, and she joined in if they were at a restaurant and a celebration was taking place at a nearby table. She'd also bring their elderly neighbors and relatives who lived alone cupcakes and candles, and she would stay to sing and encourage the traditional wish making.

Hannah was right: it was chocolate. The pieces were cut and shared, and the kids dug in. Lincoln asked for another piece before Hannah had even taken her first bite, and she was happy to have something to focus on. She could feel Joel trying to catch her eyes from across the table, but she wouldn't give in—she did her best to subtly pretend he wasn't there. There was no mention of dinner or even of the reading Lincoln had lured her down with, so once they'd had their fill, she went back upstairs, leaving Joel to clean up the mess. All she had to do now was get through the next four hours, and her dreaded birthday would be over.

"Happy birthday!" Reuben said as Hannah approached him. It was the next day, and he was standing in front of the movie theater, holding up the tickets he must have just bought.

"My birthday was yesterday," she said. "But thank you."

"Well, we can still celebrate," he said, handing her a pink envelope.

"Thanks," she said, thinking that was probably the last thing she wanted to do.

He motioned for them to go inside and pointed toward an empty bench across from the concession stand. The smell of popcorn made her think of her kids. She sat down and opened the card, which she noticed was sealed and not still wet, so he must have planned ahead. And it wasn't like he owed her a card anyway. If he hadn't had one, that would have been okay, totally fine. The front of the card said *Hello Beautiful* in yellow with a pink background, just like the mug he had chosen for her that one day. Inside, the typed message said, *Everyone is beautiful on their birthday; you are beautiful every day. Happy birthday and happy every day!*

"Um, thank you," she said, thinking it seemed awfully personal. But it was also kind in the way Reuben was always kind, to everyone. She would be lying to herself if she pretended she didn't like it. At least his compliment didn't come saturated with guilt and longing. Plus, she imagined, he probably had a stack of these in his office—it was probably his signature card to give out.

"My pleasure," he said.

Inside the theater they settled into their seats. Reuben patted a small bag he had slung over his shoulder.

"It's the-day-after-your-birthday candy," he whispered. "It is also contraband, but I'm willing to take the chance."

He pulled it onto his lap and opened it for her to see. It was full of every candy she could imagine—Swedish Fish, gummy bears, M&M's, Junior Mints. He chose the box of gummy bears and held it up, raising his eyebrows.

"Sure," she said, holding out her hand to collect some as he poured.

"So how was your big day?" he asked.

"I got through it," she said, shifting in her chair to face him. "We have this tradition that Joel makes me a birthday cake every year, and he did. I don't know why I was surprised by it. I mean, it makes sense that he would this year of all years. Everything is colored because I have an almost constant urge to be mean to him, but in front of the kids I can't be, obviously. It's like a tightrope act, and I'm constantly stressed. And Joel is miserable, no question about it."

"Does he know you're out with me?"

She took a few seconds to answer. "No," she said.

"Why not?"

"Well, I told you how all my dates are terrible, and I cut them short, and he knows it. So now at least we're seeing a movie, and I won't be home in fifteen minutes, which is when he probably expects me to walk in the door. So I guess that's a long way of saying I want him to think I'm on a romantic date, not out with a good friend."

Reuben reached out and patted her arm, some gummy bears falling to the floor in the process as the bag got turned upside down. "Your secret is safe with me," he said just as the lights went down.

The movie was entertaining and sad and full of great music, and Hannah enjoyed every second of it. Reuben sat next to her and handed her candy at ten- to fifteen-minute intervals. She really couldn't have asked for a better date. They sat for a long time after the movie was over. It was peaceful, and she wanted to stretch the time she was out as much as she possibly could. And it was so easy to sit here next to Reuben. It was comfortable.

"So we also have a tradition in my house for birthdays," Reuben said once the credits were completely over and even the music had stopped playing. They were alone in the theater. "Well, in my house growing up, I should say. Until the birthday person was of drinking age, they would get an ice-cream cone every birthday. Then once they turned twenty-one, they had a shot—one shot of tequila—which my father always thought was good luck. He still does. So are you open to it? Can we go get a shot?"

"My birthday was—" Hannah began.

"I know, I know, your birthday was yesterday," Reuben said playfully. "There is definitely a twenty-four-hour window on either side—another one of my family rules. What do you think? Are you up for it?"

"Why not?" Hannah said, thinking Joel must be wondering where she was already. This was by far the latest she had been out on a date.

They walked north toward Chestnut Street, and Reuben led her to a New Orleans–themed bar, which happened to be her favorite place to get a po'boy in the city. It was festive, with colorful lights and a buzzing crowd. She let him push his way up to the bar. He was back in a minute with two tequila shots. He handed one to her and kept the other.

"Okay, so in my family we say, 'Make a wish and drink a shot; the ice cream is gone, but hopefully your health is not,'" he said. "Ready? One, two, drink!"

They both drank the shot, and she was glad it was tequila. Anything else she would probably have refused or at least had a much harder time getting down.

"Is that really your family's birthday saying?" she asked. "Because it's sort of depressing. And what do you say if someone isn't healthy?"

"Well, this is going to sound really weird, but then they get the ice cream again, and that saying goes, 'Take a birthday lick and make a wish,'" he said. "It all seems so normal when you do it year after year, but I can see it's a little strange. Whenever someone has a birthday at Saint Martha's, I think about my traditions, but they're just so unusual I haven't dared try them on anyone. Plus, they're all pretty sick, so I think it would just be ice cream. I guess that could work."

"Families are so weird," Hannah said thoughtfully, feeling the tequila move to her chest and maybe even her head. She had not had enough to eat to do tequila shots. She knew that.

"Hey, are you okay?" Reuben asked. "You look a little red in the cheeks."

"Yeah," Hannah said. "I think so. I just haven't eaten much except for our movie snacks. I skipped dinner. Basically, I've had sugar and tequila today since lunch."

"Oh, let's eat," Reuben said excitedly. "They have the best roast-beef po'boys."

"I know!" Hannah said. "I love the debris gravy. And the bread. Really, if you close your eyes and take a bite, you would believe you were in New Orleans."

"I agree," Reuben said, leading her toward the tables. "Do you have time to sit?"

Hannah looked at her phone. It was almost eleven. Her goal had been to stay out as late as possible, but she hadn't expected it to be so easy. "Sure!"

They sat at a pretty tight table along the wall, and Reuben had to wedge himself into the space. He just did it. He didn't ask if he should or where she wanted to sit; he just took the less good seat.

"It's the day after her birthday!" he said to the server as soon as he approached. "And we'll both have the roast-beef po'boy."

"Happy birthday!" the server said, smiling. Hannah squinted to see his name tag, which read *Rex*. She wondered if that was his real name or if they had to choose New Orleans–themed names. He was pretty cute, longish wavy hair and blue eyes. Maybe Hannah could have an affair with him. But really he looked too young and, to be fair, out of her league unless he had an older-lady fetish of some sort like that awful Wiley. Plus, she had another idea, something she wanted to run by Reuben. "I'll be right back with your po'boys. And I want to encourage you to make a wish when you take your first bite. It's a little something we suggest people do on their birthdays. There's magic in the air here." When he said the last part, he whispered and winked. Hannah was going to roll her eyes as he walked away, but when she looked at Reuben, he was smiling.

"Another tradition," Reuben said, like he had proved their point, not letting Hannah say once again that it really wasn't her birthday anymore. In fact, with all this talk about her birthday, she almost felt like she was getting a redo. "But I'm a big fan of wish making. There are certain things you always make a wish on—like birthday candles or lone eyelashes—but in my family we also made a wish the first time we had watermelon for the season. Do you have any?"

"Wishes?" she asked.

"Yeah, or times to make wishes?"

"Well, when I was growing up, we always made a wish the first time we put our feet in the ocean for the year and the first time it snowed," she said. "Do you ever actually keep track of your wishes? I mean, do you pay attention to if they come true? I don't, really. Even though I love the idea of them."

"Most of my important wishes have not come true," he said seriously, just as Rex placed the delicious-looking sandwiches in front of them. He stood there, clearly waiting for her to make her wish. She lifted the sandwich, took a bite, closed her eyes, and thought, *I hope I will not always be this incredibly angry with Joel.* She opened her eyes, completely surprised by the words that had just run through her mind. Even though she had been warned, she hadn't really thought about what she was going to wish. Really, she wished for so many things: that life could go back to normal, that her family wasn't in danger of breaking up. But she knew somehow that the key to all of it was her anger, her ability or inability to soften and stop feeling such rage.

"Did you make a good wish?" Reuben asked.

"I honestly don't know. I hope so," she said. "What wishes haven't come true for you?"

"Well, when my mom got sick, I wished she wouldn't die, but she did," he said matter-of-factly.

"Oh my God, that's awful," she said, putting her hand to her mouth. "I wasn't expecting that. I am so sorry."

"And I always hoped to get married," he said, moving right along. "But that hasn't happened. I just keep dating a woman who might as well be a ghost. Really, she might as well not even be a real person. To be perfectly honest, I have a terrible time with commitment. It is just not something I'm comfortable with. And obviously, it doesn't take a great therapist to figure out that I'm just sort of letting it happen, or *not* happen, as the case may be."

"We all do strange things, I guess," Hannah said, the tequila now clearly taking up residence in her head. "Things that seem strange even to us. Which leads me to a proposal I have for you. Do you want to have a fake affair with me?"

"A fake affair?" he asked. "What would that entail?"

"Well, it would entail spending time with me, maybe one or two evenings a week, but doing stuff like this, nothing crazy," she said, thinking. "Not much more than that, really. We could play it by ear."

"So would you be open with that information?" he asked. "Would you tell Joel you were involved with me?"

"Would that be bad?" she asked. "Is there something unethical about that?"

"I mean, it probably isn't ideal," he said. "My job is to help you and your family, not to make your life and your relationships more complicated."

"I get that," she said. "I would be willing to not say it is with you. I mean, I don't see us canoodling in the lounge or the conference room."

"Would we be canoodling at all?" he asked.

"No," she said. "Of course not. We're friends. But I like to spend time with you. It's easy and fun. Really, does my affair have to be so stressful? I am so mad at Joel. I have no idea how I am going to get over that. But this—this plan—lets me not have to make any decisions yet. It would help me. Plus, it would give you some company until Lucy gets home."

Hannah took another bite of her po'boy, feeling slightly more clearheaded.

"So what do you think?" she asked.

"I think it's hard to say no to you on the day after your birthday."

CHAPTER EIGHTEEN

Joel stopped in the doorway as he came into the bedroom. It was a Wednesday night in November. Hannah had been having a fake affair with Reuben for three weeks.

Hannah was reading in bed. She waited for Joel to keep moving, but he didn't. He just stood there, one hand on each side of the doorframe like he was holding himself up.

"What?" she finally said, not looking up.

She had been out and had gotten home after the kids were already asleep, so there had been no reason to speak to Joel. She and Reuben hadn't wanted to see another movie, since they were pretty much caught up, so they'd driven around from ice cream place to ice cream place, sampling and judging. She'd had a good time, but by nine thirty they'd both been tired, their tongues numb from too many cold desserts, so she'd come home earlier than usual.

"I know I'm not supposed to ask," Joel said now. "I know that's the point, and I promise I am trying very hard to let you have this . . . time.

But clearly something is going on. Clearly you have established . . . something, and I just feel really bad. Like, sick."

She reluctantly moved her eyes from the book to Joel.

"I know you aren't doing anything—I don't even know what the word is—illegal? Not allowed?" he said, coming in and closing the door but still standing with his back to it. "I guess I just wondered . . . I mean, we haven't talked much lately; I guess I wondered if we could go back to Dr. Snow. Maybe she can help us reconnect or something. I miss you. A lot."

Hannah had continued to cancel appointment after appointment, thinking, What was there to talk about at this point? They were sort of in a holding pattern. Plus she felt sheepish, and she didn't want Dr. Snow to know what she was doing or at least trying to do.

"Not yet," Hannah said. "But maybe, at some point."

"Okay," Joel said, defeated. She knew he had lost fourteen pounds since this all had started; she could see it, and the other day she'd heard him telling a neighbor who'd asked what sort of diet plan he had been on. *The misery diet plan,* Hannah had thought in her head. *The tear-your-family-apart-and-suffer diet plan.* She looked at him now. He was way too thin, way too pale. She wondered how bad it could get without his getting really sick. She didn't want him to get really sick. She watched as he went into the bathroom and closed the door. The water ran, and in a minute he was out again and got heavily into bed, still wearing his sweatpants and a T-shirt.

"Night," he said, turning out the light and lying on his side, facing away from her.

"Night," she said.

She kept looking at her book but couldn't absorb a single word. She waited to hear Joel's breathing slow, but it didn't. Lately the kids hadn't been coming into their bed. Maybe they felt somehow that it wasn't the warm, welcoming place it once had been; maybe they sensed the hostility, even though she and Joel tried so hard to mask it. Finally, she gave up and turned out her light, facing away from Joel.

She didn't know what time it was, but at first she thought one of the kids was pushing up against her back. Someone must have come in, though she realized she'd never even gotten up to open the door, and usually the closed door meant to try their best to stay in their own beds that night. It was not a usual practice, but they had it in place just in case.

That isn't a kid, she thought as she very clearly felt a hard penis—separated by clothes—push toward her from behind. When they'd first been married, really even before that, when they were first together, she would often wake up at various stages of having sex, and Joel, too, would be only semiconscious. She'd loved it, thinking they were so drawn to each other they couldn't even keep their hands off each other while they slept. But it hadn't happened in so long and certainly not since she'd discovered the affair. Honestly, she wasn't sure how Joel was holding it together, and somewhere deep down she knew that withholding sex was not the way to keep your husband faithful. He pushed harder and groaned. Was he awake? She was afraid to say anything. She was aroused, whether she liked it or not. She pretended to be asleep and let him keep doing what he was doing, slowly finding a path around the clothes. She had a moment when she could have stopped him, but she didn't want to. She wanted to do this. She kept her eyes closed and turned toward him, letting him ease his way into her. It felt so good, right away; she couldn't hold back. And then he was groaning louder, more excited, until he let all his weight fall onto her, like he was still asleep. Was he? She didn't want to ask. She didn't want to talk. What she especially did not want to do was acknowledge this. He stayed there for a long time. Finally, she eased him away, and he moved, as if in sleep, off her and over to his side, onto his back, the way he used to sleep. She waited a minute, listening, and she guessed from his breathing that he was fast asleep. So she moved into the space next to him, letting the side of her touch the side of him, and she fell into the deepest sleep she'd had in weeks. Maybe longer.

In the morning they didn't say a word. If he knew what had happened, he didn't let on. She had a terrible thought about halfway through the morning—what if that was going to be the last time?

"Do you want to go to a hotel with me?" she asked Reuben later that day. She had planned to ask him, but now she felt she had to do something. After sex with Joel last night, she was losing her resolve, her edge. She felt the outer fringes of her rage turning into deep sadness, and she wasn't sure exactly how she felt about that.

"Do you mean a fake hotel?" he asked. "And funny you would ask today."

They were sitting in the conference room, waiting for Richard to be bathed and dressed. He was still basically the same, still quiet. For some reason, though, today he'd agreed to get up and come out to the main room, but he wanted privacy in the meantime. He had been on an antidepressant for a few weeks now, and Hannah was hopeful this was the beginning of his feeling better.

She raised her eyebrows as if to ask why, and he handed her a steaming mug of coffee. The mug was pink, and she turned it to see what it said. *Shack Job* was written in script letters next to a tiny cabin surrounded by hearts. She almost dropped it.

"What the heck?" she said. "I can't drink out of this. What does it even mean? What if someone else gets it by mistake? Does this mean what I think it means?"

"Oh, come on, let me have a sense of humor," he said. "I am nothing if not discreet. And yes, I think it does mean what you think it means. By the way, the coffee is a new blend, still that Joffrey's from Orlando, and I did go a little more Disney this time: this is the Prince Charming blend." He batted his eyelashes and put on a silly smile.

Hannah rolled her eyes and took a sip. It was rich and deep and good coffee. She shook her head and smiled. He walked over to her and elbowed her.

"I deserve it," she said, giving in. "All of it. But can I switch the mug? I'm afraid Richard is going to see."

"Richard will not see it," he said, but he walked to the shelf and scanned the mugs, choosing one with a big red heart but nothing else. He held it up.

"Fine," she said. "Real subtle, by the way, but at least that one doesn't look like it was bought at a sex shop."

Reuben smirked. "So tell me about this hotel," he said as he expertly poured the coffee from one mug to the other and handed it to her.

"Well, we would go for one night. And it would be my treat," she said. Reuben raised his eyebrows. "I don't mean in that way. But I have to go for work. It's the Dogfish Inn in Lewes, Delaware, an old motel converted into a hip boutique hotel with a beer theme and a local twist."

"You had me at *beer theme*," he said.

"I thought so," she said. "From what I've been told, it has a lot in common with the hotel I'm helping design. I think I can get some good ideas from it. So we'll go, Joel will presumably think I'm on a sleepover with my affair mate, and you, my friend, can keep me company and enjoy the Dogfish Head beer and a fireside chat with the founder and president of the company, Sam Calagione."

"No way!" he said, looking truly excited. "I have admired him from afar."

"I know you have," she said. "You've mentioned him a few times."

"So when do we leave?"

"That's one possible complication. The chat is on Saturday, and I know that's Shabbat," Hannah said, as usual not at all sure how Reuben dealt with that. She thought she had seen him at Saint Martha's on a few Saturdays here and there, but she wasn't absolutely sure.

"That's okay," Reuben said quietly. "Thank you for being aware of that. There was a time I wouldn't have considered traveling on Shabbat, but as I mentioned, I'm reevaluating and trying to figure out what works for me. I'm in!"

She was so relieved she didn't even think as she put down her coffee and leaned in for a hug. She relaxed into him more than she had expected to, letting her head rest on his chest, and when she pulled away, Richard was there in his wheelchair, looking right at them, a nurse behind him with her hands on the chair handles.

"Richard," she said, pulling back and trying to appear normal.

Richard looked at them for a moment too long before turning back and saying something to the nurse. She nodded and wheeled him away, back down the hall toward his room. Hannah followed, not at all sure what he was thinking, not sure how much to explain. But in the end, she didn't have a chance to find out. The nurse was moving fast—he must have been encouraging her to pick up the speed—and when they got to his room, the door closed firmly and decisively in her face.

She tried not to think about anything as she packed up, not about Joel lingering just outside the room, not about what Richard was imagining he had discovered. She had tried to call him, but he wouldn't take her calls. She also tried not to think about Kim, even though she generally thought about her all the time. They had seen each other twice, once when they'd run into each other at Whole Foods and once when they'd had to follow through with an already-planned activity with the kids, and both times Kim had been cool and made Hannah feel she was tolerating her but nothing more. She never would have thought their friendship was so fragile, but she never would have thought a lot of things that were proving to be true lately. At this point a night away with Reuben sounded pretty good.

Hannah told Joel she was going to Delaware partly for work—the other *partly* just sort of hung there, unexplained—and that she could be reached on her cell at any time. She'd meet Reuben at his house, where she had never been despite their ongoing pretend affair, and he would drive to Delaware. Last they'd talked, he'd said he was already packed and had a long list of questions he hoped to be able to ask at the beer chat later that evening.

Reuben was waiting for her in his car when she got there.

"Hi," she said as she got in and put on her seat belt.

"Hi yourself," he said.

He had the Waze app set, so he started driving, the soundtrack to *La La Land* playing quietly, and she tried to relax. Ridley hadn't been feeling well, and it had been hard to leave, but Joel had promised they would be okay. She'd been a little surprised by his assurance, really his kindness, but she also knew he was probably doing it for the kids, who were watching their exchange. Just before she'd walked out, Lincoln had wrapped his arms around her legs.

"Mommy," he'd said, "I don't want you to go."

"It's just for one night," she'd said, leaning down. "I'll be back tomorrow."

"Well, I hope when you come back, you will be here more," he'd said seriously. "You're here, but it's like you aren't really here."

She'd pulled back. Had Joel said something like that in front of the kids? It seemed way too sophisticated for Lincoln to come up with by himself, but then again, he did often surprise her.

"I'll be here more," she'd said, standing up. She'd been going to add something like *That's my goal* or *That's what I'm working toward*, but she hadn't—it was too much. It would raise questions. And really, she should have known there was no such thing as an easy exit.

Now in the car, she put her head back and tried not to think about her house and what her kids were doing and if she was damaging them in some permanent way. She spent a lot of time trying not to think of things these days.

"You can sleep," Reuben said soothingly. "Just rest if you want to. You look tired."

She didn't think she would actually sleep, but when she opened her eyes, they were off the highway on a much smaller road.

"Where are we?" she asked, feeling groggy. "I was really out."

"We'll be there in about fifteen minutes," he said. "I'm glad you woke up; I was thinking of waking you. It's pretty here. I didn't want you to miss it."

She looked around. It *was* pretty. There were lots of open fields and quaint houses. She stretched and sat up, expecting to feel the pull of the kids behind her, but she didn't. She felt surprisingly peaceful.

"Thanks for driving," she said. "I really feel like I'm away. I haven't felt that in a long time."

"Happy to," Reuben said. "While you slept, I updated my list of beer questions—I can't believe I'm going to get to meet the founder of my favorite beer company. He's my idol. What he does—it's my dream job. It's like . . . in all the world I can't think of something that I would want to do more. What would your dream job be, if you could choose anything, like literally anything in the world?"

"Well," she said slowly, trying to shake off the groggy feeling. "I mean, I actually really like my job and this project. It is a dream project."

"Yeah, but you know, like astronaut or pirate or something."

"Pirate? I don't think that would be much of a dream job. I think it would be scary with probably not a lot of showering opportunities, not to mention the illegal stealing aspect to it."

Reuben laughed. "You know what I mean."

"Well, I guess I always wanted to be on Broadway," she said. "But I would call that more of a fantasy than a dream job."

"And if I had to pick a second, okay, I'll call it a fantasy job, I would want to be a professional football player—an Eagle, to be specific," he said. "Speaking of which, I really want to see the game tomorrow—home or out, but I don't want to be driving. Is that okay?"

"Yeah, totally okay," she said. "We can leave right after breakfast. I wouldn't mind seeing it, either, and I know Lincoln is counting down to it. It would be nice to watch it with him. He's such a funny kid. He will wear only Eagles gear at this point in the year. We keep having to go out and buy more."

She stopped for a minute when she said *we*. She didn't talk about Joel too much to Reuben, even though she could. She guessed that was the beauty of a fake affair. You didn't have to hide anything or pretend.

"He thinks the Eagles can go all the way this year; he says he's sure of it," she continued. "I worry he's going to be disappointed."

"Well, I'm hopeful too," Reuben said. "You just never know."

"That's true," she said. "You never know."

They drove through a charming town and finally turned right into the parking lot of the inn. There was a main building with two floors, the doors facing the outside corridor like a motel, and a smaller building with an outdoor firepit surrounded by seats.

"Cool," Reuben said.

"It's smaller than I expected, but it looks nice," Hannah said.

They got out and walked to the office, which was decorated with colorful signs, rugs, a nice couch, white lights, and magnetic letters. To the right were a tiny store and a small kitchen with a big wooden picnic table. Hannah took it all in. When it was their turn, she walked up to the desk.

"Hi! We're checking in," she said. "My last name is Bent."

"Welcome, Mr. and Mrs. Bent," the young woman said. For a second it seemed like everything stood still, like somehow at the mention of those words Joel was going to appear next to her and Reuben would magically disappear.

"Oh, we're not married," she said quickly. "We're, um, business associates, and in fact we have separate rooms."

"Oh, I see that here now," the young woman said. "I'm so sorry to be presumptuous."

"No problem," Hannah said.

"You are in side-by-side rooms," she said. "On the second floor."

"Great, thanks," Hannah said, reaching over and accepting the keys, which she noticed were real keys, not electronic cards like you got at most of the chain hotels these days. *Nice touch,* she thought.

"What if I lose it?" she asked, holding it up.

"That's not a problem," the woman said. "And if you do and you find it after you get home, just drop it in a mailbox. It will find its way back to us."

"Good to know," Hannah said. "Oh, and what time is the chat? My friend here is very excited about that."

"Great! It starts at around six. Come a little early if you want a seat. And you'll find a growler in your room—it's empty now, but bring it down, and we'll fill it."

"Cool," Reuben said, and Hannah thought to herself that that was the only word he had uttered since they had arrived.

"Should we go see our rooms?" Hannah asked Reuben. "Thanks!" she called over her shoulder. They walked out and to the left, climbing the concrete stairs to the second floor. They didn't talk as they looked at the room numbers. They were right next to each other, as promised. On each of their doors *WELCOME* was written in colorful magnetic letters. On the other side of Hannah, the message on the door said *Happy Anniversary*. Hannah turned away. She handed Reuben his key, and they both opened the doors at the same time. The room was nice, with blond wood and modern platform beds. Hannah could see that the far wall held a big sink, and the bathroom was probably just off to the side. She came back out.

"How is it?" she asked. His door was open, so she walked in. He had a king-size bed to her two queens, but other than that they looked the same.

"Really nice," he said, holding up the previously mentioned growler. "I'm going to head back down. I don't want to miss the chance to get a good seat."

"Sounds great," Hannah said. "I'll just hang out in my room and take a look at the details, which is why I'm really here. After the talk we can walk around the corner and get some dinner."

"Okay," he said. "I'm happy to be here. Thanks for bringing me."

Hannah looked at him. He was wearing a Dogfish Head T-shirt, which she thought was adorable, his hair was brushed back, and his yarmulke was pinned on as usual.

"Have fun," she called as he closed his door and went back the way they had come.

Hannah spent the next hour chronicling the details of the room—including a well-appointed minibar with items, all local, that were not too expensive, which she liked, as well as things to buy or use, like a beach chair and a beach bag, which made sense since they were close to the beach. The shampoo and conditioner were in their own small bottles, and she could see the appeal, but she wasn't going to back down on that one. And the soap was amazing—a big bar made of the same grains used to make the beer. She sniffed it, taking the wrapper off, and decided to try it all. She stripped down and got in the shower, which had that rainforest feel that she hoped to be able to install in the Philadelphia hotel. She took her time, sniffing the products, and loved the soap so much she thought maybe they could stock the new hotel with it, deciding that this was still local enough. Honestly it was the best hotel soap she had ever encountered.

She got out and used one of the big, fluffy white towels—another must—to dry off. She brushed her hair and was just wrapping the towel around her torso when there was a knock at the door. She moved closer.

"Hello?" she called.

"It's me," Reuben said. "The talk was so great. I brought you some ice-cold beer. Open up."

"I can't," she called back. "I'm not decent."

"You are always decent," Reuben said. "Too decent."

Was he drunk? She doubted it, but he did sound—what was the word? Robust?

She eased the door open but kept her foot there so it wouldn't go beyond three inches or so.

"Hi!" he said, smiling. He held up an icy glass of beer. She sighed and opened the door just enough to grab it. He stood there while she took a big sip. It was truly delicious. She took another. She hadn't realized she was so thirsty.

"Can I come in?" he asked, gently now.

"In?" she asked.

"Yeah, in, to your room," he said, moving a little closer. Crazy thoughts went through her head—she was already naked, she basically had signed permission, and there was no question Joel already assumed she was having sex, which she decidedly was not, at least not with someone other than Joel himself. She guessed that was the downside to having a fake affair. Plus, she had never quite seen Reuben take charge like this. She took another sip of the beer, drinking it down. It was cold and smooth and really the best beer she had ever had, but she figured that was the point of coming to a beer-themed hotel.

"Sure," she finally said. She stepped back so he could open the door all the way, and he came in, closed the door behind him, and smiled again. Now the beer was going to her head. She felt light headed and excited. Had she even eaten anything today? She'd had a tiny bit of a cast-off cinnamon Pop-Tart this morning when she'd been cleaning up breakfast, but that had been it. That explained the buzz she was feeling.

"Do you have any more beer?" she asked.

"Actually, I do," he said, taking her empty glass and filling it with beer from the growler in his other hand. She drank some and put the glass on the desk and turned to him. He leaned in, slowly at first, and then, once he knew she wasn't going to say no, more forcefully. His lips touched hers, and she moved toward him. He smelled like the good beer she had just had and something else behind that, cedar, maybe. Whatever it was, she liked it. She responded to his kiss, then made it even bigger, opening her mouth to tell him it was okay, and he clearly liked that. He kept his mouth on her as he eased her over to the bed, where they sat on the edge, her damp towel still wrapped around her. At first she tried to hold on to it so she could keep covered, but eventually it was too much, and she wanted to put her hands on Reuben, so she let it drop. He moved even closer, still fully dressed, and pressed into her in a way that made her crazy. They kissed deeply now, not holding back at all, and she was reaching for his T-shirt, wanting to feel his skin against her skin—it seemed like the most important thing in the world—when her phone rang. For the briefest second, she thought she could ignore it, she would ignore it, but she felt Reuben hesitate just the slightest bit, and then somehow the spell was broken. They pulled away from each other, breathing heavily, the towel now across her lap, her breasts totally exposed, his T-Shirt pulled up to his neck. The phone stopped ringing.

"I don't even know how that happened," Reuben said, averting his eyes.

"I know, I wasn't expecting that. I feel so, I don't know what the word is, aroused and confused," she said. When she said the word *aroused*, her phone began to ring again. "This wasn't . . . I guess I want you to know I didn't plan this."

"Of course you didn't," Reuben said, looking at her now as he yanked down his shirt. "I didn't either. I lost control, I guess. I couldn't resist you."

She smiled. "And clearly I couldn't resist you," she said.

"But it's a good thing we did," Reuben said, more of a question than a statement. "Resist each other, I mean."

"I guess it is," she said, covering herself. She honestly wasn't sure. Her phone rang for the third time, and she finally looked to see who it was. Joel's image looked back at her—she had never changed it—and she guessed it was probably Lincoln checking in. She should answer it, but she didn't want to with Reuben here. She would call back as soon as he left.

For the first time in a long time, she let herself think about what Joel had that nobody else would ever have—the only thing that no one else would ever possess, no matter how great they were. It was that he had been there when both of their children had breathed air for the first time. But it was so much more than that. She always knew it, but she let herself *think* it now. It was hard to find someone to have an affair with, that was clear, but there were other people out there. If she had met Reuben at a different time, maybe. He was kind and smart. But he wasn't Joel. Nobody could make her laugh the way he did, or know what she needed before she even knew, or—and this was the big one—stick around even when things got bad, because inevitably, at some point, they were going to get bad in one way or another. It was fairly easy to be aroused by someone when you were in the right place at the right time, drinking ice-cold, delicious beer. It was impossible to know if that would last until the next day or the next year or beyond a decade. It was impossible to know any of these things without having the luxury of time to test them.

"I'm sorry," she said, worried now that she hadn't been nice enough to Reuben, that he might be so aroused that she would make him uncomfortable by stopping. She thought quickly about what it would mean to sleep with him, just this once, just quickly, but she didn't want to anymore. She didn't even want to do it to get back at Joel. That wasn't what this was going to be about in the end. It wasn't about who else she could be with. It was about if she could forgive Joel and move on from there.

"*I'm* sorry," he said, so kindly, leaning into her shoulder and hiding his face for a minute. "I pushed you. You've been very clear, and I pushed you. I'm just going to go back to my room, take a quick shower, and I'll be ready for dinner in thirty minutes, okay?"

She let him keep his head there, and she pushed hers back against his to let him know that yes, that would be okay. He got up, not quite looking her in the eyes, and walked to the door.

"Don't forget your growler," she called.

He turned and picked it up before pouring some more to fill her glass and then drinking directly from it.

"Whoa, slow down," she said, laughing. "All is well."

"Is it?" he asked, looking at her. "Because I think you're attractive—I always have, long before any possible fake affair or anything like that—but more than anything, I like you, I like our friendship, and I had promised myself I wouldn't do anything like that. But then I got so excited at the beer chat—it was inspirational—and I think this beer might have a slightly higher alcohol content or at the very least has some magical powers, and I just felt, I don't know, invincible for a minute. Please, forgive me."

"There is nothing to forgive, and please don't misunderstand this," she said, feeling more in control now that he was enough of a distance away from her that she could trust herself again. "This isn't because I'm not attracted to you. I am. It's just that, well, in addition to everything else, I don't want to do to Lucy what Tara did to me."

"I respect that," he said quietly. "More than you know. I'll see you in a few."

What she had wanted to say, though she thought it would be too much in the moment, was that she wanted to thank him, too, because for the first time she could almost understand how something could happen so out of context, under just the right circumstances. The big question was, What should she now do with that realization?

PART THREE—I'LL SEE YOU TOMORROW

CHAPTER NINETEEN

"We're from Philly," Ridley chanted.

"Whoa, whoa, whoa," Hannah said, interrupting the song, which, Hannah knew, continued with the words *fucking Philly*. "Rid, come on, I get that it's a catchy song, but no bad words, okay?"

"Sorry," she mumbled.

"That's okay, sweetie. I know it's an exciting night," Hannah said. She ran back into the kitchen to grab the cake she had baked, chocolate in the shape of a football with *Go Birds!* written on it. Ridley cheered as she brought it out and held it up for her to view.

"Do you think we'll see Daddy and Lincoln on TV?" Ridley asked, moving closer to the television screen.

"I doubt it," Hannah said.

"Do you think they'll get better seats if Lincoln tells someone he's named after the stadium?" she asked, tripping a little on the word *stadium*. "That's so cool that he's named after that place, and I'm named after a dumb park in Delaware County."

"That's not true," Hannah said. "That it's a dumb park. It's a great park. We go there all the time."

"Whatever," Ridley said, beginning to adopt Lincoln's ability to sound much older than she was. "But do you? Think they can get better seats?"

"I hope so," Hannah said.

The doorbell rang, and Hannah jumped up to get it. Kim stood just outside the door, looking vaguely sheepish. "Hi!" she said, raising her hand and waving half-heartedly.

"Hi yourself," Hannah said, grabbing her forearm and pulling her inside. She was so glad to see her. Hannah had called her after her time in Delaware and begged her to be her friend again. She had said those magic words: "You're my person. I am never going to find another person like you." And Kim had agreed, though she hadn't said the words back and continued to seem a little cold. Then the other day Kim had called, sounding especially sad. She'd explained that Hank had gotten tickets for him and the kids to the NFC championship game between the Eagles and the Minnesota Vikings. She had considered getting her own ticket, but she and Hannah had agreed that would be worse—sitting alone while her family was somewhere in the stadium together. That was when Hannah had felt the slightest shift back to the way things used to be between them.

Kim was wearing her Eagles jersey. She had green paint on her face and a green foam hand that said *#1*. Hannah felt sorry for her. She looked as stadium ready as a person could look.

"Thanks for coming," Hannah said, leaning in to hug her. "And for bringing so much spirit."

"I'm happy to be here," she said, hugging back before dropping onto the couch next to Ridley and patting her on the thigh. She focused on the screen. "Do you know where Joel and Linc are sitting?"

"High up, I think," Hannah said. "But Lincoln was going to tell someone he's named after the stadium with the hope that they'll treat him like a VIP. I was afraid to tell him that wasn't very likely."

"You don't think they will?" Ridley asked, alarmed.

"Oh, I don't know," Hannah said. "Maybe."

She was excited about the game, but it wasn't lost on her that the Eagles were playing the Minnesota Vikings. Somehow it seemed like more than just a football game, like it was some sort of symbolic battle, that if the Eagles could win, it would be a concrete step toward putting Minnesota and Tara and HOTEL behind them, even though she knew that was ridiculous.

Lincoln had barely slept the night before. He'd been up at three o'clock and again at four o'clock, changing from one Eagles shirt to another because he truly believed that his shirt choice might somehow affect the outcome of the game. They were all exhausted. Hannah sat down in the chair next to the couch with a big sigh, just in time to see the Vikings run away with the ball to score the first touchdown of the game.

"Oh, that's not good," Hannah said.

"It's still so early," Kim said seriously. "It's going to be a long game."

Hannah's phone rang across the room. She pushed herself up with effort and went to grab it. She was surprised to see Reuben's name.

"Hello?" she said reluctantly.

"Hannah? It's Reuben. I am so sorry to bother you, but I tried Joel, and he didn't pick up."

"That's okay," Hannah said. "What's up?"

"It's Richard," Reuben said.

"Is he okay?" Hannah asked, her eyes still on the game, imagining it would be an issue with the soap or maybe his crying.

"Well, we're taking him to the hospital," Reuben said. "An ambulance is here."

"What? Why?" Kim and Ridley turned to look at Hannah; her tone had gone from not too interested to panicked.

"When I went in to say good night, he didn't look good," Reuben said. "He was disoriented. As I got closer, I could see his lips were blue. I called for help right away."

"Where are they taking him?" Hannah asked.

"Methodist," Reuben said. "I can meet you there."

"I'll come right away," she said. "I'm leaving now."

When she hung up, she jammed her phone into her purse and looked up. Kim and Ridley were watching her.

"It's Grandpa," she said, trying to tone down her intense concern. "He wasn't feeling well, so they have to take him to the doctor. I'm going to meet him there since they couldn't reach Daddy. Kim, do you mind staying with Rid?"

Kim stood up and walked over to Hannah. She put her calming hand on her shoulder. "I don't mind at all," she said. "Is there anything else I can do?"

"No, this alone is so much," Hannah said, grabbing her coat. "What would I have done if you weren't here?"

"Well, I'm glad I am," Kim said.

Hannah walked over to Ridley and gave her a quick hug. "I'll call as soon as I can," she said. When she got to the door, she turned around and called, "Go Eagles!"

Hannah flagged down a cab and tried calling Joel, but there was no answer. Before she knew it, she was getting out at Methodist and going through the metal detector, thinking that as soon as he was well enough, they would transfer him to Pennsylvania Hospital.

Inside she told the woman at the desk whom she was there to see and was escorted back to a hectic emergency room. She found Richard in a curtained area to the right. A bunch of nurses had gathered just outside and were whispering, and at first Hannah was alarmed, thinking they were talking about his health. But then she heard someone say,

"The news anchor for NBC! I grew up watching him!" And someone else said, "I can't believe he's here," and she knew they were just starstruck. She smiled as she walked by them and toward Richard. His eyes were closed, and he looked pale. He was getting oxygen, and he already had an IV in place. Reuben came up behind her.

"Hi," he said. "They'll need you to do some paperwork."

"How is he?" she asked.

"They think it might be congestive heart failure," Reuben said. "They're still doing a bunch of tests; nothing has been determined yet. His oxygen level was very low, but they have it back up now—not all the way but to a better place, they said. They had a more aggressive oxygen mask on at first, which he didn't like, and they just switched to this, so that seemed like a good sign to me."

"Well, it was nice of you to come with him," she said. "Once again you did more than you had to."

"I wouldn't have had it any other way," Reuben said. "Anyway, they were asking about insurance and a few other things. I told them you would go over it when you got here."

"Okay," she said, not wanting to deal with that now. "And I guess you can go. You probably don't want to miss the game."

"I don't mind hanging out a little," he said. "Could you reach Joel?"

"No, he's at the game. I have a feeling the cell phone signals are completely overwhelmed. It might be hard to reach him."

Reuben nodded.

"Hannah?"

She turned and saw Richard's eyes were open. He sounded tired, but he also sounded just like himself. She went over to him and hugged him gently, placing her head on his chest for the briefest minute. She realized she thought she might not get to talk to him again, that he wouldn't be there anymore. The thought overwhelmed her, and she swallowed hard before lifting her head all the way up to meet his eyes.

"Richard," she said. "I'm so glad to see you. How are you feeling?"

"Can you please close the curtains?" Richard said seriously. "I have to tell you some things, and I am not sure how much time I have left."

"You have time," Hannah said. "They got your oxygen level back up already. You look much better than you did, I'm sure of that. Maybe you were dehydrated. You have plenty of time."

"Is Joel here?" he asked.

"No, but not because he doesn't want to be," Hannah said quickly. Richard had let Joel start to visit him again, but Joel kept saying their time together still felt strained. "I can't even reach him. He doesn't know you're here. He's at the game with Lincoln."

"Okay, that makes this all a little easier," Richard said, closing his eyes for a few seconds. "Can you please close the curtains? And close them as tight as you can. I can hear people out there whispering about me. One nurse asked me for my autograph, which I didn't mind, really. How many have I signed in my life? Thousands? More? So I figure, what's one last autograph? It's symbolic."

"What are you talking about?" Hannah asked. "Why would it be your last autograph?"

Richard raised his eyebrows and nodded toward the curtain. Reluctantly, Hannah walked to the outer edge of his area. She grabbed the curtain to pull it shut and caught Reuben's eyes as she did it. She made a face saying, *I have no idea what he wants*, and Reuben made a similar face back to her.

"Okay," she said, walking back to Richard. "All closed."

He pushed himself up as best he could. "All living things have a cycle," Richard began, using his official *I'm reporting the news* tone. "People are born, they live, but they must die."

"Richard," Hannah said, exasperated. "You are not going to die!"

"Well," he said, not sounding as official as he just had. "I am ready to. I have decided it's time to go. A new year has begun; I no longer want to be a burden to any of you. In fact, I think you will be better able to focus on your family and your marriage once I'm gone. I have sucked too much away from what's important."

"Richard," Hannah said, trying not to cry. "No. Just no. You are our family. You are what's important. As much as any of us. Richard. Please. This is totally crazy."

"And there's something else," he said.

"Something else?"

"I almost told you before, I'm sure you remember," he said.

"Oh yes, something about a regret you have?" Hannah said. "I do remember."

"Well, this is my deathbed confession," he said, and he cleared his throat.

"Look, Richard, I want to know what you have to tell me," Hannah said, talking quickly. "I have wanted to know since you alluded to it but not if it's your deathbed confession. I would rather not know if it means keeping you around longer. I don't really need to know. Tell me another time. In a few years. Or maybe not even that soon."

"It isn't up to you to determine when and how someone gives a deathbed confession," Richard said, and she caught a glimpse of the part of him that hadn't been around much for the last few months, maybe longer, the part that was authoritarian but saw the ridiculousness in it. One of the parts of him that she loved and missed. "It is only up to the giver of the confession to determine where and when that will happen. So please sit back and listen, because this is it."

Hannah looked around. There was a chair off to the side, but it seemed too far away, so she just stood there and waited.

"If one is truly lucky," Richard began, "one will find the love of his or her life. Many people think that is the hard part, the finding. It isn't. The hard part is navigating all of the circumstances, changes, shocks, tragedies, and hardships that come to everyone over the course of forty or fifty or sixty years. Of course, there are many good moments, too, and it's a matter of getting through the bad or at least finding a way to accept the bad so you can share the good."

Hannah had two thoughts. The first was that this was exactly what she had been thinking about in Delaware and ever since. Had Richard read her mind? And the second thought was that, finally, he was going to tell her.

"You barely knew Celine," Richard said, talking about his wife and Joel's mother. "You joined our family when she was already sick and not at all the person she had once been. I think that's one of the sadder things, since I believe you and she would have truly loved each other. But I also believe that your knowing her better, or at least knowing her true self before she got sick, would have been a way to better understand Joel and me and the Bents in general. She was a loving, warm, and passionate woman. She was a great mother, and I would not have wanted to have any other wife. I make that last statement with complete confidence, so I will say it again. I would not have wanted to have any other wife. But she was not perfect. Really, who is? And she did things that hurt me, very much. During the course of our marriage—and as you know, we were married for almost fifty years—she had two affairs. One was ongoing, and he came back to haunt us from time to time, and the other was rapid fire; it swelled quickly and burned out. I discovered this second affair when she was out late one night, got sick, and couldn't get herself home. I was working that night, I was a reporter for the NBC affiliate at that time, and this strange man called and basically told me he didn't know what to do with her. I thought she was at home with Joel, who was fairly young, but Joel was with a neighbor. If all had gone well, if her appendix hadn't acted up at that moment, rendering her unable to function, I might never have known. But once that came out, she told me about everything, including the man she had slept with on and off since our second anniversary."

"Richard, I'm so sorry—I have to tell you I knew about this," Hannah said. "Joel told me."

"He did?" he said. His speech was getting slower and slower; he was clearly getting tired. At times, a few of his words sounded slightly slurred. "I'm surprised. He never talked about it, I thought. Well, I'll spare you some of the details, then. And let me say that while I was always faithful to Celine in the traditional sense, I was not easy. If I was forced to put a label on it—and please bear with me, because I know this is a cliché—I would have to admit that my career was my mistress. You don't get to be the anchor of a national news outlet for twenty-four years without paying some sort of price. It wasn't that I wasn't loving, but when I look back, I remember how many times we were settling in for a quiet moment at home and something broke in the world—the Berlin Wall, the Challenger disaster, you name it—and I would have to run, just run, leaving Celine alone with Joel time after time."

"Richard," Hannah said, but he put up his hand to indicate that he was still talking. She noticed the skin on his arm was speckled with dark spots and looked so thin and shimmery, so well worn.

"What I am getting to is this—despite everything, despite it all, we never wanted to dismantle our family, and she never truly loved the other guy, the one she saw on and off from time to time—well, either of them—more than she loved me. She never wanted to be with him instead of being with me. That was the key. Things would have of course been different if she had. She liked his attention, I assume she liked his body, but she did not want to build a life with him. We had a wonderful, well-crafted life—a wonderful son, a warm home, a daily routine that we could not have managed without each other. Plus, as much as my work took away from our life together, it also added a certain cachet that would have been hard for her to give up. But Joel found out—it was inevitable—and it became part of our family discussion. At the time, I thought it proved that we are strong, but now, or as soon as Joel told me about what he did to you, I knew it had the opposite effect. I was all wrong. Instead of teaching Joel that marriage is something to be cherished, that it is sacred and not to be played with, the message

I left him with was that a marriage can survive an affair. And while I do think that is so, if all the circumstances are right, if both people are fully committed to recovering and making it work, I will never forgive myself for that or for the fallout, which hurt you."

"Richard," Hannah said. "This has nothing to do with you. This is not your responsibility or your fault."

He had closed his eyes, and now he kept them closed.

"Richard?" she said, shaking him slightly. He stirred but still didn't open his eyes. "Richard!"

"I'm not dead yet," he said belligerently. "That is decidedly not how my deathbed confession will work, unfortunately." He opened his eyes and looked right at her.

"I want to make it very clear that we don't need you to die so we can focus on our marriage," Hannah said. "That is the most ridiculous thing I have ever heard, and now I'm afraid you're going to die soon and I will always feel I didn't do enough to stop you. What can I do to stop you?"

"I promise I'm not going to die right now," he said. "It takes a little time. I have to starve myself first."

She couldn't stand it. She was crying hard now, still trying to keep the noise down but succeeding less with each passing second. Reuben pushed through the curtain and seemed relieved to find them both there, conscious and alive. He touched her forearm gently and quickly moved his hand away. She could hear quiet cheering coming from a cubicle nearby. The Eagles must have scored a touchdown.

"What's going on?" Reuben asked.

"So many things I can't even say," she said, sniffling and wiping her nose. "I need to find Joel. I have to keep Richard from giving up."

Reuben nodded in his comforting way, like that all made perfect sense. They both turned to look at Richard, who was sitting regally in bed. He had pushed himself back up, his lips pursed and his eyes just off to the side, like he was intentionally trying not to meet their eyes. Since Richard had witnessed her hugging Reuben, they had been careful not to be with him at the same time, though now it was impossible. Her affair with Reuben, fake or not, had ended when they'd returned to Philadelphia from Delaware. Hannah had moments of regret for being so in control when they were in Delaware. Sometimes she found herself fantasizing about him, and she decided, in the end, that was okay. She didn't have to feel guilty about that.

Lucy had finally come back from her African adventure, and she was ready to move to the next phase—the phase of deciding. So was Reuben, it seemed. Hannah looked at him now and thought about all the things he had done and all the things he was still doing for them—for all of them—the many roles he had played. He was like some sort of shepherd sent to them from . . . she didn't know where.

"Thank you," she said, turning to look at him now, placing her hand on his arm the way he had just done to her a few minutes before. "For everything."

Reuben didn't say anything. He was wiping tears away from his eyes. She wasn't sure which of the recent events was triggering them, and honestly, it was just too much to ask about now, especially in front of Richard.

"Listen, let's go do the paperwork quickly," he said, and once again she was grateful to him for knowing what to do next and for giving her an excuse to leave Richard for a few minutes and pull herself together. "After that we can think about everything else."

CHAPTER TWENTY

The Eagles won. They were going to the Super Bowl. It was fifteen minutes after the game when she finally reached Joel.

"Sorry, sorry," he said as he answered. "I can see you called four times. Is everything okay?"

"Yes, for the moment, but your dad was taken to the hospital. Reuben went in to check on him before leaving and said he didn't look well and was disoriented. They think he was having trouble maintaining his oxygen level. They're still trying to figure it all out. I'm here with him; Ridley is home with Kim," she said. "Do you want me to meet you at home, and then you can come?"

"No, we'll come right there," he said.

"But it's so late," she said. "And I don't know how Lincoln will handle this. It's an emergency room—with, you know, lots of emergencies. Plus, he has to be exhausted. He barely slept last night, and after the game and everything."

"We're coming," he said, interrupting her gently. "We'll be there soon."

Hannah wandered back into Richard's area. They were getting him ready to be moved to a room for the night. There was talk about him being given the last private room. She was just letting it all happen instead of fighting to get him transferred. He didn't seem to mind. They were being very nice to him here; he had so many fans and was clearly being treated as a VIP. His eyes were open, and his color was much better. He cleared his throat when he saw her.

"I've changed my mind," he said, his voice a little stronger again. "I am not going to die right now."

"Thank goodness, Richard," she said. "That was such a crazy thing you said."

"Well, you have the Eagles to thank for it," he said. "I'm not going to miss this Super Bowl, not after waiting all these years to see this—it is amazing. After that who knows? We'll just have to see."

"No, after that we won't see," she said. "We need you here as long as it is humanly and medically possible. I refuse to let you take yourself out."

Reuben came to the curtain. "I'm going to get going," he said to both of them.

"Thank you for everything," Richard said, extending his hand, which Reuben rushed to grab. "Hopefully I'll be back at Saint Martha's tomorrow or the next day."

"We will be so happy to have you back," Reuben said warmly. "Bye, Hannah."

"Bye, Reuben," she said. "Thank you."

As soon as he was gone, Richard turned to her and raised his eyebrows. *Oh no,* Hannah thought.

"Reuben? Really?"

"Richard, I know what you're thinking . . . or I have no idea what you're thinking. It was, I don't know, it was something I had to do, I guess."

"Whatever you have to do. Who am I to judge?" Richard said.

"I was just so mad, so incredibly angry that Joel would ruin everything we shared, everything we had built," she said honestly, and it felt good.

"I understand that anger," Richard said.

"And I can see now it gave me a chance to see if I wanted to stay or go."

"Time in the pocket," Richard said regally.

"What?" Hannah asked.

"It's a football metaphor, when the quarterback needs to be protected while he figures out what to do with the ball. You needed time to figure it out. Time in the pocket."

"Exactly," Hannah said, relieved that he understood. That was exactly what she had needed.

"It isn't a secret that I hope you and Joel can find your way back to each other so that this is not always a barrier separating you. As long as you can do that, I will be happy. And don't let it linger the way I did, the way Celine did. We managed, but I should have put my foot down. People can make one mistake; most people do in one way or another, but more, well, that can be too many."

They both heard Lincoln's voice at the same time. "Grandpa?" he was calling loudly. "Grandpa?"

"In here," Richard called with a forcefulness Hannah hadn't heard from him all night.

Lincoln appeared, looking tiny. As soon as he saw them, he scrambled up onto Richard's bed.

"Take it easy," Hannah said. "I don't want you to hurt him."

"He couldn't possibly hurt me," Richard said, helping him settle in next to him and rearranging his tubes. Lincoln grabbed on so tight Hannah wondered if he'd thought Richard might be dead when he got here.

"Actually," Richard said, looking at Hannah, "this is even better than the Eagles' win."

She made a mental note to make sure to bring the kids to visit him at least once a week, maybe more.

"Lincoln?" Joel called, sounding panicked.

"In here," they all shouted at the same time.

Joel came around the corner, looking rumpled in his Eagles jersey and carrying two green rally towels, one in each hand. He looked sweaty and smelled vaguely of beer.

"He got away from me," Joel said. Then to Hannah, "I'm so sorry."

In that moment it felt like he was saying he was so sorry for everything, which he had done so many times before, but it felt so real, so heartfelt, that she simply said, "It's okay."

"How are you?" he asked Richard. "How is he?"

"Better," Hannah said. "They're still trying to figure it all out, and I think they're waiting for another test result or two. He'll at least stay overnight."

Hannah and Joel watched as Lincoln told Richard about the highlights of the game.

"And then Nick Foles had the ball and he threw it to Corey Clement and then he threw it back to Nick Foles and then Nick Foles threw it to Torrey Smith and he caught it and made a touchdown! It's called a flea-flicker, Grandpa!"

"Flea-flickers are my favorite," Richard said, smiling in a way Hannah hadn't seen in what, weeks? Months?

"Can we talk out there?" Joel asked quietly, pointing over his shoulder.

"Sure," she said, following him through the curtain.

"What a night," Joel said, running his hands through his messy, thick hair. "It was emotional enough, just with the game. I didn't expect this."

"How could you?"

"Thanks for coming," he said. "For being here when I couldn't."

Hannah just nodded.

"I'll stay with him tonight," Joel said. "At least until he gets settled. Maybe longer if he wants me to. When they're finished talking, you can take Linc home."

"Okay," she said.

"It was a great game," Joel said. "The game of a lifetime. The stadium was shaking with all the energy and excitement. I have a few videos. I'll show you later."

"Did Linc tell anyone about his name?"

Joel's eyes lit up. "We went to the customer-service desk as soon as we walked in, and we waited in line. It was a crazy long line, but he didn't care. When it was his turn, he pulled himself up so he could talk to the woman behind the counter, and he told her, in his serious little man-slash-little-boy voice, and guess what?"

"What?"

"They gave us VIP seats," Joel said. "It was awesome. I mean, everyone was so happy, so excited, I think they were being way nicer than they might usually be. He kept wanting to call you—well, he really wanted to call Ridley, I think they had some sort of bet going—but you know, there was no service, so he still hasn't told her. We were just going to call when you called me. To leave there flying so high and then get the call about my dad. I'm on an emotional roller coaster."

"Shoot, I never called Kim," Hannah said, rubbing her forehead. "And now it's too late."

"It's okay," Joel said soothingly. "She'll understand. Hey, I've been wanting to ask you something again, but I don't want to push you, I don't want to put pressure on you, and most of all, I'm afraid that I'm going to scare you away."

Hannah nodded. She got that.

"But can I ask you one thing? The thing that I've asked before and I keep wanting to ask until you say yes?"

She was honestly a little scared. She knew what was coming. What if she wasn't ready? But she looked at him, all rumpled and vulnerable, having just taken their son to the game of a lifetime. She thought of how he'd indulged Lincoln, waiting in line so he could tell someone official that he'd been named after Lincoln Financial Field. Lincoln had always wanted to do that. She knew she wouldn't have had the patience for it all. She would have talked a big game and ultimately suggested they not wait in line because it was so unlikely that the staff would do anything for them. But Joel hadn't done that; he'd let Lincoln play it out. And now Lincoln was going to remember this night forever—everyone in the entire city would but especially Lincoln. She closed her eyes and kept them closed.

"Sure," she said, holding her breath.

"Will you go back to Dr. Snow with me now?" he asked. "So we can talk again, about all of this. Please?"

She opened her eyes and exhaled.

"Okay," she said. "I was thinking the same thing."

Three nights later they were on their way to the Northeast to see Dr. Snow. Hannah thought about the last time they'd come, how they'd sat outside and she hadn't been able to go in. How far apart they'd been from each other, how that moving away had seemed like the only real choice at the moment.

She wasn't sure what she was going to say once they went in to see her. The last few days had been filled with taking care of Richard, getting him back to Saint Martha's, where he hadn't even gone to his room right away but had sat in his wheelchair in the main room and talked about the pride a winning sports team could bring to a city, to a place in general. She and Joel had sat and listened as he'd talked about the history of the Eagles and the long-standing drought of Super Bowl wins. He'd referred to the infamous Curse of Billy Penn, and he'd taken on the voices of Rocky and Adrian in the clip from the Rocky movie that was played at the beginning of most Philly sports events, which never, ever failed to hype everyone up. By the time he had been talking for about fifteen minutes, Hannah guessed the entire nursing home had gathered in the room. When he'd suggested they sing "Fly, Eagles, Fly," she could almost feel the building shake, even though many of the voices were weakened by old age and illness. It was amazing. Reuben and Joel had had to take over the *E-A-G-L-E-S* chant at the end, as Richard was just too tired, and Hannah had watched as they'd stood side by side. Then she'd had to look away.

"So here's the thing," Hannah said as they took their seats in Dr. Snow's office. She looked less like Dr. Melfi from *The Sopranos* these days—her hair was longer, and her glasses were different—and it made Hannah realize that she'd been in some sort of trance in those early days after finding out about Joel's affair. Or maybe it was less that and more that she'd wanted the discovery of the affair to be a television show she could turn off, as opposed to her new reality. "Even this last week, we're so busy. I mean, there's Richard, you know, Joel's dad, who was just in the hospital and needed extra care but always needs attention—and believe me, I wouldn't have it any other way. And then our kids, who are amazing but at these crazy ages, and—I say this proudly—they are so smart and creative that they keep us on our toes, all the time. So even though I couldn't really see it before, or I didn't want to admit it, it is hard to focus on each other, and it has been for a long time. I still don't accept that as an excuse for what happened. Even with all of that chaos, there was never a time when I wasn't happy to see Joel walk through our front door—or any door, for that matter—when I wasn't happy to have him in the house or at the dinner table or in our bed, with kids between us or not. But to really stop and focus, to look each other in the eyes or, well, more . . . how do we do that on a regular basis? How can we manage to focus on each other and keep up everything else we have to do? Because I don't want to be constantly wondering if I should be paying more attention or if my focus is in the wrong place. I just want to live."

"Well," Dr. Snow began.

"Wait!" Joel said urgently. She was ready for Joel to bring up her affair; she knew it was a good possibility. "I feel I have to make this very clear: This did not happen because of anything you did or did not do. You have always been exactly what I wanted you to be, exactly who I thought you would be when I asked you to marry me, when I saw you at the diner that very first time or selling the honey. You have always been—you. And you are the person I want to spend my life with. What happened, what I did, was stupid beyond words. It was like I convinced myself that what took place there had nothing to do with us, with our family, but that was as untrue as anything could be. Right now, I can't even conjure up that way of thinking, it's so clearly false. But then it was like I was in a daze, in some sort of alternate universe. As soon as I realized it, once something clicked—and that was weeks before you discovered those texts—I ended it, not because I was afraid you were going to catch me but because it was not something I wanted to do, then or ever again."

Okay, she thought to herself, *he isn't going to put me on the spot like that.* Even though she hadn't specifically asked him to not tell Dr. Snow about their agreement, she was relieved. For one brief moment Hannah let herself remember her time with Reuben in the Delaware hotel room far away, feeling excited and buzzed from the beer and, well, so turned on. She could imagine, if they had continued down that road, how it could have felt almost separate from everything else she knew. She shook her head to get rid of the image.

"You've made that clear," Hannah finally said, addressing Joel directly. "And I maintain that whatever was lost between us, whatever fell through the cracks, was not reason to do what you did. In a million years. But if we are going to try to make this work in any way, I want to feel in control; I want to feel the foundation is stable. And I think, with some perspective, our foundation, our base that needs to be strong to hold everything else up, was crumbling just the slightest bit."

They sat quietly for a minute. Then Dr. Snow cleared her throat.

"I think just knowing this, recognizing it and talking about it, all of it, is key," she said. "And to get back to your point, Hannah, there are ways to find time to be alone, if you're creative. Maybe make a lunch date when everyone is out of the house and meet at home, or if both kids are in your bed, once they're asleep, sneak downstairs to the couch. I know that's hard; I know someone could wake up at any second and need you. Do you guys have a lock on your door?"

"No!" they both said with some horror.

"Think about it," she said. "It isn't the worst thing in the world. If someone knocks or tries to come in, it just gives you that extra moment to pull yourselves together. It might help you relax."

Joel turned to Hannah. "I promise, with all my being and heart, that I will never do anything like that again," he said. He waited a few seconds, and Hannah met his eyes. "I will never, ever, ever be unfaithful again."

Hannah nodded. Dr. Snow nodded. Now it was just a matter of Hannah's deciding if she could live with that.

CHAPTER TWENTY-ONE

"I wish he had agreed to come with us," Hannah said as she loosely wound a green Eagles scarf around Lincoln's neck. "It isn't even that cold out. We could have easily taken him in his wheelchair. It's a once-in-a-lifetime event!"

"I tried really hard to talk him into it, but he wanted to be at Saint Martha's," Joel said, placing an Eagles cap on each child's head and making sure they were on straight. "I think he plans on narrating the event as it unfolds, even though I know it will be on all the TVs in the place with plenty of official commentary."

"But you have the iPad, right?" she asked. "Because I want to Skype him from the parade." She looked around to make sure they weren't forgetting anything. She had all the flags, the rally towels, the sign Lincoln had made that read, *Flea-Flickers Rule—Thanks, Nick!* in green glitter paint. She held it carefully by the stick he had taped to the back. Ridley had decided to leave Stinker on the couch dressed in an Eagles shirt. Dune was now back in Lincoln's closet, under the shoes, of course, in case his back got itchy. The bear, too, was wearing an Eagles shirt.

"I do," Joel said. "Right here in this bag."

"Come ooooon," Lincoln whined. "We're going to miss it!"

"No, we aren't," Joel said calmly. "We have plenty of time."

"Oh, wait, I just need to get one thing," Hannah said, leaving them standing in a jumble by the front door, all green and sparkly.

She ran upstairs to the bedroom and pulled out the small bag she had stashed behind the books on her nightstand. Inside was a small piece of sea glass, and she needed it because she was planning to propose something to Joel later that day, and the sea glass was an important part of the symbolism of what she had planned. She carried the bag downstairs and shoved it in her purse.

"Ready," she said.

They stepped outside, and the air felt cool and crisp on this February day. The sun was shining, and people were out in droves. They walked west to Broad Street, where the Eagles Victory Parade would make its way north, eventually going by them and then city hall and ending up at the art museum.

"Go Birds!" people yelled.

"We're number one!" others shouted.

"Finally!" others said to each other, nodding knowingly.

And the ubiquitous "We all we got, we all we need," which meant more to Hannah on this day than she ever would have expected.

The Eagles had won the Super Bowl for the first time ever on Sunday in an exciting game against the New England Patriots with a final score of forty-one to thirty-three, and it felt to Hannah that the city was electric. They walked the way they always did when the city was crowded, Joel up front, followed by the kids in single file, and Hannah bringing up the rear. It gave her a chance to see everyone, to watch Joel in the lead, with his eyes in front of him charting the path and every few seconds looking subtly behind to make sure they were all there. Then came Lincoln with his old-man walk, so serious, his shoulders looking heavier than they had to be; then Ridley, pretty, silly Ridley, in her pink shoes and long braids tied today with green ribbons. Everyone was going to be okay no matter what; she knew that, but she also knew they were better together.

By the time they got to the corner, they were about six people deep.

"I'm not going to see them," Lincoln said like it was the end of the world. "I'm not going to see Carson and Nick."

"No, I think you will," Joel said, leaning in to see if he could spot anything coming. "I think the floats or buses or whatever they are going to be on will be high. I think you'll see everything."

But just then people shifted, and Joel very patiently, very subtly moved and found his own place in the crowd. He reached out his hand for Lincoln, then nodded to him to reach for Ridley. Hannah was off to the side, watching. It took a while, probably ten solid minutes. She knew he knew he couldn't move too fast, or someone might call him on it. But a big group of people like that shifted constantly, and he was an expert at getting his family to the front. Once they were there, he looked around for Hannah. She smiled, possibly the most open, real smile she had given him since this whole mess started. He knew it, he recognized it, and he reached out his hand for her. He was not trying to be subtle anymore. She leaned in and grabbed his hand and let herself be pulled to the front. She held her breath for a few seconds, but nobody said a word.

The crowd went crazy, and she could see big buses making their way north toward them, green confetti flying everywhere.

"Quick, Skype Richard," Hannah said.

Joel pulled out the iPad and found his name. It rang and rang, but he didn't answer.

"He promised," Hannah said, disappointed. She didn't want him to miss this, not just the parade but what she had planned for after. "Try again."

"Okay," he said, and she heard the phone ringing.

Finally, the call was answered, and the main room at Saint Martha's came into view. The image bounced up and down until it settled on Richard's face, too close, like he was holding it near his ear.

"Dad, hey, Dad," Joel called. "We're Skyping you. It's a video call."

The cheers were getting louder, and the buses were getting closer. Hannah watched as Richard rearranged his phone, placing it on his lap looking up. Then someone took it from him and set it on a table next to him. They could see Richard, and the room was full, so many people facing him, presumably soaking in his words, whatever they might be today. The television screen behind him was lit up with the image they were in the center of right now.

"Look, you can practically see us," Ridley said, pointing.

"They're coming, they're coming," Lincoln said, like he could barely stand it.

Joel held up the iPad so Richard could see the up-close version of the buses passing, though they all knew the news cameras probably had a better angle. Just then the cheers were out of control, and Hannah looked up to see Carson Wentz, the star quarterback who'd been injured during the regular season, making many wrongly think their Super Bowl dreams were over, and Nick Foles, the quarterback who'd stepped in and won it all for them. They were up there, smiling, waving, and—Hannah did a double take. Had Carson just winked at her?

The first bus was the best, but they waited and cheered as the rest went by. Finally, it was quiet. Joel turned the screen to face them, and they could see Richard was talking to the group.

"Philadelphia is a city of fighters. We never give up," he said.

She looked closer and saw he had a mug next to him that said *The Philly Special*, the now-famous play Nick Foles had used during the Super Bowl, one of the flea-flickers Lincoln kept referring to, with dots showing how the ball was thrown. She laughed to herself. That had to be Reuben's doing. Reuben and his mugs.

"Richard," she called toward the screen. It was so loud behind her she worried he couldn't hear her. But he looked at them and smiled. Now seemed like the right time for the moment she was planning. She was ready, she knew. And just to keep things in line with tradition, she had made an emergency hair appointment with Cami yesterday so that her hair was freshly cut, as it had been before all the other important events marking her life with Joel. She moved toward him now, reaching into her bag for the sea glass. As she grabbed on to Joel's elbow to get his attention, a man walked between them, and she had to let go and take a step back. They both saw his shirt at the same time. It said **The University of Delaware** in big blue letters. She watched as Joel's face lit up. He knew what the mascot was, of course he did, and as the words formed on his lips—she, too, knew they were the Blue Hens—something shifted, and he looked at her. She was pretty sure the same thought she was having moved through his mind at that moment: *Who would come to this Eagles parade and not wear Eagles gear?* Someone who did not deserve to be recognized was who. They looked at each other, and he shook his head, smiling at her knowingly, and in that moment she knew two things for sure—she was making the right decision, and now was not the right time for her surprise.

Five days before Joel asked Hannah to marry him, she got a bad cold. She didn't know for sure that he was going to ask her in five days; there had been a few holidays and a day trip here and there during the previous three months when she'd thought, *Maybe he'll ask me today,* and he hadn't. They had talked about marriage and having a family, and she was fairly sure Joel had reached out to her mother; he had asked for her number and Hannah had noticed, at a certain point, that her mother could not stop smiling when they were together.

The day her cold was at its worst, they had been planning to have dinner at Villa di Roma, her favorite red-gravy place since Joel had introduced her to it on their first official date. But she had to cancel. Her throat had been sore the last few days, but by that point she felt terrible pressure in her sinuses, and her eyes had that swollen sensation inside their sockets. Everything hurt. Joel spent a few minutes trying to talk her into still going but relented quickly and said he would bring her a simple dinner and some tea instead. They would go to Villa di Roma when she felt better.

He arrived at her door not too long afterward with a brown take-out bag and another tiny shopping bag.

"This is clean, by the way," he said as he pulled a bowl out of the second bag and held it up. "I brought it from home. I've been saving it for you."

She watched from the couch as he unpacked the brown paper bag and got her meal ready. He found a tray she kept under the stove, and when he brought it to her on the couch, it was the perfect dinner for someone who wasn't feeling well. There was chicken escarole soup, which she learned later he'd gotten at Villa di Roma, some of their bread and butter pats, a Sprite, and a cup of tea with a tiny ramekin of honey, which he also told her later was from his stash of Holy Honey. The bowl was ceramic with a blue-and-white gingham pattern. It was a little bigger and deeper than a normal soup bowl, a little more regal, if a bowl could be regal.

He sat quietly next to her while she ate. She hadn't realized how hungry she was.

"Why didn't you get food for you too?" she asked him.

"I don't know," he answered honestly. "I guess . . . this sounds silly, maybe, but I was just thinking about you."

She had smiled then, knowing she had something not everyone got, feeling like she was really, really lucky, like she wanted to grab his hand and pull him outside and show everyone. But of course she was way too tired and achy to do that. Besides, she would have appeared to be crazy.

"What's the deal with the bowl?"

"I'm glad you asked," he said, turning to face her. "I've had it for a few weeks now, and I thought of you the minute I saw it, at a little shop on 20th Street. I got it because it seems like a good, solid, usable bowl, but I also had all these crazy thoughts that made me think of us, as a couple, as a couple moving into the future together."

She held her breath. Was this going to be it? Was he really going to propose when her nose was so red and runny? She hoped not. But she also hoped so. She waited.

"But what I was thinking was that a bowl is so basic. I mean, everyone has a bowl; it's useful and important but can often be taken for granted. It shouldn't be—taken for granted, I mean—because it would be really hard to eat cereal or ice cream or, as you just demonstrated, soup without it. More than that, though, it isn't just for the good things. It's for the bad things too. I mean, you have an ice cream sundae when you're celebrating and relaxing or rewarding yourself for something, maybe just treating yourself; you might have oatmeal in the bowl to get your day started; and now, when you're sick, you have soup to try to feel better. Sort of like life or a good marriage: the good and the bad, even though of course we all prefer the good. I mean, I would always choose ice cream over soup. Please stop me—I'm totally rambling. I guess I just really liked this bowl."

"I like it too," she said, leaning her head toward him and resting it on his shoulder. "Thank you for it."

She continued to wait, thinking, *Any minute now, surely, with that preamble, he is going to ask me,* but there was nothing else. That wasn't a proposal, was it? It sort of sounded like one, all that philosophy about life and bowls and the good and the bad in one place. But there was no actual question, no offered ring. She spent the next five days wondering, not sure if she should ask him if she'd missed something. It wasn't until she was much better, and Joel was just at the beginning of the cold but not so bad that he didn't want to go out, that they rescheduled their dinner at Villa di Roma. And it was when the fried-asparagus appetizer came out, a diamond ring on one of the stalks that sat in that delicious and decadent butter sauce, that she knew the bowl conversation had not been the official proposal, even though in so many ways she thought it might as well have been.

Much later, they talked about those days, and Joel confirmed that he had shifted things because of the circumstances of her cold and the timing. He hadn't wanted to give up his idea of proposing at Villa di Roma, but he'd wanted to do *something* that night. And so he'd gotten the idea to give the bowl, and he said later that had been his favorite step. The actual proposal and the ring were important, of course, but more of an expected formality. "The bowl step," as they came to refer to it, had been . . . *pure*, he finally said. She might have added a few other words to the description—*confusing* was one of them—but she didn't. Pure seemed like enough.

"Mommy, I'm worried," Lincoln said in his serious voice, pulling her back to the parade and away from that memory of how incredibly naive they'd once been. That was her biggest takeaway from the discovery of the affair and its aftermath, though also that they'd been lucky to be naive because if they hadn't been, would they really have taken such a big chance? Would anyone? Now that she thought about it, though, in addition to being naive, they'd also been smart. Considering these last few months, that bowl metaphor was even more forward thinking than she had realized.

"What are you worried about, sweetie?" she said, leaning over so she could hear him better. Now that she knew she wasn't going to do it here, at the parade, she could relax a little.

"I'm worried that this is as good as it gets," he said. "That it will never be this exciting again."

"For the Eagles?" she asked, thinking for the ninetieth time that this kid was really something. What eight-year-old thought this way? She looked around for Joel; she wanted him to be in on this conversation. They were all right there, but they weren't in a clump anymore. Joel was leaning over saying something to Ridley. She glanced at the screen Joel was still holding, which now looked blank. She wondered if anyone had said goodbye to Richard.

"Well, yes, for the Eagles, but for everyone, for all of us," he said, sounding like he had given up. "And Mommy?"

"Yes, sweetie?" she said. She was trying to pay attention to Lincoln, but her mind was racing. Why hadn't she realized it before? She had missed a crucial step that needed to be taken before she did what she had planned to do at the parade. She had to backtrack. She had to do this right.

"If you go out tonight, can I call you like usual?" he asked. "But can we change it to every nine minutes? That last minute is always the hardest."

What she thought to herself was that it would still be hard, that last minute, whether it was between nine and ten or eight and nine. But what she said was, "I don't plan to go out tonight, Linc. I haven't done that in a while, didn't you notice? I am so sorry I went out so many nights without you and Daddy and Rid. I don't really want to do that anymore."

"You don't?" he asked. "That is great news."

"Yes, it is," she said, grabbing his hand and navigating their way over to the others. "Yes, it is."

They'd been home for just a few minutes when her phone rang. When she saw Reuben's name on the display, she froze and answered quickly.

"Everything's okay," Reuben said right away. "Richard is asking for you. Any chance you can stop over quickly?"

"All of us?" she asked, relieved that Richard wasn't being rushed to the hospital again. It would take a long time to get over that.

"No, actually, just you—specifically you."

Hannah looked around. Joel and Ridley were settled on the couch, watching coverage of the parade and footage from the Eagles' winning season. Lincoln, on the other hand, was watching her closely.

"I might bring Linc," she said quietly into the phone. "But please tell Richard I'll be there soon."

Joel looked up when she ended the call. "Everything okay?" he asked.

"Yes, apparently your father is asking for me," she said. "Do you mind if I run over quickly?"

"Should we all go?"

"No, Reuben said he just wanted me," she said, turning toward Lincoln. "But Linc, do you want to come along?"

"Sure, Mommy," he said.

Inside Saint Martha's, Eagles signs adorned the walls, and green confetti still dotted the floor. The woman behind the main desk had a **Go Birds!** shirt on.

"So exciting," Hannah said as she signed them in.

"One of the best days ever," the woman said.

Hannah steered Lincoln toward Richard's hall. She heard his booming voice as they got closer.

"As I just mentioned, for some it's their silver; for others it might be their china. But really, it doesn't always have to be something formal, and it doesn't have to be in good condition," he said as they came around the corner. He saw them, and he cleared his throat. "Take the ancient Japanese art known as *kintsugi*, for example, through which a broken bowl is mended. The cracks are filled in with a gold-infused lacquer, allowing the places that needed to be fixed to be visible and even appreciated."

There was a light gasp in the crowd from a woman sitting fairly close to Richard, and someone a row behind clapped excitedly. Hannah gave Richard a look that said, *Really?* And he looked right back and smiled, a fully present and knowing smile.

"I'll leave you with that for tonight," he said, waving to the small crowd. "But as always, I'll see you tomorrow."

Hannah looked to make sure she had heard him correctly, but she had. He waved them over.

"Hi, Grandpa!" Lincoln said, trying to crawl up on his lap. Hannah loved how he had a physical pull toward him. Richard grabbed on to him like the pull from his end was just as strong and helped him get settled in his lap in the wheelchair.

"Should I wheel you back to your room?" Hannah asked.

"No, it's okay," Richard said. "I like it out here. Let's just go over to the window."

She pushed the wheelchair over to a quiet corner and took a seat opposite Richard and Lincoln.

"I'm glad you didn't miss my little speech," Richard said like it was a big coincidence that they'd happened to catch it. She shook her head and smiled.

"I especially liked the part about appreciating the broken places," she said with a tone that might or might not be interpreted as sarcastic. "But for the record, Richard, I was there already."

He looked at her closely now. Then he turned to Lincoln.

"Any chance you can give your mom and me a minute alone?" he asked. "I know Rita at the front desk always has lollipops. And today I think they're green."

"Sure, Grandpa," he said, scooting down.

"Don't go too far," Richard called after him. Then to Hannah he said, "So you were already there. To be perfectly honest, I have been very worried."

"So have I," Hannah said, feeling the burn of tears behind her eyes. "I'm telling you this first, which is a little strange but also seems fitting somehow. I've decided I want to make it work with Joel. I want to keep our family together, but it's more than that; I want Joel to be my husband. I want him to be my—this sounds like such a cliché, but I want him to be my life partner, even though there has been some bad . . ." She trailed off, not sure how to finish the sentence.

Richard nodded, telling her to go on.

"I mean, this has been awful, and a shock, and I've been so mad, but I kept waiting to stop loving him, I thought that was inevitable, but it didn't happen. That was what I was really waiting for—I realize that now—to see if that would happen. I expected it to, but it never did."

Again, Richard nodded.

"The therapist we saw had this idea that our first marriage as we know it is over, but if we want to, we could start a second marriage together. I am finally ready to do that. And I want to say it isn't because I'm scared of the alternative, of being alone or starting over. Don't get me wrong—at first I was terrified of that. I have made this decision with my eyes wide open, no longer thinking bad things can't happen but believing *this* bad thing won't happen again. I am choosing Joel because he is the man I want to be with, for better or worse. And so I'm going to ask Joel to marry me again. Which, for the record, I had already planned to do before I heard your speech about the ancient Japanese art of . . . what was it?"

"Kintsugi," Richard said, smiling. "And Hannah, this makes me very happy. But I'm much less concerned with my own happiness than I am with yours and Joel's and those two amazing grandchildren of mine. I'm sorry you had to go through what you went through; I'm sorry Joel let you down. I don't think he will again. Earlier today when I was talking about the history of the Eagles and sports in general, and the importance of what that can bring to a city and a community and a family, I looked around. The room was packed; the group was much larger than it was just now. I know how ridiculous it is that I am regularly speaking to a crowd of old people; most of them might not even remember it the next day, but their eyes were bright, and they were listening. What struck me the most, though, was that two people, one man and one woman, were holding urns. I asked Reuben about that, even though I was pretty sure I knew, and they were the ashes of their spouses. They didn't live to see the Eagles win a Super Bowl, but their wife and husband got to take them to the parade or at least to the lounge of the nursing home to watch it on television. I wish you and Joel a long life together, but that is what I wish for you, too, a connection beyond connections, a love that never dies."

Hannah found Lincoln sitting in a chair just around the corner happily eating a green lollipop. Reuben was sitting next to him.

"Hey," he said warmly as she approached them, like there had been nothing more between them than work stuff and a few funny mugs of coffee.

"Hey," she said back, thinking once again he had stepped in to help. Once again he was in the place where they most needed him at the moment.

"It was a great day, wasn't it?" he said.

"It was the best day," Lincoln said before she had a chance to answer. "I worry there won't be another day this good again. I told my mother that."

Reuben held up his finger, telling them to wait. He disappeared into the conference room, and when he came out, he handed a mug to Lincoln.

"Here, keep this," he said. "You're probably old enough now to start drinking coffee, but if not, it's good for hot chocolate too."

Hannah laughed. The mug was white with navy-blue words scrawled across it. Lincoln tried his best to decipher it. He sighed.

"I don't read cursive," he said finally.

"Yeah, they don't really teach that in school anymore," Hannah said to back him up.

"Oh, no problem," Reuben said, taking the mug and holding it up. "It says, *Every Day Is the Best Day*, so basically it means all the days will be great. Also, I recommend learning a little cursive so you can read menus at fancy restaurants."

Lincoln reached for the mug and looked at it carefully. "There's a mug that says that?"

"Right here," Reuben said, pointing.

"I don't know if a mug has that much power," Lincoln said in his old-man way. "But thank you."

"It is my pleasure."

"Hey, Lincoln, can you give us just a minute? Maybe go wait in the lobby?"

"Again?" Lincoln said.

"Just one more time," she said.

"Fine!" he said, skulking off.

"What's that all about?" Reuben asked. "I assume you don't have time for a quick cup of coffee? I have an array of mugs, as you know, depending on your mood. And I have about thirty that say *The Philly Special.* That's a hard one to resist!"

Hannah smiled. "Well, you're right about that, but I'm going to pass," she said gently. "I wanted to tell you I've decided to make it work with Joel. I know you don't think I owe you an explanation, but I want you to know. You helped me get through this really hard time. Honestly, I don't know what I would have done without you."

"You helped me too," he said, smiling. "Things are going really well with Lucy. The worst part is that I'm back to drinking single-origin coffee at home, mostly from Nicaragua, that is severely underroasted. She keeps calling it lightly roasted, but well, you know, we can't agree on everything. Still, it's a small price to pay. And don't tell her if you see her, but I'm still drinking my Disney coffee here. There is only so much compromise a person can participate in."

Hannah leaned in and hugged Reuben, tentatively at first and then with more confidence.

"I'm really happy for you," they both said into each other's ears at the same time. She rested her head on his shoulder for one beat, maybe two, before she pulled away.

"I'll still be by for coffee," she said. "Save the *Crappity Crap Crap* mug for me, but I'll also accept that *Love Is Love* one if it's available when I'm here. Or, of course, I'll take *The Philly Special* any day. And just a crazy, unsolicited suggestion here, but I think you should take the *Hello Beautiful* mug home to Lucy. I think it would be perfect for her single-origin coffee."

"Great idea," Reuben said, smiling. "And much appreciated."

She waved as she walked away. She didn't see Lincoln in the lobby, but she caught sight of him out on the porch, sitting in a rocker surrounded by four older people, three ladies and a gentleman, who were completely focused on him as he rocked and talked.

"Very important," she heard him say as the door swooshed open in front of her, letting in the February chill. "Possibly one of *the* most important events to bring a city together and make a day great. But there will be other great days."

Like grandfather, like grandson, Hannah thought. She waited a few minutes, knowing the residents would be sad to see him go, and when there was a clear lull in his monologue, she gathered him up and took him home.

CHAPTER TWENTY-TWO

That night, after a dinner of penne pasta with pesto (to go along with the Eagles-green theme of the day) and a long, drawn-out bedtime routine, Hannah found the now-chipped blue gingham ceramic bowl in the cabinet. She had thought about getting a new bowl or choosing a different one from their eclectic collection, but this was the bowl. It just held even more history and possibility than it had when it had first been presented to her. Joel was sitting on the orange couch, reading. Even though she was around more at night these days, and even though she knew where she was heading lately, they hadn't really discussed it. He was still in the newer habit of entertaining himself at night.

"Do you want to watch a *Sopranos*?" she asked.

He looked at her with so much excitement she almost felt bad. *It's just a show,* she wanted to say. *You could have watched it anytime without me.* But she knew that wasn't the point. And then, to make things even more exciting, to raise the emotional bar even higher—she took the bowl from behind her back and placed it on the table in front of him.

His eyes went so wide, tears coming to the surface, that once again she felt bad. He was so easy. And she loved him for it.

"Is that . . . ?" he asked, but his voice cracked.

She took a deep breath.

"Yes. Step number one—the bowl step," she said, sitting down next to him. "Which is now chipped from the years of our using it. That big chip was when it rolled off the counter when Ridley's hands were so slippery from the melted ice cream and she couldn't grasp it. Remember? We thought it was a goner then, but it wasn't. And that one? That chip is from when the matzo ball soup was too hot after I filled it and it crashed to the table in front of Richard. Thankfully it didn't splatter all over him."

"I remember every single chip," he said.

"So you know how this goes: the good and the bad, ice cream and soup, celebrations and sickness. What I want to say is what you did to me was bad—I know you know that—and now it will always be a part of our history. It will always be in the mix of our bowl, but there is so much more good than bad, and here's the thing: I never stopped loving you. I waited to stop loving you, but I didn't, which makes me think I never will. If you ever do that to me again, I will leave. There will be no waiting period, no *Maybe I should have my own affair*, no anything. It will be over. But I believe you won't do that." She paused.

"I won't do that," he said. "I will never, ever do that."

"So the other thing I was thinking is that making this work isn't about removing the temptation. I mean, I know you aren't traveling so much anymore, and that's okay, but you are going to have to sometimes, and eventually the sharpness of all this is going to fade. I can't keep you here, and you can't keep me here to make sure; we have to trust. It has to be about resisting the temptation or maybe, hopefully, about not feeling tempted at all, not about avoiding it."

She paused again.

"Yes, yes, I agree," he said when it became clear she was waiting for a response. "I could not agree more."

"Okay," she said. As she rose from the couch, he touched her knee gently.

"Is your . . . are you . . . is it over?" Joel asked quietly. "Can we talk about it?"

She knew she was going to have to face this at some point, even though it had been over, and she clearly hadn't gone out at night in a while.

"Yes, it's over. It's been over," she said simply. "And the truth is it never really got started. Almost but not really. I tried for so long, using a dating app, going out on these terrible dates. There was an almost moment with Lance, the lifeguard from the Y. He was nicer than the others, by far, but that was not meant to be. And then there was—"

"Reuben?"

"Yes, there was Reuben," she said.

"I was so confused at first and then fairly sure I was right," he said. "It's such a relief to know. How long did you . . . ? Did you sleep together for long?"

She thought about not answering, just letting him wonder, but that didn't seem right. They needed complete honesty moving forward—she knew that.

"We didn't sleep together," she said. "We had one very passionate kiss, and that was all. I would be lying if I didn't say there were definitely elements of an emotional affair, but it's all over now. He is happily with his girlfriend. And I am just where I want to be."

He nodded, a satisfied look on his face. She had said everything she could think of, but she waited to make sure he didn't have any more questions. When he didn't, she got up and put the bowl back in its place. She returned to the couch and lifted the remote, finding her way to *The Sopranos* on demand, which they hadn't done since the night before the train ride, the night before she'd found out.

"What episode were we on?" she asked.

He took her hand and squeezed, and the word *pure* ran through her mind. *Pure* and also *just right.*

"We were on season six," he finally said, moving as close to her as he could. She closed her eyes for a second, feeling all of it, the comfort, the familiarity, all the things she had missed. They watched four episodes, right in a row, and that's where Ridley found them a little after two a.m.

And so the next morning over Honey Nut Cheerios and Raisin Bran, Hannah said she had an important question to ask. Lincoln was eating his cereal out of his *Every Day Is the Best Day* mug; he had insisted on it, and considering what she was about to do, it seemed like a fortuitous choice. Even though she said it twice, that she had an important question to ask, the kids barely looked up. They were running late, and though she couldn't believe it, she had already gotten a call from Saint Martha's that morning saying they had just opened the last bar of Palmolive. She would swing by the dollar store on her way to her meeting once everyone was settled, even though she had a definite feeling that Richard wasn't going to care as much about the soap anymore.

She had debated doing this when the kids weren't around but in the end decided they should be there. Even though she and Joel had been so careful to protect them, there was no question that they knew things hadn't been right, and she wanted them to know what was going on now, what she had decided. If they had questions, she would do her best to answer them, leaving out some of the details, of course.

"Step number two," she said to Joel. He put down his spoon and stood up, looking like he was standing at attention. She almost laughed.

"Will you marry me?" she asked. She stood facing him. She didn't want to get down on one knee; that didn't seem to be the way to do this.

"But you're already married," Ridley said like they were dumb, like *How could you not know?*

"Okay, then," Hannah said, moving a little closer to Joel. Both kids were watching them now. "Will you marry me for the second time?"

"I will," he said. "I absolutely will."

"And can this be the only other time we get married?" she asked seriously.

"Yes," he said, like he knew exactly what she was saying. "This will be it—our marriage for the rest of our lives."

"So you will?" she asked.

"I will!" he said.

"Does everyone get married twice?" Ridley asked.

"Not necessarily," Hannah said. "But sometimes."

"I want to get married ten times!" Ridley said.

Hannah realized they might not have relayed the correct message to her, but right now she wasn't going to worry about that. She would make sure to circle back to this later, maybe in ten or twelve years, just when Ridley was starting to date but hopefully before she fell in love for the first time, and explain what had happened here. Maybe.

"Oh, wait," Hannah said, running to her purse. She still had the bag in there from yesterday. In her mind she had thought she would do a much more corny proposal at the parade, with everyone watching and Richard on Skype. But this was so much better. She opened the crinkly paper bag and pulled out a small plastic one tied with a blue ribbon, shaking off some of the green confetti that had found its way into her purse at the parade.

"For you," she said, handing it to Joel. "And for me."

Joel looked at it through the plastic but didn't say anything. The kids were trying to get a better look.

"I was going to get a pearl, but I didn't want that idea of the bad thing—in the pearl's case, the sand or whatever brings it into existence—to be at our core, not to mention it's a cliché, so I chose sea glass because it starts as one thing before it churns and churns and churns and softens and eventually becomes something else. Also a cliché, but still, I like the symbolism. Plus, I collected sea glass when I was their age. I always loved it. It seemed just right."

Joel still didn't say anything.

"Can I have it?" Ridley asked, reaching for the plastic bag containing the smooth blue piece of sea glass.

"Sure," Hannah said. "It isn't like it's a ring. I just wanted some sort of object, but we don't have to honor it or anything. I just wanted to make my point."

"Really?" she asked gleefully, like she couldn't believe Hannah had said yes. "It's so pretty."

Ridley grabbed for it, and Joel absentmindedly handed it to her. She stuffed it into the pocket of her bright-green Bobby Lemons' Christmas Tree Stand sweatshirt fast, like if she gave them any time to think about it, they might change their minds.

"Are you going to have a wedding?" Lincoln asked. He was the only one who seemed to be fully tuned in at the moment. "A real one?"

"I don't know, probably not," Hannah said, looking at Joel. "Kids—go get your shoes on, get your backpacks." She was almost surprised when they listened to her. "Are you okay?" she asked Joel once the kids had dispersed.

"I am so okay," he said slowly. "I was so unsure, I was so scared—" He stopped and looked to make sure the kids weren't listening. "Now I am so happy. And here is something that I've wanted to tell you for months, but I wasn't sure how to. I was planning a surprise party for you. It was all set, invitations were about to go out, I scheduled it for a little more than a month before your birthday to completely throw you off. It was going to be so much fun. But then, well, everything happened, and I postponed it. I could have just cancelled—they offered to give me the deposit back—but I didn't want to. I hoped we would still be able to have the party at some point. In fact, when things were at their absolute worst, that's what I would imagine to try to feel better or to punish myself. I'm not sure which. Night after night when I couldn't sleep, I would picture you walking in and being surprised and being mine, still mine, but I didn't know if that would ever be true again. So let's do it. I can call today; we can have your no-surprise surprise party. It will be a great way to, I don't know, get back to normal, not to pretend it didn't happen, that we aren't different, but to celebrate that we're here, that we're still a family. For me it will be like living that fantasy I imagined so many times."

"Where would it be? Where did you plan to have the party?"

Joel smiled his confident, slow smile.

"Villa di Roma," he said proudly. "Perfect place for a first date, a proposal, *and* a birthday party. Your birthday party."

"It could also be the perfect place for a wedding celebration," she said, moving in to hug him. She rested her head on his chest.

"That's true," he said, wrapping his arms around her. "But will we tell people? I don't know that I want to have to tell everyone what I did and what we've been through these last few months."

"I agree," she said. "But let's do it anyway. We don't have to explain anything—we'll know—but we'll just call it a celebration, with meatballs and cannoli and a huge banner that reads *I'll See You Tomorrow*."

"Really? Why?" he asked.

Those words had run through her mind so much lately, ever since Richard had said them to Reuben, and especially more recently when she'd really been deciding—for so many reasons—and then to have him say them yesterday, in a way he hadn't in so long . . . they were Richard's words, and they were such hopeful words. That was the thing about being married: there were exceptions, of course, work trips and other reasons to be out of town here and there, but the basic belief was that you would see that person tomorrow. She'd never wished for that to not be true with Joel, and she quietly thanked Richard for helping her realize it.

That was too much to explain right now. The kids were back, waiting at the door. They were already late.

"Because I always want to see you tomorrow," she said, keeping it simple because finally, for them, it was again.

ACKNOWLEDGMENTS

I will begin where I always do, by thanking my outstanding, kind, creative, intrepid, and brilliant agent, Uwe Stender. This book is dedicated to you because, really, I couldn't have done any of this without you. I am so proud to be a part of Triada US. Thank you to everyone there for your strong and continued support.

I also could not have done this without my amazing, caring, smart, and patient editor Jodi Warshaw at Lake Union Publishing. It is a great pleasure to work with you again on this fourth book together. I am grateful for your unwavering guidance. Thank you to my developmental editor, Jenna Free, who, as usual, could see the whole of my novel more clearly than I could and helped me navigate it to the right place. To everyone else at Lake Union, including Nicole Pomeroy, Rosanna Brockley, Riam Griswold, Haleigh Rucinski, Kelsey Snyder, Gabriella Dumpit, and, of course, Danielle Marshall, I thank you all so much!

My continued gratitude goes to Dennelle Catlett and Kathleen Carter for doing so much to help get the word out about my books. You are the best!

Thank you to Melissa DePino for being a constant touchstone as I write and for your early feedback about this book. Thank you to Elisa

Ludwig for reading this novel early and offering invaluable insight and suggestions. Thank you to Greg Pinchbeck, fellow Hackley Hornet and NBC Page, for talking me through the ins and outs of using the overhead flags at a swimming pool so Lance could show Hannah how to successfully do the backstroke. Thank you to Leah Kellar for your friendship and your insight into the details of the online dating world. Thank you to Cynthia Mollen for your willingness to answer my most random medical questions. Thank you to Carmela Amore Calderone for over twenty years of great haircuts and even better conversation. Thank you to Ivy Gilbert for your rapid late-stage proofreading and great catch. Thank you to Don Friedman for introducing me to *kintsugi*. Thank you also to Jennifer Weiner, Simona Gross, Dawn Davenport, Nika and Dave Haase, Mary McManus, Jane Greer, Kathleen Woodberry, Andrea Cipriani Mecchi, Jennifer Mansfield, Margie McNaughton Ford, and Doug Cooper for your seemingly endless support.

Thank you to the Philadelphia Eagles for the amazing Super Bowl win and memorable season—here's to many more! Fly Eagles Fly!

And finally thank you to my family, especially my husband, Craig, and my children, Alice and Arthur. For the record, given the choice between a quiet train car and a regular one where we can be together talking and laughing—I would always pick the noisy one!

ABOUT THE AUTHOR

Photo © 2016 Andrea Cipriani Mecchi

Elizabeth LaBan is the author of *Not Perfect*, *The Restaurant Critic's Wife*, and *Pretty Little World*, which she wrote with Melissa DePino. She is also the author of *The Tragedy Paper*, which has been translated into eleven languages, and *The Grandparents Handbook*, which has been translated into seven languages. She lives in Philadelphia with her restaurant-critic husband and two children.